ACT OF AVARICE

Also by John Bishop

ACT OF MURDER

ACT OF DECEPTION

ACT OF REVENGE

ACT OF NEGLIGENCE

ACT OF FATE

ACT OF ATONEMENT

ACT OF MERCY

ACT OF AVARICE

A DOC BRADY MYSTERY

John Bishop, MD

MANTID PRESS

Act of Avarice

A Doc Brady Mystery

CONTENTS

CHAPTER 1

THE ROLLS

I was standing on the sidewalk outside the HEB in Marble Falls, Texas, waiting my turn to cross what some drivers must have been pretending was the Indy 500 raceway, considering how fast they were traveling. Finally, a nice gentleman waved across several of us who were waiting to enter the parking lot with our grocery carts, prompting honks from those behind him. He rolled down his window and gave them the universal salute with his middle finger and continued to wave more shoppers across the lane until there were no more in sight.

One has to be a little careful in Texas. Most everyone is carrying or concealing a weapon of some sort, and I have not seen any groceries yet that are worth dying for. I gave the man a wave, and he returned the gesture with a half salute. As I walked in front of his red Chevy pickup, I noted he wore a WWII cap. He was part of the Greatest Generation, according to Tom Brokaw, which meant that he probably shouldn't be driving, as he had to be in his nineties. But this is Texas, where you don't give up your guns or your car without a fight.

My own mother had a valid driver's license until she passed away in her mid-nineties, which I discovered only by accident in going through her things after her death. I opened a letter from the Department of Motor Vehicles, which was allowing her to renew her driver's license by mail, by email, or in person, with no driving test or vision test required. Amazing. I pondered how many folks in their nineties with auditory and visual impairments and a pistol on the passenger seat were out there driving and creating havoc on the roads. The thought made me consider shopping for groceries online at a store with delivery service.

I'm not a very good shopper. I tend to wander around and try out the food samples. You can make a meal off the bite-sized morsels at the HEB. There were lines at every food station. I loved their small-sized hot dogs, especially with fresh hot mustard. There were also the miniature beef Wellington bites, which were out-of-sight delicious. So I would usually load up the cart with frozen versions of the sampled bits, along with Nacho Cheese Doritos, ice cream sandwiches, Cheez-Its, Jimmy Dean breakfast sandwiches with sausage and pepper jack cheese, and an array of other items that should be accompanied by a coupon for a cardiovascular exam. Mary Louise would ask upon my return home about the missing bottled water, paper towels, Kleenex tissues, and toilet paper, those items that were on my original mission list, but that had lost priority somewhere between the barbecued pork ribs and the canapés with smoked salmon.

Mary Louise knew better than to send me to the grocery store, but that day she had no choice. She had driven to Austin for a charity board meeting; for which cause, I had forgotten. It was a Friday, the day I take off from my orthopedic surgery job at Hill Country Medical Center and hit the links with my golf-junkie buddies. I normally make rounds on hospital inpatients in the early morning then head to one of the four courses we are privileged to be members of as part of our membership at Horseshoe Bay Golf Club. This morning it had been the Summit Rock course, a

Jack Nicklaus Signature design with outstanding vistas of the Hill Country and Lake LBJ. Because of a dinner party we were having at the house, I had to decline libations after golf and attend to my shopping duties for my bride.

As I was loading the rear of my Chevy Tahoe with the day's shopping bounty, I noticed an ancient Rolls Royce across the aisle from my car. It was one of the models with the sloped rear end, four-door, and with an odd color combination, brown on the top and hood, with cheesy yellow sides and trunk. I loved the style of the car, but who in the world would choose those two colors? Most of the Rolls I had admired over the years were a combination of silver and burgundy. But brown and yellow?

As I was staring at the Rolls and pondering the colors, a tall, thin man with slicked-back silver hair and carrying a grocery sack walked up to the vehicle, opened it, and sat his shopping bag in the trunk. He sensed me staring and turned my way.

"That is some automobile," I said. "What year?"

"1958 Silver Cloud, left-hand drive. I inherited it from my grandfather some years ago. I loved that man more than life itself and have been unable to part with it. It's of course a service nightmare, and only worth around $35,000 now, but back in the day, can you imagine what a chick magnet this car was?"

I laughed at that. "I can't help but notice the way you are dressed. You match the car."

He had on yellow pants, a yellow shirt, a brownish-yellow corduroy jacket with elbow patches, and matching western pointed-toe boots in a yellow tint.

"I only take her out once a week, usually Friday, sometimes Sunday, and I feel she deserves the respect of my trying to match her in color. That's the only time I wear this outfit. Probably seems silly to you, huh?"

"No sir, not at all. I had an old 1982 Mercedes Benz 300 Turbodiesel I drove for twenty years. I understand the attachment."

"Have a fine day," he said, closing the trunk and boarding the Rolls. I went back to my business of loading my sacks chock-full of great items to eat—all bad for you—and hoped that I had managed to gather the necessities Mary Louise needed to prepare appetizers and dinner for our guests.

I heard the crunch of metal against metal, turned back toward the aisle, and saw the vintage Rolls crushing its left rear fender into a huge black GMC Denali. I yelled in the direction of the driver, but his window was up and I couldn't see within. I strode over to the car and noticed the Rolls was still in reverse, push-ing against the SUV. I knocked on the driver's window, with no result. I grabbed the driver's door handle and pulled, and I saw him slumped against the steering wheel.

"Are you okay? You've run into another vehicle across the aisle," I said, with some desperation. He didn't respond but was coughing severely, and he had a gray tinge to his face. I reached in front of the driver, managed to grab the gear shift, forced it back into neutral, and shut off the engine. As I gently pulled his shoulders back against the seat, I noticed his skin color was wors-ening, and he had spittle coming out of his partially open mouth. It appeared he was in the midst of a stroke, a seizure, or a coronary artery occlusion, commonly known as a heart attack. His carotid pulse was thready, so I pushed him down into the seat and started cardiac massage. I attempted mouth-to-mouth resuscitation, but his airway wasn't clear, due to froth coming out of his nose and mouth, and my attempt to initiate respirations failed.

I backed out of the car, dialed 911 on my cell phone, gave the operator the location, and went back to trying to revive the driver. Several other folks appeared, asking me questions to which there were no answers. I made an attempt to clear his airway with a grease-stained towel I found in his glove box, but to no avail, then returned to my resuscitation efforts.

It seemed like forever, but the EMTs arrived within ten minutes, and we three hoisted the dying man onto a gurney. The medics brought the device up to waist height, quickly intubated the driver, started an IV line, and ran a portable EKG.

"He's in ventricular fibrillation," one said. "Get the defibrillator."

The other EMT went back into the fire department emergency vehicle, brought out the requested device, told everyone to stay clear, and shocked the driver's heart. The patient jumped several inches off the gurney during the shocking procedure, after which the other EMT determined the patient was back in sinus rhythm.

"Thanks for your help," the EMT said to me. "You might have saved this man's life. What's your name?"

"Jim Bob Brady. I'm an orthopedic surgeon at Hill Country Medical Center."

"That's where we're headed, Doc. You might consider following us over there, in case the E.R. docs and the cardiologist have any questions for you."

With that, they loaded the unknown patient into the ambulance and, sirens screaming, headed out of the parking lot.

"Hey, did you see what happened? That guy wrecked my truck," said the GMC owner.

"All I know is that he and I were having a conversation about his Rolls, he gets in the car, starts backing up, doesn't stop, and his fender met your bumper guard, which looks to me to be way oversized and made out of stainless steel. I see a little paint damage at the contact point, but it looks to me like his vehicle fared much worse than yours."

"Well, it's not my fault. Somebody has to pay!"

"Well, if the driver survives, I'm sure he'll try and accommodate you. If he doesn't, well maybe you can find a lawyer around here who will represent you against a dead man."

I left that jackass behind, walked back into HEB, and found a help counter. I asked for store security. The clerk looked at me like I had arrived from another planet. There was a nameplate in front of her station that read "Christie."

"Store security. You have security cameras in the store. I notice them whenever I shop here. If you have cameras, you have security. How about a store manager, Christie?"

She smacked her gum and blew a giant bubble, making me wonder how in the world she got a job at the help counter. So far, she was anything but. Her hair was dyed green on one side, blond on the other, although I couldn't tell if the blond was dyed or natural. She had several piercings in both ears and a small ring in her left nostril. I thought it likely that all that metal was causing a conductivity problem in her frontal lobe.

"Christie? Store manager, please?"

"You're that doctor, aren't you?"

"Excuse me?"

"That doctor at the hospital who got involved with those missing women last year. Brady, right?"

"Yes, Christie, I'm Dr. Jim Brady. I don't see what that has to do with—"

She got up from her chair, walked around the counter, came right up to my face, and hugged me. "Thank you for what you did. For all of us who used to let our partners kick us around and do what they wanted. You gave us individual strength, and even more strength in numbers. You changed my life, Doc. You, and Dr. Buck, and Sister Mads." She hugged me so tight I couldn't take a deep breath.

Christie finally released me, went back to her chair, and paged "Scott" to the help desk.

Scott, the store manager, who looked barely old enough to shave, arrived shortly thereafter. I related the events in the parking lot and handed him the keys to the Rolls Royce.

"My advice is to call the Marble Falls Police Department and tell them what happened. They can follow up with the owner at the hospital, provided he survives. They will probably impound the vehicle, for no other reason than to keep it safe."

"Thank you, sir. I've not encountered a situation such as this before. I appreciate your advice."

Scott left for the parking lot, and I bid Christie adieu. I was reminded of a saying that we all need to remember: you can't judge a book by its cover.

Last year I had become involved in a search for six missing women who had been abused by their spouses. Once again, I had wedged myself into a situation that I had no business involving myself in, which of course did not stop me. It was a complicated scenario, one which was eventually resolved but involved the untimely deaths of four individuals: two abused women and two abusers. Mourning Doves, a residential facility for abused women, run by a former nun, Madeline O'Rourke—Sister Mads, as she was called—was at the epicenter of the problem as well as the solution. But then, that's another story.

CHAPTER 2

DINNER PARTY

By the time I arrived at the hacienda, it was almost 4 p.m. Guests were arriving at 5:30 for cocktails, followed by dinner at 6:30. There was no time for me to return to HCMC and check on my unknown and unnamed patient with the Rolls Royce Silver Cloud. Hopefully the Marble Falls PD went there, checked on the patient, and got his car put in storage, things I should have done but had no authority to do. Not that having no authority has ever stopped me from doing what should be done. I've found it's better to ask for forgiveness after the fact rather than ask permission.

I got into the shower, telling Tip, my golden retriever, that I would take him for a walk after. He barked, but I didn't know if that meant "Okay" or "Hell no, I'm not waiting."

My biggest worry was that I had once again failed Shopping 101, and Mary Louise would be unable to construct her dinner as planned. So it was that when I heard the loud clamor of the engine of her Porsche SUV, I leapt to attention and opened the kitchen door that led to the garage.

"Hey, mama, what's happenin'?"

She exited the car, stood behind the driver's door, and looked at me. "What are you up to, Jim Brady?"

I had to laugh. She knew me so well. She'd had a long day, I knew, but there she was, all five foot ten inches of her, blond mane up in some sort of fashionably messy style, decked out in a white cable-knit sweater and white slacks. She could have modeled for Saks Fifth Avenue just like she was.

"What? Are you talkin' to me?"

"Yes I am, husband, and you have that look. Did you go shopping as I asked?"

"Yes, ma'am, I did as instructed."

"Really? Did you get those items I requested, or did you wander the store and nosh on all the free goodies?"

"Well, I might have had a bite or two, because I was starving after golf."

"Uh huh. Come help me with the packages, please."

I walked around to the trunk and saw boxes and sacks with Trader Joe's labels.

"What's all this?" I asked.

"Dinner, darling."

"Oh, I thought you were cooking." I was starting to feel relieved.

"I wouldn't put the burden of buying cooking ingredients on you. I'm sure you were able to free up the appetizers from their hidden locations in the HEB freezers, but I wouldn't expect you to find all the items for a dinner that I needed to cook. No, we're eating with the Trader tonight."

We carried everything inside. She turned to me in the kitchen and put her arms around my neck.

"Have I told you today how much I love you?" she said.

"I don't think so, and I'm glad to hear it." I kissed her on her full red lips and started to feel a little frisky, as I sometimes do.

"Save that for later, young man. Now, pour yourself a glass of your favorite libation and take yourself and your dog for a walk while I work."

We lived in a house that Mary Louise had remodeled last year, on Lake LBJ but high enough up the hills to discourage the insects that loved to hang around water. We had looked at houses right on the water, with boat docks included, but I just couldn't stand the bugs. We were at a friend's house last fall, trying to watch a football game, but we couldn't see the television due to the black mass of insects crawling around the brightly lit screen. Thanks, but lake-level living was not for me.

So our lovely home high in the hills above the lake had spectacular views of the water and the Hill Country, inside a gated community with only five houses. I took my Macallan twelve-year-old scotch in a to-go cup and let Tip run through the community unleashed. It was against the rules, I'm sure, but a man—and yes, even a gelded doggie-man—needs his roaming space from time to time.

We had six guests for dinner that evening. Susan Beeson, the former Houston chief of police and current assistant special agent in charge of the Austin division of the FBI, and her husband Gene, a CPA, were in attendance. We had been friends with the Beesons for years. She and I had collaborated a number of times in the past on various murder and mayhem cases in which she was official, and I was the amateur sleuth. Susan's father, retired Houston Chief of Police Stan Lombardo, had been my patient. I first encountered him in the emergency room at University Hospital in Houston, Texas, after he had fallen from an elevated deer blind and fractured his hip after having consumed three Bloody Marys beginning at seven in the morning. He later required a replacement of his hip due to a disruption of the blood supply from the fracture, but he still complained about his painful hip and blamed me for his predicament. Susan had aged significantly in her job as chief of HPD. She seemed to have shrunk, and now had a full head of gray hair. But she still wore what she called her "sensible shoes," black brogans fit for the convent.

Dr. Buck Owens, chair of the board of the Hill Country Medical Center, was present. He and I had become good friends over the past year or so. Buck had brought me on staff, having convinced me that slowing down my orthopedic surgery practice by moving from the fast-paced academic world at University Hospital in Houston to HCMC in Marble Falls would reduce my stress level and allow me to enjoy my patients again. He had been right on. His wife had passed away a few years back, so he came stag for dinner.

Michael Reardon, a cardiovascular surgeon at HCMC, and his wife Phyllis were also invited. Mike and I had become friends over a case we shared, and we found that we had in common that fickle mistress called golf, aptly named since all the other four-letter words were taken. We played in the same Friday–Saturday golf group at Horseshoe Bay Golf Club, provided there were no emergencies that required our attention. And honestly, sometimes we played so badly that we prayed for our respective beepers to go off and rescue us from our misery. Mike was over six feet tall and was slender, with large hands but very thin bony fingers, which apparently was an advantage in sewing cardiac vessels back together. Phyllis was a statuesque blonde, probably the same age as Mike but, as it was with Mary Louise and I, much better preserved than her husband.

Last was Shelly Wood, who began our relationship as my part-time nurse but gradually assumed full-time duties as we worked successfully together. Shelly worked in my office on Tuesday and

Thursday, which were clinic days for me, and on surgery days, normally Monday and Wednesday, covered the office phones, coun-
seled patients before and after surgery, wrote prescriptions, and in
general performed admirably all those duties that are necessary
to run a surgeon's office. She was a nurse practitioner as well, so
she "moonlighted" in the emergency room on occasion when the
E.R. was short on staffing. Shelly was five feet four inches or so,
small, not more than 110 pounds, with unruly black-turning-gray
hair. She had been married early on in life but now was single, and
childless. Her trademark was wearing differently colored large-
framed glasses.

It was a pleasant evening in early May, warm but not hot
yet. The group gravitated to the terrace to enjoy cocktails and the
changing of the light as the sun slowly sank behind us. The house
had an easterly view, which produced beautiful sunrises. Mary
Louise and I had avoided buying a house facing into the Texas setting sun due the summer sun's intensity. Mary Louise and Susan
Beeson stayed behind in the kitchen, allegedly to work on dinner,
but more likely to catch up with each other's lives.

As the rest of us exchanged pleasantries and enjoyed our libations, I mentioned to the rest of the group about my experience at
the HEB earlier that afternoon with the Rolls Royce and its presumed owner. "I was running behind, and although felt I should
accompany the gentleman to the E.R., you all were coming over,
and appetizers that Mary Louise had me purchase were in the car
and needed to be refrigerated, so I came home. Did any of you
hear about what happened to him?"

I gathered some strange looks from my friends and colleagues.
Shelly Wood spoke first.

"Dr. Brady, after I finished up in your office, I headed down
to the E.R. for an overtime shift. They were short-handed due

to a staff member calling in sick, so the supervisor called me and I agreed to work. The patient in question was brought in by the EMTs just as I arrived. He was in ventricular fibrillation upon arrival. The EMTs told me they had shocked him back into sinus rhythm at the HEB parking lot, but that he kept vacillating between sinus rhythm and V-fib on the way to the E.R. They shocked him a couple of more times in the ambulance. We tried using drugs to revive him—epinephrine and vasopressin—since he had been shocked three times by the time he arrived, but to no avail. We couldn't get a functional heartbeat."

"You don't know who he was, Jim?" asked Buck Owens.

"No idea, Buck. That encounter in the parking lot was the first I had seen him. Who was he?"

"G. Sanford Lowell III. Ring a bell?"

"Sorry, but no."

"His family is the reason we have the Hill Country Medical Center. His grandfather, George Sanford Lowell, was one of the richest men in Texas. He was a participant in the discovery of the Spindletop oil fields in the Beaumont area in the early 1900s. After he made his first fortune there, he moved to Midland and started drilling in the Permian Basin. He made another fortune there. Lowell II, his son, and Lowell III, the grandson, have continued to manage the family finances all these years. I'm surprised you haven't heard the name."

"Remember, Buck, I've only been here for a year. Prior to that, I lived in Houston for many years, where names like Cullen, Richardson, Blaffer, and Farish dominated the oil business and social columns there. And those folks I only knew from name recognition. It wasn't like I was out playing polo with them."

"Well, I hate to see Sandy pass away. His father died some years ago. He had a younger sister who basically drank herself to death, died at fifty-two of cirrhosis of the liver. Sandy never married and had no children, at least that I know of."

"Was he healthy, as far as you know?" I asked.

"Yes. Mike, do you know anything about Sandy's health?" Buck asked.

"No, I don't. He was never a patient of mine. He had no prior cardiac problems that I know of. I do remember that when he would come in for his annual physical he would create quite a stir in the hospital. I mean, he was an ultra-wealthy man, good-looking, and single. He always had 'the works' during his annuals— total body scan, cardiac imaging, treadmill testing, and a colonoscopy every five years. The procedures would take a couple of days. He would stay in one of the suites on the hospital floor while his tests were being run. His primary doc was Billy Stevens. He could tell you more, although I'm not sure it matters, now that he's passed on."

"Wasn't he a big contributor to the hospital, Buck?" asked Phyllis Reardon.

"Yes, our largest. I will need to have a discussion with his CPA and his personal attorney to see if his demise will impact our finances. I hate to seem callous, but Sandy Lowell has been very good to HCMC. Hopefully there will be a bequest for the hospital from his estate.

"Gene, you're a CPA," said Buck. "How long before we would have some publicly available data regarding Sandy's finances?"

"Well, since most financial records are computerized, about as long as it takes to hit a couple of keystrokes on the computer. That kind of information will have to come through his attorney, of course, but if his will is up to date and no one contests it, not very long."

Mary Louise opened the door leading to the patio and told the group that dinner was served. "Get your plate and serve yourself."

Our hostess had placed name tags on the table next to each place setting. I noticed she sat Shelly next to Buck. That would be a May–September romance. He was in his early seventies, she might have been in her early fifties. I wondered if there'd be an issue with him being admin and her being medical staff, but that was probably premature anyway.

I didn't want to be morbid, but I was curious, so I had to ask, "Won't he have to have an autopsy? Isn't that the rule when you die within twenty-four hours of arrival at the emergency room?"

"Yes," answered Mike.

"Hmmm. I wonder who'll get that duty?" I said.

"Don't know," said Buck. "They have a rotation down there. We'll know in the morning."

"Now don't be shy, friends," said Mary Louise. "We have Caesar salad, chicken piccata, and a fresh vegetable medley. Eat up. Cheers," she said, raising a glass to our friends.

"Cheers!" we all said.

Our dining area was part of a "great room," with a large seating area off to the left adjacent to the bar, open space in the middle, and the dining area off to the right. A wall of floor-to-ceiling windows fronted the great room, with spectacular views of Lake LBJ and the Hill Country, albeit from a distance. As we stood in the short line to load our plates, Phyllis Reardon made a comment that turned a few heads.

"I used to see Sandy on occasion at the plastic surgeon's office. We went to the same doctor over in Austin, Dr. Robert Warner."

No one said anything for a moment, being as how going to a plastic surgeon and keeping that information confidential was sacrosanct; at least that was the case in Texas. Phyllis had her blond mane up in some sort of "do," exposing her ears and neck. I was standing next to her in line and immediately started surreptitiously inspecting the flat post-auricular area (behind the ear) for the telltale scar of a rhytidectomy (face lift). I needed more light to know for sure—then I felt a poke in my ribs, and noticed the familiar yet loving glare from Mary Louise, standing behind me and giving me the signal to stop staring at our guest's face and put food on my plate.

We sat down and started the eating process and made small talk for a bit, and during one of those silent moments at the dinner table, Phyllis continued.

"I've had a facelift, a tummy tuck, a boob job, and a bleph," she said, bleph short for a blepharoplasty or eyelid lift. "I think Dr. Warner did a wonderful job, don't you all?"

By then, Mike, her husband, was looking for a hole to crawl in. Susan, Shelly, and Mary Louise nodded in unison, made comments like "absolutely," "a wonderful job," and "you look years younger."

"I saw Sandy in the waiting room at Dr. Warner's office sometime before the holidays. He was there for a post-op visit. Sometimes after a face lift, the skin incision behind the ears doesn't heal well, and the tissue there turns sort of a black color and dies, and that takes a while to scab over. Sandy had the procedure ten years prior, and this recent surgery was a repeat, so that's why he was having healing problems, or so he told me. He was getting better, and his face looked great. You wouldn't know he was in his early seventies."

I almost choked on a broccoli spear. "You're telling me he was in his seventies? I only saw him the one time, in the parking lot, but I estimated his age as mid-fifties. I can't believe that."

"Isn't that right, Mikey? Early seventies?"

"I think so, Phyllis. I'm not sure Sandy would want us to be discussing his plastic surgeries. That is a very private matter."

"Well, it's not like he's going to object now, is it?"

None of us could argue with that.

CHAPTER 3

AUTOPSY

"**A**ll that talk of plastic surgery started me thinking that I might need something done. What do you think, Jim Bob?"

"Is that a trick question? Sounds like a lose-lose situation for me."

"Of course not. Come in the bathroom with me and look at my face under the lights."

We were lying in bed enjoying a relaxing Saturday morning and recapping the evening's activities and conversations until Mary Louise "popped the question" about plastic surgery. I moaned and groaned, got out of bed, slipped on my boxer shorts, and padded into the master bath with its array of Hollywood lights around a large vanity mirror. I stood very close to her, seeing as how she was scantily clad in a short nightie that was almost transparent. She was a full-figured woman, and it was difficult for me to concentrate.

"Keep to your job, young man," she said. "I know that look of yours all too well. Tell me what you think about my face."

I turned her face this way and that, moved her upper and lower eyelids to check for skin turgor, tested the elasticity of her neck, then moved my surgeon's hands delicately in a southerly direction and palpated her full breasts.

"What are you doing?"

"You asked me to inspect you for cosmetic issues that a plastic surgeon would deal with. The breasts are included in that milieu." By that time, Little Jim Bob had taken over by shunting blood from Big Jim Bob's brain and internal organs to himself. I was almost dizzy.

"I think your anatomy is fabulous, an impeccable specimen," I said, hoarsely.

She moved up against me and said, "Well, look what I've started."

With that, what few items of clothing we wore were removed and to the bed we returned.

I was awakened by Tip's whining, which evolved into a frantic bark, after which he jumped up onto the bed and started licking my face, a sure sign of urinary desperation. I slipped my boxers back on and took him into the backyard for relief. Although it was May and still not too hot, you could feel that stillness in the air that comes with summer in the Hill Country. Tip frolicked for a bit, found some delectable item in the grass, and began rolling in it, a sure sign that it was poop—from what creature, I didn't know.

"Tip! Stop that right now!" I yelled, which brought him up to attention briefly, but then he began to roll in the substance again, its fragrance so delectable he couldn't stand it. I finally had to pull him up by his collar and swat him on the rear, after which he made a mad dash toward the back door and, once there, set to barking at me, I wasn't sure for what offense. Was he hungry? Was he mad about my taking him away from his delight? I didn't know, so I gave him his kibble and filled his water dish and hoped that would satisfy him. I then wondered if I had gone completely nuts with my trying to read Tip's mind. C'mon, man, I told myself, he's a dog!

"Good lord, Jim Bob, what's that smell?"

"Your dog. I let him out to do his business, and before I knew it he was rolling around in bird or critter poop. It's bad, isn't it?"

"He can't stay in the house. Put him in the garage. We'll have to take him to the groomer, tell them it's an emergency."

"Can you take him? I have a tee time."

My bride of many years put her hands on her hips and gave me "the look," the one so diametrically opposed to the look she had given me an hour or so ago.

"Tell you what," I said quickly, "I'll drop him off, go play golf, and pick him up after. I'm sure he'll have to wait, since we don't have an appointment."

"Great idea. I have a Child Advocates board meeting, so that will take up most of my day. See you this afternoon with a clean and odor-free canine?"

"Yes, ma'am. You can count on me. See you later. I love you, and thanks for the morning."

"The pleasure was all mine, sir."

I kissed her, put the leash back on Tip, and headed out.

We lived in Granite Falls, one of the many small communities around the Lake LBJ area. Doggie Day Care and More was in Marble Falls, only fifteen minutes away. Their facility housed several veterinarians, a pet boarding "hotel," and multiple grooming bays. As expected, their grooming schedule was packed, but when the clerk smelled Tip, she assured me they would find the time to spruce him up. She allowed as how I might take better care of my dog, keep him away from the nasty items he so loved to cavort in. I didn't see how Tip could get any better care than he was getting, but I took the high road and thanked her profusely, all the while trying to avoid staring at the purple hair and her array of lip rings. Not that there's anything wrong with that . . .

I headed for the golf course after dropping Tip off. Apple Rock was on the schedule for the group that day, one of my favorites. On the way, I called HCMC and asked to speak to someone in the pathology department. Dr. Jerry Reed was on duty that day. He and I had become acquainted with each other the previous year after the murder of an employee.

"Tell me you're not on the way to play golf, while I'm stuck here with this formaldehyde stench."

"Okay, I won't tell you. Sucks for you, man, but hey, that's why they pay you the big bucks."

"Jim Bob, stick it where the sun don't shine. What the hell do you want, anyway?"

"G. Sanford Lowell III. Sudden death from yesterday. I was at the HEB parking lot talking to him about his vintage Rolls Royce, next thing I knew he had backed into a pickup truck. I opened the driver's door to see what was wrong and realized he was unresponsive. I assumed he was in cardiac arrest and I tried to resuscitate him, but to no avail. The EMTs were there pretty damn quick and shocked him out of ventricular fibrillation, but apparently further resuscitation efforts at the hospital failed."

"How well I know. I have him on the table right now. His medical history from our records here at HCMC does not reflect any history of heart disease. And it looks like he is—was, rather—faithful in getting annual physicals with blood work. I've got his internal organs separated out, and grossly they look entirely normal. I'll have to look at the slides under the microscope to confirm that, though. His heart shows a massive infarction, as does his brain. That's odd because on his last physical he had an echocardiogram which was normal, and a cardiac catheterization which was normal. And it's tough to get a cardiologist to do a cath without symptoms of chest pain, which according to his records he definitely did not have."

"He was a big donor, and those folks sometimes dictate their own treatment."

"How well I know, my friend. At any rate, it looks like sudden death due to an unexplained arrhythmia, followed by cardiac and cerebral infarcts with complete system shutdown. I'll check the cardiac chambers, coronary arteries, and aorta before I complete the autopsy, but he looks like a perfectly healthy guy until his heartbeat went haywire. We'll probably never know what triggered it. I'll talk to you tomorrow or Monday, give you the final analysis."

"Thanks, Jerry. Enjoy your day at work."

"Jim Bob, go f—" he said, but I hung up before he could complete his sentence. I had an inkling of where he was going with that, though.

Apple Rock was in superb shape, although my golf game was not. I had a grand time with my friends and lost a little money, which is what you should do when you play like you've never held a golf club in your hands. If you can't hit the green from 100 yards out with a pitching wedge, you deserve to accept whatever punishment the golf gods hand you. The highlight of the day was a cold beer and a hot juicy burger from the Caprock food truck after the round.

On the way to pick up Tip, the mobile car phone rang. It was Lucy Williams—administrative assistant to Dr. Buck Owens— who had lost her daughter, and my patient, last year in a senseless act of violence. While I presume one never gets over the loss of a child, Lucy had brought herself out of a severe depression and was pleasant and functional again, at least on the surface.

"How's my favorite orthopedic surgeon?" she asked.

"Licking his bad-golf wounds. What are you doing there on Saturday?"

"Jim Bob, you know this is a twenty-four-hour-a-day job. When Dr. Buck Owens calls, the world listens."

"Glad to hear you're . . . better?"

"Much, thanks to you and many other good friends who have helped bring me back from the depths of despair."

"Well, Lucy, I assume you didn't call me on a Saturday afternoon for chit chat? We had your boss over for dinner last night, so I've talked to him very recently."

"Yes, I know. He wanted to talk to you about Mr. Lowell. Have you by any chance talked to Dr. Reed in pathology today?"

"Maybe. Am I in trouble?"

"No more than usual. Hold for Dr. Buck."

"Jim Brady," said our chair of the board, "thanks for a wonderful evening. That Mary Louise is something special. You'd better stay healthy and mind your Ps and Qs, otherwise I'll be charging down the path to happiness with your wife."

"Buck, I don't think I have a friend that hasn't told me that. She is a find. Why she latched on to me back when I was a mere medical student, I'll never know. She was working in a retail store when I went in to buy my mother a gift for Mother's Day. She told me she hated medical students, but I slowly wooed her into loving me."

"Temporary insanity on her part is more like it. Anyway, she's a jewel and I had a swell time."

"Buck, nobody says 'swell,' do they?"

"Yes, back in an Eastern Seaboard boarding school a hundred years ago. But, after four years at the University of Texas at Austin, I got words like that out of my system for the most part. Still, sometimes they sneak out. The other day I used the words 'splen-did' and 'noxious.'"

"Buck, I'm not sure we can be friends any longer."

"Good, you go away and I'll make Mary Louise my own."

"Buck—"

"Just kidding. About Sandy Lowell, I want you to help me with whatever comes down the pike about the circumstances of his demise and his last will and testament. I heard you spoke to Jerry Reed this morning."

"Yes, I was curious about his autopsy since I was the inadvertent initial responder to the beginning of his demise. Looks like an undefined arrythmia of some sort, with secondary cardiac and cerebral ischemia, basically a heart attack and a stroke, due to loss of blood pressure and subsequent blood flow, and organ shutdown. Unless some lab data or the tox screen give us a cause of the arrhythmia, Jerry said he has no clue of what initiated the ventricular fibrillation the EMTs saw on their monitor in the HEB parking lot. As I understand it, the arrhythmia became less defined in our emergency room and became a ventricular flutter, which soon progressed to asystole. Once he flat-lined and didn't respond to the defibrillator, he was essentially a goner. Jerry went over the EKG tracings at length."

"Well, that's just too damn bad, my friend. At any rate, you will be my right-hand man henceforth on the Sandy Lowell business."

"'Henceforth'? Have you lost your mind?"

CHAPTER 4

SUNDAY

Mary Louise and I decided to take a drive to see if we could find any bluebonnet stragglers in the Hill Country. Prime blooming season for the lovely wildflowers is around the end of March to early May, depending on weather conditions. The arrival of spring in Texas means a sea of blue spreads across the state. If there is a good deal of rain in the winter, the blooming process is heightened. This was the second week of May, and prospects of bluebonnet blooms usually are diminished by then. Even so, a Sunday drive around the Hill Country was still a pleasant experience.

We took the Tahoe, which had plenty of room for Tip in the backseat. I cracked the window for him, since being able to put his nose out into the wind seemed to be the thrill of a lifetime for my aging golden retriever. We headed east on Highway 71 then turned south on Highway 281 toward Johnson City. We found some bluebonnets there, at the site of Lyndon B. Johnson National Historical Park. I pondered whether his legacy would end up being the establishment of Medicare and Medicaid, or his acceleration of the Vietnam War. Historians would argue that subject ad infinitum. We stopped at a McDonald's drive-through for coffee, then wandered the Pedernales Falls State Park. Tip frolicked while we sipped and walked. A few more bluebonnets lingered there, though their vibrant blue color had faded.

Moving on, we drove down Highway 290 to Fredericksburg, famous for its German heritage and wineries. We strolled the downtown area, full of antique shops and small restaurants, which made us hungry. We returned to the SUV and made a side trip of thirteen miles over to Luckenbach, a venue for country music. That reputation began when Jerry Jeff Walker, backed by the Lost Gonzo Band, recorded a live album, *¡Viva Terlingua!*, at the Luckenbach Dance Hall in 1973. The town's reputation was further enhanced by the hit classic from Willie Nelson and Waylon Jennings, "Luckenbach, Texas, Back to the Basics of Love." We ate outdoors at Hondo's, named for Hondo Crouch, a previous town owner, and enjoyed fresh-off-the-grill cheeseburgers with all the trimmings, and Shiner Bock beer. Tip delighted in his own cheeseburger, albeit it sans cheese, pickles, lettuce, tomato, mayo, mustard, purple onion, jalapeños, and bun.

There was a young woman on stage, sitting on a stool and playing acoustic guitar. Her voice was on the raspy side in a good way, like a younger Bonnie Raitt. She was plunking a blues riff, but the words to the song were definitely country. Her microphone needed to be turned up, or I needed hearing aids. The words sounded something like "the best songs come from broken hearts," definitely a country music motif. She had long brown hair topped with a straw cowboy hat. She wore a white long-sleeved western-cut shirt and faded denims tucked into high cowboy boots decorated with roses of various colors along the shaft. What a package. She looked to be in her late thirties, although I'm a lousy judge of age.

On our way out, I stopped at the stage, told her we enjoyed her music, bought a couple of CDs from her, and dropped a $50 bill in her tip kitty, which sadly was empty. Her eyes widened when she saw the $50. She called herself Bonnie Bishop, but in this day and age, who knew what an artist's real name was. That girl had to be going places with her talent, and here she was, playing a Sunday lunch gig at Hondo's with maybe twenty souls in attendance.

And that set me to pondering about how vocal artists make it, who does and who doesn't. There had to be a world of local talent out there, and having lived in Houston and lately the Hill Country, we had seen quite a bit of it. And yet, as I understand it from friends of mine with grown children still trying to make it in the music business, it was a hard road, regardless of the level of talent. I admired this young woman's stage presence, this so-called Bonnie Bishop. More than likely her real name was Brenda Smith, something straightforward. Bonnie Bishop. Catchy.

On the way home, Dr. Jerry Reed called me and interrupted my listening to one of the albums I had purchased at Hondo's from the bluesy girl singing country music.

"Where are you, Brady?"

"Leaving Luckenbach, on the way back home. Why?"

"Just wanted to know how much more fun you're having than me, that's all. Did you eat at Hondo's?"

"Yep."

"And is that beautiful wife with you?"

"Yep."

"Put me on speaker phone."

"Why?"

"Just do it."

Reluctantly, I did as he requested.

"Mary Louise, Jerry Reed here. I just wanted you to know that if you ever tire of that sorry husband of yours, I'm your man."

"Thanks, Jerry. I'll keep that in mind. I wouldn't hold my breath if I were you, though."

"Jerry, did you have a reason to call?" I asked.

"Yes. Sandy Lowell. All his coronaries checked out fine, no plaque buildup, no occlusions. Also, no aortic or mitral valve problems. His heart was clean, except of course for the massive heart attack he had due to loss of his heartbeat. He also sustained a massive stroke, again due to loss of blood pressure. We're back to this mystery arrhythmia as the source of his demise."

"No clue as to the origin of that, huh?"

"Nope. Zip, nada, nothing. His tox screen was clean, no drugs in his system, lab values within normal parameters, except of course his potassium levels were high, but that would probably be due to the cardiac arrest. It's possible the patient had high potassium levels prior to the incident, and that triggered the ventricular arrhythmias, but those levels also rise after a myocardial infarction. It's like which came first, the chicken or the egg?"

"But you can't tell from the autopsy and the blood chemistries which came first, high potassium resulting in arrhythmias, or an arrhythmia resulting in reduced blood flow to the heart that caused a heart attack which the produced high potassium levels?"

"Not at this time."

"What does that mean? Might you possibly have an answer at some later date, Jerry?"

"I might if I had more information, but I don't right now. I'm leaving the door open."

"Okay, well, thanks for calling."

"Enjoy the rest of your day, Jim Bob. Goodbye, Mary Louise."

In my days as an academic orthopedic surgeon at University Hospital in Houston, I would make the trek into my office on Sunday afternoon and go over the charts and X-rays of the patients on my operating schedule for Monday. There would be six or eight cases in two operating suites, with an orthopedic resident in one and an orthopedic hip and knee fellow in the other, with plenty of opportunity for mistakes to be made. I ran a massive schedule back in those days, with a Monday-Wednesday-Friday surgery schedule, and a Tuesday-Thursday office schedule. I burned myself out. Then I was blessed with an inheritance windfall from a grateful patient, which allowed me to take a three-month sabbatical and reassess my life. The revenue from the investment principle was three times what I was making as an orthopedic surgeon, so slowing my life down became an affordable necessity.

I ended up at Hill Country Medical Center, a first-rate Level 4 trauma center in Marble Falls, Texas. Although Marble Falls is a small town, the drawing area for the hospital included several counties around the Lakes area in the Hill Country, such that the population of the draw area was around 150,000 people. A Level 4 center provides advanced life support prior to a patient being transferred to a Level 5 or 6 center. Level 4 care provides evaluation, diagnostic capabilities, and stabilization of patients prior to transfer.

My new schedule consisted of three surgical cases on Monday and Wednesday, and office hours Tuesday and Thursday, followed by three days off to rejuvenate. I was happier, healthier, and able to enjoy my patients once again. I was able to provide the same quality care as before, just on a smaller scale. My golf handicap, however, did not descend into the single-digit range, as I expected with the career change.

Tip and I dropped off Mary Louise at the house, then headed over to HCMC. Business looked to be good—good from the hospital board's point of view, bad from the patients required to be there—as the hospital parking lot was packed. I pulled into a PHYSICIANS ONLY slot and parked. I leashed Tip and we entered through the main lobby of the building. The lobby contained a few folks sitting and waiting on loved ones being evaluated in the emergency room, since there was no elective surgery on Sundays, or waiting for visiting hours for the hospitalized to begin.

I looked down the left hallway toward Dr. Buck Owens's office and conference room, and noted that Lucy Williams, his admin assistant, was not present. We greeted Fred the security guard at the central desk.

"Hey, Doc Brady," Fred said, shaking my hand. "How's our boy today?"

He kept treats for Tip, which endeared him for life with my canine. Tip put his paws on the front of his desk, accepted his treat with humility, and enjoyed the head rub from his current best friend. Golden retrievers aren't at all prejudiced. They love anyone who feeds them, pets them, and takes them for walks. They don't care about skin color, hair style, where you find religion, or who you vote for. Hmmm. We humans could learn a lesson from that.

As we were walking away toward the entrance to the clinic side of the building, which housed physician offices and the exam rooms where we saw patients, I heard a shrieking behind me.

"NO! He's not DEAD!!!"

Tip barked. I didn't blame him. The woman's voice grated on me like sandpaper on stone. Fred jumped from his chair, walked toward the woman, and tried to calm her down. I guessed her to be in her forties, with lank dishwater-blond hair, dressed in sweats and athletic shoes. She had a companion, older than the screaming woman by twenty years. Could be her mother, an aunt, maybe a caretaker of some sort.

"Just tell me he's not dead! Tell me!" she screamed.

"Who, ma'am? Who are you talking about?" Fred yelled.

"His name is Sandy! Sandy Lowell!"

I didn't know if Fred knew who Sandy Lowell was, or even that he was dead, but he dutifully returned to his desk, picked up the phone, and called someone, probably a nursing supervisor on duty, or a hospital administrator on call, or even the morgue to see if this patient had been a recent entry. He made a second call after he hung up from the first, then returned to the woman's side.

"Ma'am, I have a nursing administrator coming down to talk with you. I'm in charge of security, so I can't tell you about the status of the person you're asking about. If you could just please quiet down and sit down, we can get to the bottom of this for you. Please?" Fred walked with her and her friend over to an isolated couch and had a few more words with her that I couldn't hear.

She did quiet down, and she sat with her companion but continued to sob. I felt I should walk over and see if I could do anything to help, but I had learned over the years to try and not involve myself with situations over which I had no control. And the manner in which the woman had been shrieking was not something I wanted to see recur, so I walked over to Fred's desk and sat down in a chair reserved for his security partner, who was absent.

"Who'd you call besides the nursing supervisor?" I asked.

"Admin on call. I knew Sandy Lowell, everyone did. And I know he died. But telling that woman is way above my pay grade, so I'm waiting for reinforcements."

"Did she say who she was?"

"Yes, although I have a hard time believing it."

"Don't keep me in suspense, man, who is she?"

"She said she was his daughter."

"What? Buck Owens told me he was a bachelor and had no children! Has she lost her mind, Fred?"

"I don't know, Doc, but I'm stayin' out of this one."

CHAPTER 5

A DAUGHTER

I wanted to stay in the lobby and find out what happened, but I thought it best to carry forward with my appointed duties. I went to my office and reviewed the charts for tomorrow's surgeries. I had a virgin hip to replace, a virgin knee to replace, and a redo hip replacement. The latter was the most difficult of the three cases due to the necessity to hammer and grind out the cement in the hip that was used to fix the previous prostheses in place. Some of the newer model hips had non-cemented components, such that one could unscrew the acetabular cup and replace it and remove the femoral stem and replace that as well. This particular patient's prostheses had been cemented in place, so I would do that procedure first. "Best to get the most difficult operation done while you are still fresh" has been my motto over the years.

I went through the mail, signed off on a few charts of discharged patients, dictated a few discharge summaries, and wrote a couple of letters to insurance companies explaining why I needed to operate on my patients and their clients who had severe arthritis of the hip or knee, and who had been paying insurance premiums to their companies for years. Insurance companies in my humble opinion ran the greatest scam on the planet. Their customers pay premiums for years, the company invests and makes money from the premiums, then when it's time to pay out a claim, it's deny, deny, deny. I would hope not every insurance runs their business this way, but there are enough out there who do to get our attention.

With a clean desk comes a clear conscience, so Tip and I wandered back downstairs to the hospital lobby to see what was going on with the alleged daughter of G. Sanford Lowell III. The lobby was empty except for a few visitors and Fred the security guard.

"So what happened, Fred?" I asked.

"Lucy Williams came in to handle the problem. She escorted the two of them back into Dr. Owens's conference room. He just showed up five minutes ago."

"Buck? Must be a big deal if he came in on a Sunday."

"Yep. Big money in that Lowell family, Doc. Sandy has been a big contributor to the hospital over the years, at least that's what I hear through the grapevine. Probably there's going to be lots of scrambling around—a real-life version of *Dialing for Dollars*, if you ask me."

"Funny, Fred. I think you might be right. Well, Tip and I are going home. I need a nap so I can be ready for cocktails and dinner. Thanks for the info," I said, and shook his hand. Fred gave Tip another doggie treat and another head pat, and we went on our merry way.

"So tell me about this girl, the one who claims to be Sandy Lowell's daughter. What was she like?" Mary Louise asked. I had completed my nap successfully, and we were having a glass of chilled Rombauer chardonnay on the deck. Or terrace. Or patio. Mary Louise had explained the difference to me a number of times, but it just never made sense.

"Screechy voice from hell, M.L. It grated on my nerves so badly I couldn't stand it. As curious as I was, I went on up to my office to get some paperwork done to get away from the sounds she made. I mean, really, you wouldn't believe the unpleasantness of it. My impression, which could be wrong, was that she had some sort of mental impairment. When I say she didn't seem to act in an appropriate manner, would that make sense to you?"

"Of course. I'm surprised that Buck didn't call you, since he put you second in command for all things Sandy Lowell."

"Me too. I was glad to get out of there."

About that time, my cell phone started humming to the tune of the Allman Brothers Band's rendition of "It's Not My Cross to Bear." I liked to change the ring tone often. Last month it was "Tennessee Whiskey" sung by Chris Stapleton.

I looked at Mary Louise and mouthed "Buck."

"Hello, oh great leader," I said.

"I need you here, Brady."

"Mary Louise needs me more. It's Sunday afternoon, almost dinner time, and I have three cases to do in the morning, so I need to have a quiet evening and go to bed early."

"Fred told me you were here this afternoon, that you encountered the so-called daughter?"

"Yes. She was hysterical."

"I had to admit her to the hospital and sedate her. I called in one of the psych docs to see her. Could be she's telling the truth about being Sandy's daughter, although I've known him for years, and nothing about his paternity has ever surfaced, to my knowledge. This will require some investigation, Jim Bob."

"I agree, Buck, but you will have to wait until tomorrow or the next day for my help. Sorry," I said, and hung up.

"That won't make him happy," Mary Louise commented.

"True, but I need to set some boundaries with Buck. He needs to know that I'm my own man, that I don't answer to him except in a very professional sense in that I'm an orthopedic surgeon employed by the hospital of which he is chair of the board. That does not give Buck the right to dictate to me what my actions are to be on a daily basis. He's the sort of megalomaniac that will take over your life if you let him."

"He's one of your best friends, Jim Bob."

"True again, but I still have to set boundaries. Don't forget, Mary Louise, that we are now independently wealthy. I'm working here for enjoyment, and for the opportunity to continue to help folks, to give back what I've been given. We don't need the money I'm making, so I don't have to take anyone's shit for any reason, and that includes Buck. I'm happy to help him out with this Sandy Lowell business, but while no one likes a good mystery to solve any more than I do, I have to stand firm."

Mary Louise stared at me for a moment, then smiled and said, "Wow. That little speech of yours just turned me on, young man." With that, she stood and walked toward our bedroom. At the door, she turned to me and asked, "Coming?"

The cases Monday morning went smoothly. The longest and most difficult, as expected, was the redo hip replacement, which I performed first. I was done in the operating room by 2 p.m. I stopped by the waiting room and checked in with the patients' families, then headed over to my office.

One of the smart things that Buck Owens and the board of HCMC had done was to begin hiring nurse practitioners to work in the O.R. as surgical assistants. When I started doing cases here last year, and you had a procedure that required an assistant, you had to arrange for another surgeon to assist you. While it was nice to have an able surgeon to assist, it was sort of a waste of time of the surgeon's talents to hold retractors when they could be doing their own procedures. These new nurse practitioners were being used all over the state as "near physicians," working in underserved areas and acting in the capacity of a physician. This was not unlike a member of the secular clergy who functions as a priest in an underserved area.

The nurse practitioner who had assisted me this morning was delightful, well-trained, and quite capable. Her name was Charlotte Stone. She grew up in Ft. Worth, graduated with a nursing degree from TCU, and had completed her two-year nurse practitioner certification at Texas A&M in College Station. Her husband was in veterinary school at A&M and had two more years to complete his training. They were doing marriage by commute. She was a find, and I hoped he might consider setting up shop in our part of the Hill Country so that, selfishly, I wouldn't lose her as an assistant.

Shelly Wood was at her desk outside my office, talking on the phone, and she waved as I entered the area. My desk was surprisingly clean, probably because of my trip yesterday. I made a couple of calls to patients with questions, signed a few dictations, put my size-12 boots on my desk, and leaned back in my office chair and reflected on a good day.

Shelly knocked on the open door and said I had several insistent calls from Dr. Buck Owens, who wanted to speak to me as soon as I arrived.

"How will he know when I'm here, Shelly?"

"I am to call him when I see the whites of your eyes, I believe he put it."

"Do you see me yet, Shelly?"

"No, sir, I do not."

"Great. Give me ten minutes, please."

She shut the door, and I closed my eyes and thanked the good lord for Mary Louise, who had suggested—maybe insisted—that this job at this point in time of my life was ideal for me and my state of mind. She had been right, as always. I actually dozed for a moment, dreaming I had a hole-in-one during the opening round of the upcoming member–guest golf tournament at Horseshoe Bay Golf Club. What was clapping in my dream turned out to be someone slapping on my office door, which was my impatient friend Dr. Buck Owens.

"I told your girl to tell you to call me the moment you arrived. She apparently did not do as instructed."

"First of all, she's not my 'girl.' She is a highly qualified nurse practitioner, with whom you had dinner Friday night at our house, and who followed my instructions perfectly, which were to give me ten minutes with my boots on my desk before I had to deal with you."

"I don't think you appreciate the gravity of the situation, Brady. Millions of dollars are at stake here, and we have to ensure that Hill Country Medical Center is still going to receive its fair share of the Lowell estate."

"Isn't that already decided, Buck? I mean, there is a will some-where, and maybe a codicil, and the hospital is either in or out. It's been determined by Sandy Lowell, at some previous point in time. There really is no urgency that I can see."

"Brady, there are things you don't know about. So please, as a favor to me, come down to the conference room next to my office. I called an emergency board meeting. You'll be enlightened."

I followed Buck down to the first floor of the hospital side of the complex, where the opulent conference room was located. The cabinets were dark wood, with a matching table surrounded by well-padded chairs with purple fabric. We found several folks sitting around the conference table. There was Bill Porter, CEO of HCMC; Dr. Jackson Morse, chief of surgery; Dr. Dan Burns, chief of anesthesia; Lynn Abbott, head of HR; Del Anderson, publisher of the local paper, the *Highlander*; Madeline O'Rourke, former nun but still referred to as "Sister Mads"; Louann Simms, nursing supervisor at HCMC; and my bride, Mary Louise Brady. These, including myself, were the majority of the board members of HCMC and they, along with Buck Owens, the chair of the board, were in charge of making decisions in the HCMC's best interests. Mary Louise winked at me as I entered. That always put my heart in a brief palpitation mode.

There was a man at the table I didn't know. He was dressed in a fine suit and had manicured nails and perfectly groomed silver hair. I could spot a lawyer a mile away.

"This is our chief counsel, Darrell Bledsoe. I believe you all know him, except Dr. Jim Bob Brady and Mary Louise Brady. Darrell is part of a large firm in Austin, Bledsoe, Boone, and Barbour. They do insurance defense work primarily and provide in-house counsel to hospitals, schools, and governmental agencies. Some of your attorneys even serve on hospital boards, isn't that right, Darrell?"

"That's right, Buck. We're the lawyers in the white hats."

Lawyer Bledsoe and I shook hands. "Pleased to meet you. I've heard some good things about you, Doctor. I understand that if my hip or knee needs to be replaced, you're the man."

"Well, I appreciate that, Counselor. On the other hand, I hope I don't need your services anytime soon."

"Amen to that, Doctor, amen to that."

He spoke in a deep baritone voice, with perfect diction in spite of what sounded to me like an upbringing in Texas or Oklahoma. I felt there had been a little seasoning with a Harvard Law influence to achieve that effect on his speech.

"Why don't you bring us up to speed, Buck, and then I'll put my two cents in," said Lawyer Bledsoe.

"All right then. The issue today is the passing of our major benefactor, G. Sanford 'Sandy' Lowell III, and the woman admitted upstairs who claims to be his daughter. Sandy died on Friday, victim of a massive cardiac arrest and concomitant stroke due to an uncorrectable ventricular tachycardia. It just so happened that Jim Bob Brady was in the parking lot at HEB when this occurred. He initiated CPR seconds after the event, and continued until the EMTs arrived on the scene, estimated to be only ten minutes. They defibrillated Sandy, got him back into sinus rhythm, got an IV line in, intubated him, and had him here in the E.R. not more than ten minutes later. Unfortunately, his heart slipped back into V-tach, and repeated defibrillations were unsuccessful. As his blood pressure collapsed, he had a heart attack and a stroke simultaneously, and then flat-lined in spite of our efforts.

"Dr. Jerry Reed performed the autopsy on Saturday, and Dr. Brady was in attendance by phone for part of that. According to my records, and correct me if I'm wrong, Jim Bob, his internal organs were intact. His coronary arteries and cardiac valves were clean. He had no evidence of a pulmonary embolism, or blood clots in his legs that would initiate some sort of embolic pathology. His liver, kidneys, and pancreas were pristine. He obviously had pathological damage to his heart and brain due to lack of blood flow, which in turn was due to the persistent ventricular tachycardia. And the only abnormal lab value was a highly elevated potassium, which could be a result of the cardiac failure, or which was present prior to these events and was the source of the arrhythmia, which in turned caused the cardiac failure. Dr. Reed said he couldn't make a decision based solely on the autopsy findings. He did say, however, that based on Sandy's medical records, and his medication records, he had no health issues that would predispose him to develop an elevated potassium level. And that if he had to make an educated guess, he would say that the initiating factor for these events was an arrhythmia of undetermined etiology. We see these things in young athletes on occasion, and in folks with a history of heart disease and hypertension, but this was not the case with Sandy Lowell.

"In summary, we have a perfectly healthy man who develops a fatal arrhythmia for no apparent reason and dies. Any questions?"

There were none.

"All right, then, I'd like to discuss some financial issues with the hospital.

"It costs about $2,200 per day per bed to run the hospital. That's $132,000 per day based on sixty beds, which translates to a little over $48 million per year. That's a staggering amount of money. As you all know, revenues are declining because reimbursement from private insurers and governmental programs such as Medicare and Medicaid are declining. Last year we had a profit margin of 3.4 percent, based on $46,000,000 of revenue and $1,564,000 of profit. This year it's going to be 2.7 percent, based on $48,000,000 of revenue and $1,296,000 of profit. Our revenue comes primarily from patient care such as hospital admissions, surgical procedures, MRI and CT scan studies, laboratory testing, etc. We have ever-expanding employee costs and are constantly battling the insurers for reimbursement of the costs of taking care of their clients. As a result, we have little or no margins for capital costs such as new equipment and improvements to the facility.

"So, where does the money come from for extras after we have provided patient care with that small of a profit margin? People

like Sandy Lowell, who donate money for those costs of improv-
ing medical care to our patients that we cannot afford based solely
on patient-oriented revenues, that's who. And if any of you are
wondering why we're so involved in finding out the terms of his
will, it's because without his and other patrons' donations, our
needed medical center would not stay in business.

"Darrell?"

"I'll be meeting with Sandy Lowell's personal attorney tomorrow, and hopefully I'll have news for you all then. I've explained to
Buck that once I have numbers in hand, we'll need to call another
meeting of all the board members and have another discussion."

CHAPTER 6

DR. BILLY STEVENS

Buck pulled me aside after the meeting.

"I need you to get working on Sandy Lowell's background. Maybe get that son of yours involved."

Our son J.J., with his long-time friend and former college roommate Brad Broussard, ran a company known as B&B Investigations. I always referred to their firm as a detective agency, but J.J. constantly reassured me that he was no Sam Spade, a fictional character and private detective created by Dashiell Hammett for his book *The Maltese Falcon*. J.J.'s business was so much more than the stereotypical "private eye" business as depicted on television and in movies. His clients included attorneys, police departments, and governmental agencies involved in cybercrime investigations. He never mentioned any of his clients by name and alluded to them only in generalities.

"I'll give him a call this afternoon, Buck," I said. "Also, think I'll call Sandy's family doc, maybe stop by his office, see if he can enlighten us on Sandy Lowell. I'm a little surprised at you, though. You told me you have known the family for years, even his father and maybe the grandfather? You're acting as though you were a stranger to Sandy. What's that about?"

"Jim Bob, Sandy and I were at the University of Texas in Austin at about the same time. I graduated in 1969, and he was a year later or earlier, I can't remember. I had to work my way through school. Sandy was a BMOC. Big man on campus. Rich boy, good looking, drove a convertible Corvette. He was the darling of the UT campus back then. We came in contact through a bulletin board at the frat house. We were both SAEs. I was advertising myself as a math tutor. I was a geology major with a secondary in pre-med studies, but there wasn't much market for tutors in geology. Identifying rock formations was mostly a memory skill. But math, that was a whole different thing. Sandy was trying to major in petroleum engineering at the insistence of his family, but he wasn't a good student. No study habits. And too much opportunity to party. He was failing calculus, not a subject you could afford to fail as an engineering major.

"So I got him through a couple of semesters of calculus, and he passed. Then I helped him with chemistry and physics, courses I needed for my pre-med studies. At the time, I wasn't sure what I wanted to do with my life. Geology and drilling for oil always intrigued me, but going to medical school assured you of a steady job and a good living. Sandy graduated on time with his petroleum engineering degree and was grateful. He was always giving me extra money, inviting me to parties where most of the kids in attendance were wealthy like Sandy. I never felt comfortable around his friends, and he could never understand why.

"We lost track for ten years, while I went to medical school, then internship and residency, then my military service required by the Berry Plan, which paid my way through school. I eventually set up shop in Austin as an internal medicine physician. Sandy was one of my first patients and sent all his friends to see me, which is why I was successful so quickly. I had a huge practice, but after ten or fifteen years, I just got burned out, not unlike someone else I know," he said, and looked hard at me for a moment.

"Sandy got me involved in the oil business, and as you know, we drilled some very productive wells in the Permian Basin, and I became a wealthy man. And ultimately, when I decided to undertake this project of building the Hill Country Medical Center, he was my major contributor. I owe an enormous debt of gratitude to Sandy Lowell."

"I understand, but you've known him so long, and have had so many business dealings with him, I would think you would be one of his best friends."

"You've obviously never had a really rich acquaintance who had done major favors to improve your life, have you?"

"Can't say that I have, Buck. I did have a patient whose generosity changed my life, but we weren't friends, though we had a memorable doctor–patient relationship."

"Well, it's like this. Sandy grew up in a different world, a world that I could never really be a part of. No matter how many parties he took me to, or how many patients he sent me, or how many oil wells he helped me drill, I could never really be a part of that world of the ultra-rich-from-birth. Those folks are a different breed of cat. You know it, and they know it, and it has always been that way and always will be that way. Which is why, even after all these years, I am not intimate with Sandy's personal life, and to some extent, I was always arms-length detached from him as a friend. And that's why you have to take this, shall we say, "evaluation" over, find out what you can about Sandy Lowell's life and his so-called daughter. I can't in any way, shape, form, or fashion be seen as ungrateful for what Sandy did for me."

"But Buck, he's not a criminal. He's just a guy that suddenly died from an arrhythmia, who may or may not have left a bundle of money to your hospital."

"True, but you know how these investigations go, since you've been involved in plenty of them. Something unsavory always turns up in the underbelly of these situations, and I can't be seen as the one turning over the rocks."

I hadn't been able to speak to Mary Louise after the meeting, since Buck had pulled me aside for his talk. He probably knew something unsavory about Sandy Lowell but wanted me to "discover" it.

"Hey, sorry I didn't get to visit with you after the board meeting. Buck grabbed me."

"I saw. You okay?" Mary Louise asked.

"Sure, another day in paradise."

"How did your cases go?"

"Excellent. I feel young again, enjoying the patients and the work."

"Are you coming home, or are you on 'Buck duty'?"

"Turns out I'm his lead investigator on all things Sandy Lowell."

"What do you want to do about dinner?"

"I'm going to call Sandy's primary doc, Billy Stevens, see if I can stop by and visit with him. He has an office in Marble Falls. Why don't we meet at River City Grille? I'm in the mood for a chicken-fried steak."

"I don't think your coronary arteries are in the mood for the cream gravy onslaught, do you?"

"I've done some research, Mary Louise, and the steak and gravy will only shorten my life by ten minutes."

"Provided you don't have a coronary during dinner. How about the country-fried chicken, no gravy and no batter?"

"What's that called? Grilled chicken? That's no fun."

"Perfect."

I called J.J. from the car. He and Brad had begun their business in Houston. Brad now ran that office, and J.J. ran a new office in Dallas. His wife, the former Kathryn Hicks, was from Dallas, had attended the business school at SMU, and had followed her father's footsteps into the banking business. Mr. Hicks's many connections influenced J.J. to open a branch of B&B Investigations there. J.J.'s administrative assistant, formerly termed a secretary, said he was on a plane, but she could patch me through via satellite phone.

"Hey, Pop. Is this a social call?"

"Of course. How are you? And are you flying private? Most commercial flights don't have satellite phone access for the weary airline traveler."

"I chartered a Gulfstream jet for my trip to Kansas City. I have to be back in Dallas for a meeting and needed to be able to make this trip in one day. Incredible aircraft."

"How many people on the plane?"

"Pilot, co-pilot, me, and our chief financial officer."

"You could have taken a Citation Jet at a much lower cost."

"Our CFO here arranged to use the Gulfstream at a nominal increased cost. We've been using a charter service out of Dallas, and the marketing director wants our business. The Gulfstream line from the 280 to the 650 holds anywhere from ten to eighteen passengers, so we would have a selection of aircraft to choose from. What's the reason for your phone call?"

"You always think I want something, and I don't usually, but this time I do."

"Pops, you always want something. What can I do for you?"

"George Sanford Lowell III. He died this past week. I need whatever you can find about him."

"Is that the Sandy Lowell playboy-guy?"

"I guess."

"He's been written about by most every national magazine in the country. He's dated some incredible women—movie stars, heiresses, Saudi princesses, you name it. I would think his life is an open book."

"No one's life is a totally open book, J.J. A so-called daughter turned up here at the hospital after he passed. Allegedly he was never married and did not father any children. I've been tasked with the job of finding out if he might have a child, and if so, what the child's origins were. Plus anything possibly unsavory that his friends here might want to keep under the radar. Think you can handle that for me, pal?"

"You know me, Dad. My company specializes in learning the unknowable and discovering the undetectable. Paying job?"

"Yes, sir."

"Atta boy, Pop. See you soon."

Dr. William "Billy" Stevens had an office overlooking Lake Marble Falls, a reservoir on the Colorado River formed by the construction of the Max Starcke Dam. His building was only a block from River City Grille. When I called and spoke to his nurse, she said he could see me in an hour, so I stopped on the way, filled the Tahoe with gas, and detoured through the busy little town of Marble Falls. I drove up Highway 281, stopped in at Sewell Motors, and looked at the new Lincoln Navigator. There was plenty of storage room in the rear, in front of which were two captain's chairs that rotated. I had never owned a Ford. I was a Chevy Man now, having been an ancient Mercedes Man for years. The salesman offered to let me test drive the giant SUV, but I declined for lack of time. My SUV was only a few years old, new compared to the Mercedes I drove for over twenty years.

It would be difficult for me to get any work done in Billy Stevens's office. The waiting room had a wall of windows facing Lake Marble Falls, whose water was a clear blue today. I noted a few boaters, Jet Skiers, and water-skiers, who were either off on Monday or playing hooky from school or work. There were only a couple of patients in the Stevens waiting room, but it was after 4 p.m., so that wasn't unusual. The receptionist was young, with light-brown skin and a head full of stylish braids. Her teeth were so white, she must have spent a lot of time in the cosmetic dentist's office. The young lady's name tag read Maureen.

"Afternoon, Maureen, I'm Dr. Jim Brady. I have an appointment with Dr. Stevens."

"Hello. Have you been a patient here before?"

"No, I'm not a patient. I'm here to see him about another patient."

"Do we have the patient's HIPPA privacy law waiver on file?"

"No, but whoever I spoke to earlier didn't seem to have a problem with my making an appointment to talk to your boss."

"That would be Abigail. I was probably on break. She doesn't quite know the rules."

"Maybe you can just check with the doctor." I realized I was in scrubs, fortunately clean ones after my earlier surgeries. And I had on boots, so I presented the prototype picture of a Texas surgeon. Who wouldn't trust me?

Maureen uttered a frustrated sigh, stood, and went through a side door that led to the inner sanctum of Stevens's office. She returned momentarily and pointed me around her desk, where I went through another door into large room with a series of cubicle offices. There was a fellow in a white lab coat waving me toward the back of the room. I counted six women working in the space. That would be seven employees at least. Expensive, I thought.

Billy Stevens was taller than me by a few inches, and thinner. He also had on scrubs, a popular work outfit among Texas doctors. Of course, it could be a universal phenomenon, but I was unknowledgeable of the current medical dress code of doctors in locations beyond Texas.

"Howdy," he said, and extended a fist to bump. "Got a cold, and the old fist bump is a pretty safe way of greeting. Have a seat. You go by Jim?"

"Jim Bob, actually, but Jim is fine. Nice setup you have here."

We walked into his office, which had a large wall of glass, also looking right down on Lake Marble Falls. There were two large etageres in the office, both filled with all sorts of Texas memorabilia. There were boots, cowboy hats, longhorn steers, bulls, cowboys, horses, even a wild turkey in flight, all sculptures in various combinations of wood and metal.

"Thanks. I love it here. I grew up in Austin, went to UT, then UTMB in Galveston for med school and residency. Been out here ever since."

"You seem to have a large office staff. You do internal medicine, right?"

"Yep. It takes a lot of staff to take care of internal medicine patients. People need lab work every time they come in, plus EKGs, chest X-rays, Doppler venous studies, the works. Takes a lot of staff to do all that."

"How did you manage to get a permit to do all that testing in your office? Most of that sort of testing has to be done at the hospital or some central location, doesn't it?"

"Well, when I first came here twenty-some years ago, there was no hospital facility. The closest was Austin. So I applied for a permit to perform all those tests in my office. Think of the runaround patients have to do these days to get those tests run. I make it easier for them. One-stop shopping. I have a Medicare certification to perform those tests, so the private insurance companies can't do much about it. I was legacied in to perform in-office testing, but you couldn't get that sort of permit these days. No sir. Let's make those patients travel to three or four different locations every week or two to get their testing done. Crazy system. What's your story?"

"Baylor undergrad, Baylor med school and residency, hip and knee fellowship in New York, then back to Houston for twenty-five years. I've only been out here a year. Sort of a retirement job for me. I'm working four days a week and enjoying the hell out of myself. I didn't realize what a rat race I was in until I took a three-month sabbatical. Buck Owens recruited me, which, by the way, is why I'm here."

"Yeah, he called me about Sandy."

"Good, so I don't have to explain myself."

He laughed. "I've known—knew, I guess now—Sandy for years. He's a little older than me, around my brother's age. They were SAEs at UT. I was a legacy pledge. Seems to me Sandy came to see me when I first opened up shop. He was my patient until he died."

"The pathologist couldn't find any physical evidence of cardiac, or lung, or any internal organ pathology, at least on the autopsy. Was he really that healthy?"

"He was a physical specimen. Worked out all the time, ran, did not consume much alcohol, no smoking, not even a cigar after dinner with a brandy. I heard a doctor found him in his car and tried CPR. Was that you?"

"Yes. I was admiring his Rolls and had a brief conversation with him, next thing I know he's crashing into a giant pickup truck behind me. The EMTs were there in ten minutes, found him in V-tach, shocked him and got him into sinus rhythm, but they lost him at the hospital. His blood pressure couldn't be sustained, and he had a massive myocardial infarction and a stroke at the same time. By then he was history."

"Wow, that's the last method of dying I would ever have guessed for Sandy Lowell. More likely he would die of some sort of terminal STD in my opinion," he said, and laughed.

"A player?" I asked.

"A cocksman of the highest degree. He didn't play tennis and he gave up golf when he couldn't maintain his former low handicap. He worked out and chased pussy his entire life. He came in every month to see me for his prescription of the little blue pill. He spent an enormous amount of money courting women. Large, small, skinny, fat, young, old, it didn't matter to Sandy. It was like a game of conquest, or a sport of some sort to him. Don't get me wrong, he was a great guy, and the women he slept with, they seemed to know they were in it for the short haul. I couldn't handle that. Maybe in my younger days . . . maybe, but not to the extent Sandy experienced."

"Did Buck tell you there was a woman admitted to the hospital claiming to be his daughter"?

"He did. And in my opinion that is entirely possible. I mean, he talked to me a lot about his sexual escapades. Not that I'm some sort of voyeur, but when he was on the schedule, he used the time to discuss his . . . activities. He always used a condom, he said; never once—what did he call it? Never once did he ride bareback."

"Did he ever talk to you about a last will and testament?"

"No, nothing but sex, sex, sex. He always came in late in the afternoon, and he would get me so worked up I'd make a beeline to the house and hope my wife was in a willing mood. I never told her what was prompting those feelings, but she started calling me her Wednesday man. That was because Sandy always came in on the last Wednesday of the month around 4 p.m. I hope you can see fit to keep that between us docs. I don't know if the HIPPA laws about a patient's privacy continue after death, but I do not want to have to deal with any more government entities."

"My lips are sealed, Billy. Any suspicions about who the mother of a daughter might be?"

"Anyone walking planet earth, my friend."

CHAPTER 7

JENNIFER LOWELL

Mary Louise and I sat at an outside table at River City Grille. It was a nice evening, warm but not humid. The water in Lake Marble Falls was still a clear shade of blue, and we were mesmerized by the early evening boat traffic. There were a couple of ski boats with skiers attached, but also a couple of small catamarans and a few pontoon boats. When I was younger, I was all about speed. Now, the pontoon boat was more my style. Cruising around the lake with a drink in hand at 20 mph was just a fine way to begin or end an evening.

"Did you learn anything today?" Mary Louise asked. She was dressed in white capri pants with low-heeled sandals and a white linen shirt with the sleeves rolled up to just above her wrists. Her hair was done up off her neck in a complicated arrangement, probably held together by hidden pins and tiny elastic bands. She looked ready to embark upon a sailing vessel with a crew of eight. Instead, she was sitting with me on a faded deck watching me eat a piece of chicken fried chicken with cream gravy. We had compromised; I had a double portion of vegetables, and not their tasty french fries.

"Yes. Too much information from Dr. Billy Stevens. Seems that our deceased Sandy Lowell was a sex addict, at least according to Billy." I rarely felt that keeping something "between us docs" meant I couldn't share with Mary Louise. "It was like a sport for him. He said he thought it was more likely for Sandy to die from a complication of a sexually transmitted disease than any other medical problem."

"Was he serious?"

"He sounded serious. He said Sandy was in great physical shape and had nothing wrong with him medically. But he didn't seem surprised to hear that a potential daughter has surfaced."

"Have they done a DNA test on the woman? That would solve that question immediately."

"I don't know. I went to see Stevens right after the board meeting, so I haven't heard anything. I wonder if there is any legal issue with testing for paternity after someone has died?"

"I have no idea. Who would be in charge of making that decision?"

"In the absence of next of kin, I guess an attorney."

"But the woman claiming to be the daughter may be the next of kin, but only a paternity test will decide that. I don't know how long the body DNA is good after death to even allow a paternity test."

"I could ask Dr. Jerry Reed, who did the autopsy. I'll bet he knows. Maybe I'll call him on the way home."

We finished our meal as the sun set. By then I was tired. It had been a long day. Once home, I had just enough energy to take Tip for a brief walk, then showered and crashed into the bed. I forgot all about DNA testing and Jerry Reed. I remembered the sex talk in Billy Stevens's office, and for a brief moment had stirrings that in my younger days could not have been stifled. That was no longer the case, as I rolled onto my left side and very quickly fell fast asleep, the idea of being a stud muffin only the stuff of dreams.

I was up, showered, and dressed by 5:30 a.m. Tip was sleeping at the foot of our bed, and as I walked by, he opened one eye, then quickly closed it, his signal that he would wait for the rising of the queen of the household. Atta boy.

On morning rounds, the three post-ops from Monday were doing well. No fevers, no excess drainage from their respective wounds, and all happy with the function of the morphine pump. Better living though chemistry is my mantra for post-op patients.

I worked through lunch in the office and triaged patients into three groups. The first group were those that had arthritis of the hip or knee who were getting by on medication and wondering if it was damaging their particular joint problem even further by delaying surgery. "No" was the answer to that question, and "see me when the meds no longer work" was the recommendation. The second group comprised those for whom the medication was no longer effective but who could still function in a more-or-less-normal fashion. The answer was "wait until you are ready." The third group were those begging for relief of symptoms, who were then scheduled for surgery. I had always approached joint replacement in that fashion. If a joint is hurting badly prior to an operation, then the pain and suffering you have to go through to get relief from it was worth it.

After seeing patients, Shelly and I returned to my office and I completed my dictation and answered a couple of phone calls.

"Shelly, would you call down to pathology and see if Dr. Jerry Reed is in? Also, would you find out where the powers-that-be are housing the supposed daughter of Sandy Lowell, please?"

"Yes, sir. Give me a moment."

I had told Shelly a number of times that she didn't have to call me "sir," that we were both employed at HCMC, and we were social friends, and that Jim or Jim Bob would suffice. She said her problem with that was she always wanted to show me respect in front of the patients and was afraid that she would slip into casual mode at just the wrong time. In her experience, nothing good ever came from a patient hearing a nurse called her doctor-employer by his first name. That faux pas conjured up all sorts of negative vibrations on the part of the patient. So, "Thank you, sir, but no thank you" was her response.

"Dr. Reed is in the morgue doing an autopsy. He said feel free to drop by but suggested you use two masks. The specimen he's working on is particularly odorous, something about an intestinal rupture."

"I get the picture. And the woman?"

"Third floor, hospital side, northwest suite."

"Thanks much, Shelly. See you tomorrow."

"Yes, sir," she said.

Jerry was right about the smell. It was unbelievably bad. Fortunately he had already removed the large and small intestine and the other internal organs by the time I arrived. But the pungent scent of internal corruption due to a bowel rupture lingered in the air.

"Brady, what's that line that Robert Duval has in *Apocalypse Now?* 'I love the smell of napalm in the morning.' Well, I can say that I love the smell of—"

"Jerry, you don't need to finish it. I get the point. I don't know how you can stand the smell, day after day."

"It's like anything else. You get used to it. My olfactory nerves have probably atrophied. I can't smell a thing anymore. Did you want something specific or were you just missing me?"

"I wanted to ask you about post-mortem DNA testing."

"Is this about the woman upstairs claiming to be Sandy Lowell's daughter?"

"Is there anything that can be kept a secret around here?"

"Nope. Hospitals are like little Peyton Places. The juicy items get spread around fast."

"Can you talk and work at the same time?"

"Of course, I'm a pathologist, the unsung hero of the medical profession. We eventually figure out everything down here. We determine how and why people succumb to their disease. We discover why some surgical procedures didn't work. The buck stops here, Brady. We're the last train station on the patient's way home."

"Man, you are on a soapbox today, friend. I hate to rush you when you're so full of wisdom and in the mood to share it, but DNA testing post-mortem?"

"All right, all right. You can get DNA from a dead body, but it can be difficult. You would need bone—femur or humerus, ideally—or teeth if the body has been buried, provided one has legal authority to exhume the body. If the body has been cremated, the ashes are useless because DNA is destroyed in the burning process. Occasionally you might find a bone or tooth residue after cremation, but it's not reliable. It's interesting to note that recent studies have shown that the half-life of DNA—the point at which half the bonds in a DNA molecule would be broken—is 521 years. Which means that under ideal conditions, all the bonds would not be broken for 6.8 million years. Remember in *Jurassic Park*, the DNA fossilized in amber? They built dinosaurs from that ancient DNA. Of course, that was a novel, then a movie, but still, the possibility exists."

"So, Jerry, what are you saying exactly?"

"Has the body been disposed of? Cremated or buried?"

"I'm embarrassed to tell you I don't know. There hasn't been a funeral to my knowledge, but then I didn't even know the deceased, so I wouldn't be invited anyway."

"Well, none of that matters, Brady. I got you covered."

"What do you mean?"

"I saved his DNA with hair samples and buccal mucosa smears, just in case."

"You could have told me that from the start, Jerry."

"But our repartee was much more fun."

I sighed. I wasn't sure I was cut out for this investigative business any longer.

"One thing I forgot to ask you when you did the autopsy, which was when? Saturday?"

"Yes."

"Did you notice any scars indicative of Sandy having had plastic surgery? Scars behind the ears, scars in the lower or upper eyelid, anything like that?"

"Let me get my notes." He walked over to a desktop computer, punched some keys and found what he was looking for quickly. "Yes. There were very thin scars behind each ear, with some scarring, as though he had had the procedure done more than once. I couldn't tell about the eyelids. If he had a blepharoplasty in the past, the scars weren't visible. He did have liposuction scars around his abdomen, though, and those looked fairly recent, meaning within the last six to twelve months."

"Okay, thanks much, Jerry. You've been very helpful."

"See you around, Brady. Don't be a stranger."

I decided to make the trek up to see Sandy's self-proclaimed daughter. The third floor of the hospital was the patient floor. It was designed in a large U-shape, with a central nursing station. The architects had designed four corner rooms as large suites, such that a family member could sleep in the adjacent space on a pull-out sofa. The suites had numbers like all the other rooms, but we called them by their location: Northwest, Northeast, Southwest, and Southeast. I knocked before entering; there was a NO VISITORS sign on the door. I didn't see any nursing staff nearby, so I walked on in.

She was in the hospital bed and appeared to be dozing. The lady who had accompanied her on Sunday was sleeping as well, positioned on the sofa bed, but it was not pulled out in sleeping position. The caretaker person was startled by my presence, waking almost immediately once I walked in. I had on the scrubs I wore to the office, so it wasn't as though I just walked in off the street.

"Who are you?" the caretaker said.

"I'm Dr. Jim Brady. We met Sunday when you came to the hospital. In the lobby?"

"Oh, yes. What can I do for you, Doctor?"

"Just a social call. How is she? I'm sorry, I don't know her name, or yours, for that matter."

"I'm sorry, I didn't mean to be rude. I'm Cynthia Stiles. Her name is Jennifer Lowell."

And there 'twas. She had Sandy's name. Where had she been? Did no one know that Sandy Lowell had a daughter?

"Cynthia, I've been entrusted by the powers that be to get some information about Jennifer. No one around here seems to be aware that Sandy had a daughter."

"She's not his daughter, silly. She gets a little confused about that. Jennifer is his sister, actually half-sister. Sandy's father, G. Sanford Lowell II, was married a number of times. Jennifer is the only offspring of his last marriage. Two died when I think Jennifer was five or six years old."

"Two?"

"That's short for Lowell II. I called him Two and Sandy, Three."

"Sounds like you know the family pretty well."

"Let's see, Jennifer is forty-three years old, and I went to work for the family before she was born. When it was determined that Jennifer had mental differences, they paid for my training and hired me full time as a caretaker for her. Her mother was not exactly, how shall I put it, the mothering type?"

"Is her mother still alive?"

"Oh, no. She had a bit of a drinking problem, like Sandy's sister. She died when Jennifer was in her twenties. I've been her caretaker all this time."

"What are Jennifer's mental issues? Do you know?"

"The doctors tested her multiple times over a number of years, but no one could agree on the diagnosis. She very emotionally labile, and her IQ is below 70, so she is considered to be intellectually disabled."

"Was she able to attend school?"

"We tried, but between her more-limited mental capacity and her emotional outbursts, it just wasn't practical. Her mother brought in tutors early on, but it was never successful. Jennifer can't read very well. Mostly she looks at the pictures. We've tried a number of enrichment programs, but none seemed to resonate with her. Her happy place is simply watching her shows on TV, mostly game shows. She loves *Law and Order* and *Blue Bloods*, but I'm not sure she can really follow the plots. I leave the closed captioning on all the time because she is able to read some things, and if it helps her follow what's going on, then all the better for her. She also likes kid shows with music, like *Toy Story* and *Frozen*, movies like that."

"I see. Well, I need to be going. Thanks much for your help. By the way, I assume you get paid for your services, and you have a home somewhere, correct?"

"Oh yes, we're quite well taken care of. Two left money in a trust for her and me. And we have a real nice home here. I just pray to God that I don't pass before she does. I don't know what that child would do."

"How did she find out about the passing of her brother, Sandy?"

"She looks at the pictures in the newspaper. She saw the death notice with his picture and went ballistic. And then his passing was discussed on the local news. Sandy and his father resembled each other, and in her chronically confused state, she somehow thought that Sandy was her father. He's been gone so long I can't imagine she remembers him, but something about Sandy's photo triggered some past memory. I'm really not sure if she distinguishes the difference between father and brother, Dr. Brady. She is locked in a world of her own."

"Why is she still here, in the hospital?"

"I don't rightly know, Doctor. She's been on different medications from the usual since her admission, and I think the doctor that's taking care of her is trying to balance out her meds to a level where she's not so agitated all the time. That would be a blessing, to have her mellowed a bit. She's a handful."

"Do you remember the doctor's name, the one that's taking care of her medications?"

"It's a funny name . . . I think it's like Dr. Begoins, or something like that?"

"It wouldn't be Dr. Buck Owens, would it?"

"Yes! That's it."

CHAPTER 8

WINDFALL

"You have some explaining to do, Buck. You've got that woman Jennifer Lowell sequestered up in the Northwest suite, fiddling with her medications like you're a psychiatrist. You knew all along who she was, didn't you?"

"Yes, Brady, and I'm sorry for that. I'm trying to protect the family best I can."

"What's there to protect? They are all dead except for Jennifer, who couldn't begin to understand what that means."

"I'm trying to preserve a reputation, and the family name."

"Buck, every family has skeletons in their respective closets. Jennifer is the half-sister to Sandy Lowell, the daughter of his father's union with his last wife."

"That wife was unsavory, no doubt about it. I'm trying to protect the reputations of all concerned."

"Well, that's all going to go out the window because my son J.J. is involved, at your request, and as you know, he will leave no stone unturned. You should have left him out of the picture. He's like a dog with a bone when it comes to an investigation. Any chance you had of handling this privately and without fanfare is history."

"Any chance you can un-hire him?"

"Not on your life, friend. I can't wait to see how all this turns out. Oh, what a tangled web we weave . . ."

I was glad to get home to the wonderful and vivacious Mary Louise. Tip greeted me as though I had been on a safari for a month. My bride met me at the doorway with an iced-over Tito's dirty martini, a welcome refreshment after a long day.

"How was clinic today?" she asked, as we sat on our terrace and sipped.

"Clinic was fine. I missed lunch and worked straight through so I could do some of Buck Owens's bidding."

"And what was that today?"

"I talked to Jerry Reed about DNA testing, in order to determine if the woman in the hospital—her name is Jennifer Lowell, by the way—is really the daughter of Sandy Lowell. But that's a moot point, because I went to visit Jennifer Lowell and got the scoop from her caretaker, a woman by the name of Cynthia Stiles. Turn out she's not Sandy's daughter; she is his half-sister from a late-in-life marriage of his father's."

"Why isn't Buck handling this? Didn't he allege he has been close to the family for years?"

"I don't know. He even had me get J.J. involved in getting background information on Sandy and the Lowell family. That doesn't make much sense if he's known all along that Jennifer was a sister, not a daughter."

"Buck has something in mind; he's just not sharing it with you. But he does have you running in circles. You're supposed to be enjoying your life, slowing down your schedule, playing golf on Friday and Saturday, and playing with me on Sunday. You're getting yourself all involved in an investigation that really has nothing directly to do with you, other than your being a member of the board. You were just an innocent bystander when Sandy had his medical problem in the parking lot of HEB. You're not a family friend, just a guy who applied CPR in a stranger's time of need. Too bad you just can't leave it behind and tell Buck to find another gopher, or better yet, let him take care of the problem himself."

"You're right, of course, as always. Once my curiosity gets piqued, I have a hard time backing off. You know I've always had a knack for figuring out mysteries, and I really enjoy that. It's just that this pesky day job gets in the way. But I love that work as well. If there were only twenty-eight hours in the day. That would be perfect."

I opened a chilled bottle of Newton unfiltered chardonnay, and we enjoyed fresh crab Louie salads at an outdoor table by the firepit. A beautiful meal on a beautiful Hill Country evening with a beautiful woman. Who could ask for more?

Wednesday and Thursday of that week were a blur. I had to add on a fractured hip to the Wednesday schedule, which meant four cases that day. That took me until 5 p.m. or so. Clinic on Thursday was heavy, so we broke for lunch to keep up our strength and didn't finish up with the last patient until after 4 p.m. By the time I made post-op rounds, dictated my charts, and cleaned off my desk, it was nearly 6 p.m.

"You have one more call to return," said Shelly Wood.

"I don't think I can do it."

"You have to. It's Dr. Owens."

"Now I KNOW I can't do it."

"It will only take a minute. I have him on line 2 in your office."

I sighed deeply. "Hello, Buck."

"Long day?"

"Yes, and you're making it longer."

"I'm meeting with Sandy Lowell's attorney tomorrow, along with Darrell Bledsoe. I'd like you to attend. There will be news of Sandy's last will and testament, and a discussion of plans for a memorial service for Sandy."

"It's about time. The body has been here in the freezer for what, seven days?"

"Yes, but there have been . . . issues."

"You know, Buck, you could just call me tomorrow after my standing golf game and let me know what happened at the meeting. I don't really have to be there."

"I thought you'd be interested. We're meeting here at 8:30 in the morning. I already checked, and your tee time isn't until noon. You'll have plenty of time. Aren't you curious in the least?"

"Of course I am. I'm just worn out. You're not carrying a full load of patients and surgery like I am."

"But I'm running a large medical center with a bunch of employees, and if that's not work, nothing is. See you in the morning."

Mary Louise and I met at Julie's Cocina in Cottonwood Shores. I was starved for Mexican food, and Julie's crispy beef tacos and chicken enchiladas with tomatillo sauce fit the bill. Mary Louise had cheese enchiladas with a chicken tostada. We washed our food down with Modelo Especial beer. I almost fell asleep on the drive home, even though it was no more than fifteen minutes to Granite Falls. I took Tip out for his nightly constitutional, then took a hot shower and slipped on a pair of boxer shorts. When I opened the door to the master, the bedroom was unusually dark, and I smelled the scent of flame and fragrant candles. Once my eyes adjusted, I noted several lit candles scattered about, and my wife laying on her side on the bed, propped up on one elbow. She had not a stitch of clothing on except for a sombrero. She greeted me with "Olé."

I was moving a little slow the next morning, but since Shelly Wood was making rounds for me as per usual for a Friday, and all I had scheduled was the meeting with Buck and the lawyers, followed by golf, I relished my time off and reflected on the evening past.

"Morning," said Mary Louise, as she exited the house and joined me on the terrace.

"Morning yourself," I responded. "Feeling all right?"

"Splendid. I feel refreshed like a wildflower after a spring rain."

"Wow. You're waxing eloquently for this time of the morning."

"Yes. Yes I am."

We sat in a comfortable silence for a bit, then together made a breakfast of scrambled eggs with fresh peppers, chiles, and pepper Jack cheese, plus thick-cut bacon and crispy hash browns.

Mary Louise returned to bed after breakfast. I showered, shaved, and dressed for golf. If Buck and the lawyers didn't like me in sporting attire, that was their problem, not mine.

There was a back entry to Buck's office and conference room, which allowed me to bypass the lobby and any patients or patients' families that happened to be there. In my experience, patients didn't like to see their doctors parading around the hospital in golf shoes while they were recovering and bedbound.

I greeted Lucy Williams, Buck's administrative assistant, who sat outside his office and conference room like a security guard at a government building. No one got past her that wasn't supposed to. She smiled at me, stood, and gave me a hug.

"What's that for, Lucy?"

"Just for you being you, Doc Brady. You're a good man. They're waiting for you in the conference room. Coffee?"

"Yes, black please, and thank you—for the coffee and the hug."

The three men rose as I entered. It was easy to distinguish the attorneys in the conference room from the doctors. I had on golf shorts, a golf shirt, and athletic shoes. Buck had on a blue blazer, white shirt sans tie, and khakis. Darrell Bledsoe wore a beautiful dark-gray suit with thin pinstripes, a crisply starched white shirt with thin purple stripes in it, and matching tie. The chairs around the table were done with purple cushions, so Darrell actually looked like part of the furniture.

"Jim Bob, meet W. Hamilton Bowles, attorney for the Lowell family."

I briefly pondered why so many successful lawyers have an initial before their name. I extended my hand;, we shook, then sat down. Lawyer Hamilton also had on a fine suit, his in black with wider pinstripes, a plain white shirt, and a solid red power tie, or so I've been told about those red ties.

"Jim, first of all, thanks for attending this meeting of the minds. I spoke to Dr. Jerry Reed this morning. As you know from your meeting with him, he collected Sandy's DNA from hair samples and a buccal mucosal smear. The lab put a rush on the testing, and I have confirmed just a few minutes ago that Jennifer Lowell and Sandy Lowell share DNA in a pattern compatible with both of them having the same father, Sanford Lowell II. Both attorneys present have agreed to stipulate that they are half-brother and half-sister respectively.

"Ham?" Buck said.

"I've reviewed Sandy Lowell's last will and testament. He has been my client ever since I finished University of Texas law school. We were fraternity brothers at UT and had been friends since. I have a son who joined my practice after he completed UT Law, and he worked on some of Sandy's legal issues as well. Sandy did not make provisions for a memorial service. He had no living relatives that he knew about other than Jennifer. His desire was to be cremated with as little fanfare as possible. His will instructs that his assets be sold and distributed as part of his will. Other than the automobiles, his house and its furnishings are about it.

"Sandy had been a golfer in his younger days, but as he aged and his swing changed, he couldn't perform at the same level as he had in the past. He couldn't stand the thought of a former golfer with a handicap of 7 transitioning to a hacker with a handicap of 18, so he quit. He did, however, specify that he wanted his ashes scattered at the Links at Spanish Bay in Pebble Beach, at sunset while a bagpiper plays. He also set aside money to have the bagpiper play "Amazing Grace." That surprised me somewhat, since I never knew Sandy to be a religious man."

"My dad," I replied, "told me that he spent four years in the European Theatre in World War II, mostly building and rebuilding bridges in France and Belgium that were constantly being blown up by the Germans to prevent the Allies' supply lines from delivering food, water, and ammunition to the troops. In all that time, he said, he never met a single atheist in any of the many foxholes he was in."

"So, I guess the point is, Sandy was covering his bases," said lawyer Hamilton.

"Did he specify who was to spread his ashes in Pebble Beach?" asked Buck.

"No, but he provided money for the transport, either by car or private plane."

"What about the Rolls he was driving the day we met?" I asked.

"That was one of five he had. He wanted his cars donated to the Rolls Royce Foundation and museum in Cumberland Valley, Pennsylvania. He provided money for all the cars to be transported in enclosed trucks."

The room was silent for a moment. Then Hamilton Bowles spoke again. "The issue that concerns this institution is whether or not Sandy left money for the Hill Country Medical Center Foundation, which is the arm that handles donations, which in turn allows the procurement of new equipment and upgrades to the hospital and office buildings. That's the sort of money necessary to keep a hospital in business, and current with the times, and competitive.

"According to my records, Sandy Lowell has been a major donor since the HCMC opened. He was one of your 'angel' investors, and his funds helped build the hospital, correct Buck?"

"Yes, that's correct. He and several other longterm friends of mine made all this possible."

"Also, according to my records, Sandy continued to contribute to the hospital on a yearly basis, to the tune of one million dollars."

"That also is correct, Ham. Sandy was very generous."

"With that in mind, in his will, he wanted to ensure that the hospital would have enough funds to keep HCMC a premier medical center in the area, long after he was gone. He updated his will last year, and there have been no changes to the will since then, so I would say, seeing as how all the paperwork is intact, his last will and testament as it applies to this facility is unchanged.

"I'm being fairly informal with divulging this information, since Sandy was a friend of mine and Buck's for near fifty years. Hell, after a couple of drinks, Sandy would talk about his net worth to just about anyone. He didn't mind regaling stories of his failures and successes, didn't mind telling a listener how much money he had lost, and then made back in the oil business. I digress with this information because I wanted you, Dr. Brady and Mr. Bledsoe, to realize that I'm not breaking a confidence with my deceased client. I know the rules and regulations about legal disclosure and all its ramifications, and I'm simply sharing this information in an informal manner because it's how Sandy would have wanted it handled.

"Sandy's estate was revalued last year, when his will was updated, at $400 million. He had no living relatives other than Jennifer. Her longterm care is guaranteed through a trust his father set up for her, so Sandy did not feel obligated to add to that trust, or to start a new trust for her. He had a few favorite charities—Pet Rescue, Child Advocates, First Baptist Church of Austin, Mental Health Research Fund in honor of Jennifer, and the University of Texas Athletics Foundation. He left each entity $50 million. The rest of his estate he left to Hill Country Medical Center in the amount of $150 million."

A quiet silence fell over the room. That was an astounding amount of money. I knew Buck would be thrilled and was probably about to wet his pants. The lawyers had a discussion about receipt of the funds, and legal issues regarding last will and testament distributions, during which I tried desperately to stay awake.

After Darrell Bledsoe and Hamilton Bowles left, I thought Buck was going to break out in song while dancing an Irish jig. He was hopping around the conference room like a young boy at Christmas who just received his first BB gun from Santa Claus.

"Have you no shame, Buck? The man is dead, after all."

"Jim Bob, you have no idea how many sleepless nights I've had since Sandy passed away."

"It was only a week ago."

"I know, but it seems longer. Just to know that our endowment will be secure for generations to come is such a relief. You remember, I built this baby from scratch with the largesse of my friends. This hospital is like my child. I want her to be healthy and provide quality medical services to the people of this part of Texas long after I'm gone. And this bequest of Sandy's will do that. I am so excited!"

He continued hopping around and humming. I worried he might have a stroke or a heart attack, or break something in his foot or ankle. Finally, he slowed down, and sat down, and seemed exhausted.

"I still want to know why he died," I said.

"What? You know why he died. Persistent ventricular tachycardia and all its downstream complications."

"I know that, but WHY did he get V-tach? He was a perfectly healthy man of seventy-two years with no demonstrable cardiac disease either clinically or at autopsy. He was in perfect health, except he wasn't. That is just not normal and doesn't sit well with me."

"Jim Bob, why can't you just leave things well enough alone? We're going to get our needed funding, and I don't want you to do anything that might possibly impact that negatively."

"Buck, finding out why the man died will not affect Sandy's bequest. I didn't even know the man, but I think he deserves to be heard from the grave. That's the least we can do."

"You are a piece of work. Can't you just enjoy our newly found fortune?"

"No, not without finding out what killed Sandy Lowell. And I intend to do just that."

CHAPTER 9

B&B INVESTIGATIONS

I arrived at the golf club just in time to hit three practice balls, each of which I chunked, and I missed four putts. Golf-wise, the day was looking dismal. The good news was that Michael Reardon was in my foursome, so we put our bags on the same cart and headed to the first tee. I wanted to question him, tactfully of course, about the plastic surgeon in Austin that both his wife and Sandy Lowell had used for cosmetic surgery. There were four groups in our game that day, sixteen players, each throwing twenty dollars into the kitty to award the winning teams. We were to be the third group to tee off. While we waited, I broached the subject with Mike.

"The plastic surgeon that Phyllis used in Austin, what was his name again?"

"Warner. Robert Warner. Why do you ask?"

"Our buddy Buck Owens sort of put me in charge of medical issues involving Sandy Lowell, so I'm just following up potential avenues that might lead me to some clue as to why he developed that fatal arrhythmia."

"I heard his estate has been settled, with a hefty sum to HCMC."

"I don't think the estate is settled, but there was a settlement conference I attended this morning at which his estate attorney divulged the amount he had left to HCMC. How did you hear about it already?"

"The medical gossip rumor mill is intact and active."

"Mike, I was there, Buck was there, and two lawyers were there, including our in-house counsel, Darrell Bledsoe. I don't see how anyone else could possibly know already."

"Jim Bob, the walls have ears."

"Seriously?"

"No. One of the admin assistants from our office had gone down to Buck's office to pick up a copy of the new HIPPA guidelines, and she overheard Buck's assistant Lucy telling someone she was talking to on the phone about a huge windfall for the hospital."

"Buck must have told her. He was definitely walking on air after the meeting."

"How much did Sandy Lowell leave HCMC?"

"I'm not sure I should say, but news travels so fast in our business, everyone will probably know by dinner time. $150 million."

Mike whistled. "That will put us in pretty good stead as far as the competition is concerned. That really is fantastic news."

It was our group's time to hit. Fortunately, a mulligan was allowed on the first tee, and it was a good thing, as I watched my brand new Titleist golf ball sail out of bounds after a duck hook. My next tee shot was short, but in the fairway. Mike and I and two fellow competitors slogged on, trying to keep our wits about us as we chased the little white ball—or yellow ball in some cases—around. No one got hurt during the round, but Mike and I did comment that if we operated on our patients like we played golf, we would be in jail for malpractice and negligence.

I called Mary Louise after the round, telling her I was alive and having a beer with Mike Reardon and waiting for the results of our efforts on the golf course. "And what are your potential losses, should you not win?" she asked.

"I'll be out twenty dollars."

"Big stakes, huh?"

"We play just as hard for twenty dollars as we would for two hundred."

"A two-hundred-dollar bet would make me very nervous. We have dinner reservations at seven at the Waterfront Grill. Will you have time to come home and shower and change?"

"Yes. I'll be out of here in fifteen minutes. See you at home. And by the way, if I was playing for two hundred dollars, I'd be shaking so bad I would miss the ball."

Waterfront Grill was a fairly new venue in Horseshoe Bay and had indoor and outdoor seating both on the entry level and also on the second level. The upper level provided expansive vistas of the marina and Lake LBJ. We ordered cocktails: a Tito's cosmopolitan for her, a dirty Tito's martini for me. As we sipped and enjoyed the view, she mentioned that J.J. had called her earlier in the afternoon.

"He said you had hired him for some sort of investigation?"

"Yes. Buck asked me to hire him to acquire information about Sandy Lowell."

"Why in the world? Sandy is deceased, and I heard through the grapevine that HCMC is slated to get a large inheritance."

"How did you hear?"

"The medical grapevine, as usual. I heard $150 million. Is that right?"

"Yes. I was at the meeting this morning but didn't have time to call you. I had to rush to the course to make my tee time."

"If Sandy is indeed deceased, and HCMC is going to be a beneficiary of that kind of money, why investigate him?"

"I think that Buck was so worried that the hospital wouldn't get the money he was hoping for that he decided to pre-empt the situation by investigating Sandy, before he even knew what was in the will. After the meeting he asked me to call J.J. off and try and close Pandora's box, but I told him it was too late. I had spoken to J.J. a few days earlier, and you know how fast he and his firm work."

"That's why he called me. He has data ready for you to review."

"Oh, man. I just don't see how any good could come from looking into the affairs of a dead man after he has already generously donated a massive fortune to the hospital. That's just asking for trouble. On the other hand, I'm interested in why he developed the cardiac arrhythmia that killed him."

"How can investigating Sandy's background lead to any conclusions about his medical condition?"

"I don't know, Mary Louise, but one never knows, does one?"

We had a nice meal, followed by a return to the Brady manse and a timely walk for Tip. I tried to watch an episode of a series on Netflix about the consequences of three suburban but financially needy women having robbed a bank, but sleep overtook me.

Dallas to Granite Falls is a three-hour drive, depending on traffic, so J.J. and I decided to communicate via Skype Saturday morning. I was no wizard when it came to computer skills, but when he called and I picked up, it was eerie to see his smiling face on the screen.

"Hey, Pops, how's it going?"

"Good, son. You? And Kathryn?"

"All is well on the home front, although I'm traveling more than I wanted to. Plus, if truth be told, she feels like her window of opportunity to have children is closing. She has a nice career, having taken over some of her father's banks, and is earning quite a bit of money. So am I, for that matter, so we're in stellar financial shape. But we're trying to work out the timing on her getting pregnant. She feels like it's now or never."

"Well, good luck with that, son. As I remember, you were an accident. I came home from work one day, and your mother told me there was a bun in the oven. I asked her what kind, and she just shook her head."

"So you didn't plan to have me, I was simply a result of you and Mom having a lot of unprotected sex?"

"Yes, emphasis on 'a lot.'"

"Pops, I don't want to think about that. You and Mom? Gross."

"Okay, good luck with your baby-planning issues. Let's get down to business. What do you have for me?"

"I've sent you the file via FedEx overnight, so you should have it this morning. After you've reviewed the information, let's Skype again."

"That's it? Read the documents and call me in the morning? Sounds like a doctor's line, son."

"I've got way too much to do to recite data to you over the phone. Read it at your leisure, and we'll talk about specifics. Besides, Kathryn just texted me, and I've got an hour to get home and do my business. Seems her temperature indicates she is at prime-time ovulation. Later, Dad."

I opened the FedEx from B&B Investigations with some degree of trepidation. I didn't want to be responsible for creating any sort of problem that might negate HCMC's share of Sandy Lowell's estate proceeds. All I wanted to do was to pursue possible causes of his demise through his ventricular arrhythmia. And why was I like a dog with a bone? I didn't know. It was simply the way I was wired.

George Sanford Lowell III was born in February 1948 in Midland, Texas, only son of George Sanford Lowell II. The grandfather, George Sanford Lowell, had made a fortune in oil by investing and drilling wells in the old salt domes around Beaumont, Texas, location of the famous Spindletop oil field. In 1901, a well at Spindletop struck oil and blew 100,000 barrels of oil per day before the roughnecks got it under control. That provided the impetus for the onset of the oil age for the United States. Prior to Spindletop, oil had been used primarily as a lubricant and for lighting. As a result of the quantities of oil discovered, burning petroleum as a fuel for mass consumption became economically feasible.

I didn't see how all this fit into the bio of Sandy Lowell, but B&B was thorough, so I was sure it was important.

Lowell I moved to Midland, Texas, after his success in the Beaumont area, and he was instrumental in drilling wells in the Permian Basin in the 1920s and 1930s. The Permian Basin extended for over 80,000 square miles in West Texas and Eastern New Mexico. The wells Grandpa Lowell drilled were mostly shallow, less than 5,000 feet in depth, due to long distribution distances in West Texas and Eastern New Mexico, and lack of pipes for transmission. Later, around the time World War II began, oil was in significant demand and justified the cost of deep oil drilling and expansion of the pipeline systems.

Lowell I called his company Lowell Petroleum, and it was taken over by his only son, Lowell II, in the late '40s after illness overtook Lowell I, which led to his early death. Lowell II expanded the company further by drilling deeper wells at higher costs but at much greater reward. Sandy's father was a heavy smoker and died prematurely of lung cancer. Sandy Lowell then took over the company in the '70s, after obtaining a petroleum engineering degree from the University of Texas and an MBA from Harvard Business School.

Sandy continued to live in Midland and expanded the company even further by continuing to drill wells, but also by investing in, and trading, oil futures, a commodity like orange juice and pork bellies. Sandy was very successful at oil trading and seemed to enjoy that aspect of the business more than the exploration and drilling business, which had been the hallmark of Lowell Petroleum since his grandfather started the company. Eventually, Sandy sold off the production to larger oil companies and cashed in his oil futures contracts. The data was a little sketchy, but B&B estimated the Lowell Petroleum had amassed a fortune of about $950 million.

Sandy quit the business and started to enjoy life as a near-billionaire. He had a sister, who had never worked due to the largesse of her father and grandfather, drank to excess, and died in her fifties of cirrhosis and liver cancer. That left the company fortune to Sandy alone. His half-sister Jennifer Lowell had been taken care of by her father, Lowell II. B&B's records did not include any information about that particular trust.

Sandy moved to Horseshoe Bay, Texas, and built an enormous home overlooking Lake LBJ. The main house was 18,000 feet, complete with a movie theatre and bowling alley. There also were two guest outbuildings, each with a bedroom, bath, and living room. He began to entertain lavishly and invited his friends from Dallas, Houston, and Midland for long weekends of drinking and partying. He was instrumental in building the Horseshoe Bay Airport, a facility for the discriminating private aircraft owner. He would provide Suburban limos to transport his guests to and from

their Cessnas, Leers, Falcons, and Gulfstreams. He arranged elabo-
rate dove hunts on those weekends and provided entertainment of
all varieties for his guests, depending on whether it was a couples'
weekend or a stag weekend.

According to B&B, Sandy purchased a private jet for himself,
to the tune of $65 million. He hired two pilots to be on standby
at all times, in case the urge to travel came over him in the middle of the night. An addendum that J.J. included, in case I wanted to learn more about private aircraft ownership, revealed that
Sandy had paid for many repairs as part of jet ownership, such as
a blown tire, which cost $3,000 to replace, and a new windshield,
which cost around $60,000 to replace. All in all, with crew sala-
ries, required maintenance and replacement costs, hangar fees, and
aircraft insurance, he was spending $1 million per year in operat-
ing costs. There was no debt to service, as Sandy had paid cash for
the plane.

All of this expense was totally affordable for a billionaire,
until the stock market crash of 1987. Sandy's fortune fell to $400
million overnight. And while that is a lot of money for us average
Joes, he couldn't maintain his lavish lifestyle. He had a "come to
Jesus" epiphany. After the market recovered to some degree, Sandy
started selling assets. The airplane went first, then the house, both
at significant losses. He downsized to a smaller, 8,000 square foot
house, still in Horseshoe Bay and still with the Lake LBJ view, just
not as grand. He started giving some money away to his favorite
charities and was instrumental in helping Buck Owens develop
Hill Country Medical Center.

There were reams of paperwork included in the packet, much
of which I had no interest in. Evaluating his checking account and
credit card accounts was not part of my task. I reminded myself that
I was interested in finding out what caused his cardiac problems.

And while spending vast sums of money on mansions, private air-craft, and lavish entertainment would predispose most normal humans to a heart attack, that had not been Sandy's problem.

I thumbed through the pages, then came to the back of the main binder and saw a tab labeled PATERNITY SUITS. Probably not a cause of arrhythmia, but of interest. There were four of them, and in each, the attorney of record was W. Hamilton Bowles, the gent I had met Friday morning at the conference about Sandy's last will and testament. The first three I reviewed had been dis-missed out of hand by the judge. Turns out Sandy Lowell had a vasectomy prior to these three suits. The attorney had a letter from the operating urologist filed with each affidavit, and in addi-tion, he had submitted to a sperm count as well. In each case, the sperm count was a big fat ZERO.

The fourth case had not been dismissed. This one had been filed prior to the other three, apparently before the vasectomy era of Sandy Lowell's life. There had been a settlement in this case, to the tune of $50 million. Wow. Some child, this one. Sandy had submitted to DNA testing, and he was in fact the father. The recipient of these funds went by the name of . . . holy shit. The Jennifer Lowell Trust.

Jennifer was his daughter after all? And not his half-sister by a late-in-life marriage of his father, Lowell II? I thumbed back through the records and searched for the mother's name, but it was not listed in the legal documents. Who was the mother? And why had everyone lied to me? Buck and Cynthia had both lied to me about Jennifer's origins. Buck had even lied at the conference with Bledsoe and Bowles, saying the lawyers would stipulate that Sandy's DNA was compatible with Jennifer from a sibling stand-point, information he said came from Dr. Jerry Reed. And notably, there was no provision made for Jennifer in Sandy's will. What the hell was that about?

I realized the need to pay a visit to Cynthia Stiles, Jennifer's caretaker. She would know all. But would she divulge all? And what about Jerry Reed? He was an expert and would not make a mistake about paternity determined by DNA sampling. Something was amiss.

CHAPTER 10

COINCIDENCES

I called J.J. to ask if he had reviewed the documents he had sent me.

"No, Pops. I don't have time to review the dossiers we prepare unless my firm is involved in more than just information gathering. Is there something amiss?"

"I don't know. Long story short is that Sandy Lowell, subject of your search, apparently fathered a child. I was told this child, named Jennifer Lowell, was his half-sister through a late-in-life marriage of his father. But DNA testing at the time of the paternity suit proved that she is in fact his daughter. And he settled the suit for $50 million. Pretty valuable child, if you ask me."

"Sounds like it. Anything else I can do for you? I'm sort of . . . occupied."

"Still working on that ideal-temperature issue, son?"

"Yep. Working on round two. Kathryn feels that—"

"J.J. Too much information for me. Just remember one thing. What you're doing now will turn out to be the easy and fun part. The hard part begins when the little critter actually arrives. Happy baby-making."

Mary Louise looked beautiful in her cream-colored silk blouse with spaghetti straps and matching pants which billowed as she walked. It seemed to me the trouser legs were extra-full, which was probably called something special by a designer, but for a man from the 1960s, bell bottoms came to mind. Her hair was done into a series of braids, and with her matching turquoise bracelet and necklace, she was a sight to see.

As the hostess escorted us to our outdoor table at the yacht club, I saw several "thumbs up" from my fellow diners as we passed. Mary Louise seemed, however, oblivious to the admiration, and continued on to our table. We had a nice view of the lake, and although three four-story condominium buildings blocked our view of the setting sun, we could see the light changes clearly.

I ordered a bottle of Rombauer chardonnay, and we toasted to yet another beautiful day in the Hill Country of Texas.

"I wanted to ask your opinion about the data I went through this morning, Mary Louise," I asked after the server had poured our wine and informed us of the specials of the day.

"I'm happy to help as always, husband."

I glossed over the financial aspects of Sandy Lowell's life, a treatise worthy of that show on television entitled *Lifestyles of the Rich and Famous* with Robin Leach. I was more interested in her opinions about Jennifer Lowell.

"So, the caretaker named Cynthia Stiles told you, and the family lawyer confirmed at the meeting, that Jennifer was Sandy's half-sister by a late-in-life marriage of his father, but now you have evidence of a paternity suit that implies she is his daughter?"

"All I have is the name 'The Jennifer Lowell Trust.' It could be a different person altogether, although that seems highly unlikely that Sandy would have a half-sister named Jennifer and also a daughter out of wedlock by the same name. I don't know where to go from here. I thought you might have some advice."

She gazed at me longingly—at least that was my interpretation. But then, I'm of the opinion that all her looks imply that she wants to go home and make mad passionate love to me. However, she did on occasion get the same look when she had indigestion.

"Jim Bob, let's look at this from my perspective. I don't see that you have any need whatsoever to be involved in some sort of post-mortem investigation of Sandy Lowell. But for the sake of argument, here's how I look at the situation. You have an adult child, Jennifer Lowell, who is either the half-sister of Sandy Lowell, or the daughter of Sandy Lowell. Either way, she is financially taken care of, either by her father Lowell II, or her father Lowell III. And let's just assume a trust was endowed with $50 million that will provide for her needs, and her caretaker's needs, until she dies. Case closed.

"Secondly, you're trying to find out what killed Sandy Lowell. It is well-documented that he died of an arrhythmia of some sort. No one is questioning that. An arrhythmia of undetermined etiology is, I think, what you told me Dr. Jerry Reed's diagnosis was. You are not a cardiologist, so determining the reason for the 'undetermined etiology' is far outside your realm as an orthopedic surgeon. So, that's settled.

"Thirdly, HCMC has the money that Buck Owens so desperately wanted, and needed, for the future success of the hospital. That is also settled.

"My question back to you is, what—are—you—doing? Everyone's needs are taken care of. The case, if there is one, is open and shut. All parties involved want to be done with the Sandy Lowell matter, except you, a non-relative and non-party to all the issues involved. You just happened to be unloading groceries near his car when he had his fatal heart problem. You didn't know the man. You have no stake in this matter, honey. Surely working four days a week, and playing golf on the weekends, and taking care of me, your wife, who adores you, is sufficient to keep your interest."

She made some great points. What in the hell was I doing?

"You're right about everything, Mary Louise, as usual. I don't know what makes me take on these crazy problems. Some sort of intellectual curiosity, I guess. I just keep pondering why a healthy man his age would develop an arrhythmia of that nature. Something had to cause it."

Our food arrived: crab cakes for her, shrimp scampi for me. We finished our wine and wanted to have a nightcap but decided that would best be served on our terrace at home. I left a generous gratuity and we departed, arm in arm. Once in the car, she leaned over, turned my head toward her, and planted a big wet kiss on my lips.

"What's that for?"

"Just for being you."

"I thought you gave me plenty of reasons at dinner why being me is not so good sometimes."

"One of the many reasons I married you is because you not only go that second mile, you go the third, fourth, however many miles it takes to make things right."

"So you're saying?"

"Do what you need to do, after you take me home and do all kinds of bad things to me."

"Bad things?"

"You know, good bad things. And do not speed. I don't want to have to stop and have the moment spoiled by Officer Friendly."

Forty-five miles per hour had never seemed so slow . . .

We lazed around on Sunday morning and fixed a breakfast of salmon and bagels with all the trimmings—purple onion, boiled eggs, capers, tomatoes, cucumbers, sour cream, and real butter. After, we took Tip on a long walk through the neighborhood within and outside the gates. There was a small dog park just down the hill that overlooked the lake, and he cavorted with new friends. We made small talk with other dog owners, strolled around the area, and enjoyed Tip enjoying himself. After a time, we wandered back home, took a sleeping nap, then decided after a burst of energy to go play nine holes of golf.

My cell phone rang while I was teeing off on the eighth hole. I ignored it and didn't listen to see if there was a message until we had finished the ninth hole and were headed toward the clubhouse. It was from Buck Owens. I listened, then hung up.

"What's wrong? Jim?"

"That was Buck. He got a call from a lawyer buddy, telling him that Hamilton Bowes, the lawyer for Sandy Lowell, had just died."

"Really? Was he elderly or sick?"

"No, I don't think so. I only met him that one time. What's strange is that he died in the emergency room. He had a ventricular arrhythmia of some sort and didn't respond to treatment."

"Wait, Jim. Isn't that what—"

"Yes. That's what Sandy Lowell died from as well."

CHAPTER 11

JENNIFER LOWELL, REVISITED

I had only two cases on Monday, a virgin hip replacement and a virgin knee replacement. I had skipped coming in on Sunday to review charts, which had been my usual custom all the years I had been in practice. In the old days, in Houston, working at the University Medical Center, I might have had up to eight cases on a surgical day, which brought about the need to review the operations to be performed the day before. With only two, I went in early on Monday and cleaned off my desk of dictation and chart signings, reviewed the X-rays on my two patients, had a light breakfast, and went to work at 7 a.m.

Both patients were on the thin side, making the surgical exposures a little easier, so, with Charlotte Stone as my assistant, we completed the cases by 11:30 a.m. I spoke to the families, dictated the operative reports, and headed upstairs to my office.

Shelly Wood was at her desk, on the phone, and I overheard her explaining the recovery time of a surgical procedure to a patient. Once she disconnected, she popped into my office.

"How did the cases go?"

"Smooth as glass. How is your day going?"

"The usual, fighting the good fight against the insurance companies. I will say one thing for you, your patients are generally very happy with your work. I have worked for other surgeons where I had to spend half my day allaying their worries and fears about the post-surgical recovery process. Your patients seem to be prepared, know what they are getting into, and realize that this too shall pass and things will be all right in time. I think, Dr. Brady, that perhaps you're too modest about your surgical abilities. There are surgeons, and there are SURGEONS, and the latter have better techniques, which make for easier recoveries and better results for the patients."

"I just make my patients wait for their operation until they are so crippled with pain that they feel better in the recovery room than they did before the operation, even with the post-operative pain. As for technique, I can't say. I haven't spent a lot of time observing other surgeons recently. Back at University Medical Center, when I trained residents and fellows, I saw a lot of house staff that I quite frankly told they should be in another field, preferably non-surgical. That used to get me in a lot of trouble with the powers that be, but better the bad apples get weeded out before they get out in practice and start maiming the general public."

"Say what you will, Doctor, but I think you're a cut above. And don't try and change my mind. What will you do with the rest of your day?"

"I have a lot to do, mostly unrelated to medicine. I'm delving into some issues that may require me to confide in you from time to time. I hope I can count on your discretion, Shelly."

"Absolutely, Dr. Brady. If there is something I can do to help, research an issue, whatever, I'm available."

"I appreciate that. I'll be moving on now. Call if you need something."

I stopped by the recovery room and checked on my two patients. Both were awake and doing fine. The hip replacement, a middle-aged woman who had broken her hip in a motorcycle accident years before, told me her hip felt better after surgery than it had in years. And people wondered why I kept practicing.

I sat in my car, opened the storage compartment between the seats, and took out a pen and notepad I kept there to jot down ideas and epiphanies. I made a list.

Sandy Lowell died of a fatal ventricular tachycardia, even though he had no previous heart disease.

W. Hamilton Bowles died of the same illness, although the information I had was second or third hand, and I would need to get the details myself. Was this a coincidence, or meaningful?

Was Jennifer Lowell Sandy's half-sister from his father's last marriage? Or was she his daughter from a relationship he had, and had been discovered through DNA testing?

And did Sandy Lowell's passing have anything to do with him having plastic surgery by the fellow in Austin, Dr. Robert Warner?

The Jennifer Lowell Trust was funded with $50 million by Sandy Lowell years before. Sandy was thirty years old when the paternity lawsuit was filed. Jennifer was now forty-three years old. Was the trust viable? How much money had been spent on custodial care for her and the caretaker? Was there enough money left to continue that care?

And did Sandy's bequest of $150 million to HCMC have anything to do with any of the above?

I decided, after all those mental gymnastics, that it was close to noon, and I had worked up an appetite. It was a Bluebonnet Café kind of day. I called Mary Louise to see if she wanted to join me, but she said she was in Austin for the day for a charity board meeting, and for me NOT to eat the chicken fried steak.

I was eating the chicken fried chicken, the next best thing, with gravy, mashed potatoes, and the best green beans on earth, when I saw a woman I recognized enter the restaurant with two other women. They didn't quite look like the Bluebonnet Café type: more like a salad and hummus trio.

Phyllis Reardon stopped by my table and gave me an air kiss. She had dressed down for the occasion, wearing tight faded denim jeans and white Keds. In contrast, she wore a white silk blouse and lots of gold bangles, so she wouldn't be mistaken for a regular at the Bluebonnet. Her blond hair was leashed by neither braid nor clip, so it fell about her shoulders like a cape.

"Jim Bob Brady, what are you doing in a place like this?"

"I could ask you the same thing. I'm much more suited to this environment, I would think, than you are. I grew up in a small town outside Waco, where this kind of country place served our staple sort of food. You look like you grew up in Dallas, daughter of a wealthy oil baron."

She laughed. "You'd be surprised. Eating alone?"

"Yes. I finished surgery early and have some errands to run. Mary Louise is in Austin for the day, so I'm sneaking off for my fix of cream gravy. You?"

"Two friends from my hometown are here visiting, so I thought I would show them a local restaurant that depicts the flavor of Marble Falls."

"I see. Sorority sisters from SMU?"

"You're right about that. Anyway, have a pleasant day. And by the way, I grew up in Cleburne, Texas, outside of Fort Worth. And I was no daughter of wealthy oil people. My dad was a pharmacist, and I got a scholarship to SMU. Being married to a heart surgeon allows me some privileges, Jim Bob. Like plastic surgery, which reminds me, have you been in touch with Dr. Warner yet?"

"No, but I will be soon, I'm sure. Nice to see you. Enjoy lunch."

"Ta," she said, and sashayed over to her friends and sat down.

I finished my meal, left a generous tip, and exited.

I called Lucy Williams, Buck Owens's admin assistant. "Lucy, good morning—or is it afternoon?"

"My favorite doctor. I'm better now. Still morning, barely. What can I do for you?"

"I would like to go and visit Jennifer Lowell, and her caretaker, Cynthia Stiles. I was hoping you had their contact information."

She paused for a moment. "Is this something that will get me in trouble with Dr. Owens?"

"Of course not. You know me."

"I know you very well, that's why I'm asking."

"You know, your boss put me in charge, at least to some degree, of gathering information about Sandy Lowell and his family. I'm just following up."

"I thought that was before we knew that he had left all that money to the hospital."

"Well, yes, but there are a few loose ends, and I'm just doing what Buck requested me to do."

She sighed, and I heard her fingers tapping the computer. She gave me the requested information, phone numbers and address. "Don't make me regret this, Dr. Brady."

"Never," I said, and hoped I was right.

I decided to show up unannounced at Jennifer Lowell's home. I could have called ahead, let them know I was coming, but then, the element of surprise is good to throw off one's preparedness. I had a little trouble finding the place. The house was in Granite Shoals, on the north side of Lake LBJ, on a street named Hill Circle. I pulled into the circular drive, got out, and stretched from the drive and the massive cholesterol intake at lunch. There were gates on either side of the two-story dwelling, which appeared to be well maintained. The limestone exterior wasn't pristine white, but then again, it wasn't speckled with green mold as can happen in this part of the country. I rang the doorbell, heard some yelling in the background, then the clomping of feet running toward the door.

"Hello?" Jennifer Lowell asked as she opened the heavy wooden door. She was dressed in blue sweats and white socks with no shoes, and her hair was cut short and done in pigtails.

"Good morning, Jennifer. I'm Dr. Brady, from the hospital. Do you remember me?"

"No." She turned and yelled, "Cynthia! Dr. Brady from the hospital!"

She turned and ran off. I waited on the porch for a few minutes, then carefully stepped inside. There was a stairwell to the second floor off to my right. There was a hallway to my left that was darkened, possibly leading to a bedroom. I moved into the entry hall, then into a great room with paned windows that faced the lake. To the left was a kitchen, and to the right was a walk-in bar and a sitting room, more of a library with shelves full of books. I just stood there for a moment and listened to the sounds of a television in the background with an audience laugh track.

"May I help you?" asked Cynthia Stiles as she entered the room from behind me.

"I'm sorry to barge in like this. I'm Dr. Brady, from—"

"I remember you from the hospital. What are you doing out here, Doctor?"

"Well, Cynthia, some issues have arisen about the, shall I say, parentage of Jennifer, and I've been assigned the task of sorting them out." I lied proficiently.

Cynthia stared at me, then walked into the great room and sat down on a leather sofa. I followed and sat across a coffee table from her in a wingback chair.

"Coffee?" she asked.

"Sounds great, if it's no trouble."

"I just made some. Black?"

"Perfect."

She walked into the kitchen area, poured the aromatic liquid into two large mugs, and returned to the sofa.

I sipped the coffee. "Excellent. What kind is it?"

"Brazilian blend. Thick and strong. Now what can I do for you?"

"When we spoke at the hospital, you said that Jennifer was Sandy's half-sister, from his father's marriage late in life. Unfortunately, however, I have come into some documents that refute that. They record a paternity test in which the DNA of Sandy Lowell and Jennifer Lowell appears to indicate they are father and daughter. This contradicts our previous conversation, so I'm hoping you can enlighten me."

"Tell me again how and why you are involved in all this?"

I reiterated the origin of my involvement with the Lowell family through Buck Owens, careful to omit the part about how Buck wanted me now to let sleeping dogs lie.

"So you never knew Sandy?"

"No, ma'am."

She sighed. "Sandy, what a piece of work he was. Generous to a fault—would give you the shirt off his back if you needed it—but just couldn't keep it in his pants, if you know what I mean. He never married because he just couldn't settle down with one woman. He would get involved with one, then after a few weeks or months, move on. Someone called him a serial monogamist, whatever that means. But there were always women. He had several paternity suits against him, all but one after he had a vasectomy. That one, when he was still able to father children, was what brought about Jennifer.

"The family tried to keep it under wraps best they could. We were all instructed to let folks who asked be informed that she was Lowell II's daughter from a late marriage. Truth be known, Sandy and the mother were related. It was an embarrassment to all concerned."

"What? Related how?"

"Sandy's father, Lowell II, had a sister who lived in Dallas. She died young of cirrhosis due to alcoholism, just like Sandy's sister. Must run in the family, which is probably why Sandy was never much of a drinker. But his aunt, she had this daughter from a failed marriage. And that gal was a head-turner. She and Sandy were always close, but when he reached the age of twenty-nine or thirty and she turned eighteen, Sandy and she changed the relationship from friends to lovers. They were inseparable. Then she got pregnant."

"This would be what, Sandy's first cousin? Good grief!"

"That's right, Doc. The simplest thing would have been for him to acknowledge the relationship, own up to what he'd done, and pay up. But he got all high and mighty, and his father got involved, and because of the animosity between Lowell II and his sister, they let it get to a point where Jennifer's mother had to file a lawsuit over paternity. And of course, she won, because that DNA doesn't lie. That pretty much ruined the relationship between Sandy and his cousin. And then, of course, came Jennifer, who was intellectually disabled. I took over her care early on; the mother didn't want anything to do with a child who had supplemental needs. Sandy always took good care of us and visited us often. Good lord knows what will happen to her when I'm gone, or no longer able to care for her."

"What about Jennifer's mother? I understand Sandy's sister and his aunt are both deceased, but is the mother still around?"

"Oh, yes, still lives in the area, some big fancy house on the lake. She has a life of her own and doesn't want anything to do with us. She's married to a bigtime doctor."

"Would you happen to know her name?"

"Of course. She goes by Phyllis Reardon."

CHAPTER 12

QUESTIONS

Over a home-cooked dinner of Caesar salad, pan-fried pork chops, and fresh green beans with bacon, Mary Louise listened to the story of Jennifer Lowell's origins as told to me by Cynthia Stiles.

"Jim Bob, I don't even know what to say. Having a child with your first cousin? That is a notable cause of mental disability, is it not?"

"I think so, but I would have to research it."

"Wouldn't that have been an indication for voluntary termination of the pregnancy back then?"

"I would think so, but I can't say for sure. I'm almost speechless about the whole mess. Makes me wish I had listened to Buck and just backed off. Maybe he knew I would find out about the sordid past of Sandy Lowell and warned me off for my own good."

"I can certainly see why he might have done that. You know how you are."

"How am I?"

"Well, you have this burning desire to find out all kinds of information which you may or may not be privy to, but once you discover deep truths about a situation, you often wish you had never delved into the matter in the first place. Sometimes, perhaps you might think about treading lighter, and save yourself from the knowledge of sad circumstances. You really don't have to know everything about everybody, do you, Jim Bob?"

She was spot on. "No, I don't, and I totally understand what you're saying, and completely agree with your position. I just can't help myself from turning over rocks, just to see what might be laying beneath."

"You've got your practice, you have golf, you have me . . . That should be enough for any one man, wouldn't you say?"

"Absolutely, Mary Louise. By the way, this meal is sumptuous. What kind of sauce did you sauté the pork chops in?"

"Tequila lime."

"Wow. It is spectacular. Mind if I have another?"

"Help yourself. The chops are much better for you than the chicken-fried whatever you probably had for lunch."

That didn't warrant a comment, so none was forthcoming.

I ate silently for a moment, then said, "I saw Phyllis at lunch today, at Bluebonnet. She was entertaining two former SMU sorority sisters."

"At Bluebonnet? I'm surprised. She seems like a tofu sort of girl."

"I agree. Maybe hummus?"

She laughed. "Did you speak?"

"Yes, for a moment. I was just about finished with my meal when they arrived."

"Phyllis Reardon, matron of the arts, wife of a prominent cardiovascular surgeon, first cousin of Sandy Lowell, and mother of his love child. I wonder about the will, having this information."

"What do you mean, Mary Louise?"

"I believe you shared with me that the attorney for the Lowell family gave you and Buck a laundry list of his bequests at the conference. I don't remember you mentioning any gifts to Jennifer, his daughter, much less to Phyllis Reardon. In fact, didn't you tell me that Sandy's father, Lowell II, had bequeathed money to Jennifer upon his demise?"

"Yes, I did, and I believe that information came from B&B."

"Well, Lowell II was not Jennifer's father, as per that paternity test from years ago, so did he actually pass that money down to her? And if he didn't, and if Sandy Lowell didn't leave her anything in his will, how in the world is she going to be taken care of? She's only forty-three, and from what I've gathered talking to you, has no medical illnesses that would shorten her life. Does she have any money? And if she doesn't, what would she and her caretaker do? And what about Phyllis? When Sandy allegedly settled that paternity lawsuit for, what, $50 million, did she actually get the money and use it to take care of the daughter she has nothing to do with? And if she didn't get money back then, would she be looking to try and get some now, from Sandy's estate? And for that matter, how much money is left in the Jennifer Lowell Trust? It was established over forty years ago. A lot of things can happen in forty years. There are many unanswered questions."

Yes, there were.

I called Buck Owens on Tuesday after clinic patients were done. Lucy Williams, as usual, answered the phone, and put me through immediately.

"Afternoon, Jim. What can I do for you?"

"I wondered if I could drop by for a few minutes, like now?"

"Sure, come on down."

The lobby was full of patients and families. The din was about the level of a dull roar. Good for business, but no such thing as a quiet zone at the hospital any longer.

I greeted Lucy and went back to the conference room. For reasons unknown to me, Buck preferred his meetings there rather than his private office.

"So, Buck, I've been looking into the Sandy Lowell matter, as requested. And, I have J.J.'s report from B&B Investigation's findings into the background of our benefactor."

"And I was in such a good mood, Jim Bob."

"I think you may have misled me about some issues, Buck. Like for starters, how Sandy fathered a child when he was thirty years old or so, named Jennifer, and set up a $50 million trust for her. You told me Jennifer was his half-sister, fathered by his father Lowell II in a late marriage. In fact, at the meeting with the lawyers regarding Sandy's bequest, you brought up the DNA issue and said it was compatible with he and Jennifer being half-brother and half-sister. And, Mr. Bowles and Mr. Bledsoe both agreed to stipulate at that meeting that Sandy and Jennifer were related in the manner you described, which wasn't true at all. Somehow you've convinced two attorneys to circumvent the truth."

He leaned back in his chair and sighed. "I didn't really want you to get involved in all that mess. It was forty years ago. Sandy was sowing his wild oats back then, and I was a fledgling doctor . . . it was a long time ago. There is no need to reopen old wounds."

"Buck, while that may be true, the fact remains that the trust for Jennifer was established over forty years ago, and she, and for all I know, her caretakers, have been living on that money ever since. Mary Louise brought up the fact that—"

"Mary Louise? She knows about this? Why in the world would you share it with her?"

"I share everything with her, Buck. She is my sounding board, and my best advisor. As I was saying, she brought up the fact that a lot can happen over forty years, and she wondered how much money is actually left in the trust. With Sandy not leaving any money in his will to the trust, or to Jennifer in a new trust, does she have the funds that will allow her to continue living as she has in the past? And this thing with Phyllis Reardon, my god!"

Buck sat straight up in his chair. "How in the hell did you find out about that? Your son?"

"No, through Cynthia Stiles, Jennifer's caretaker. I went over to see her. She mentioned Phyllis's name like it was no big deal. Is it common knowledge that she is the mother of Jennifer Lowell?"

"Not only no, but HELL NO! The only living people that know are Phyllis, me, and Cynthia. Sandy of course knew, but he's gone. Ham Bowles knew, but he's also gone."

"So Mike Reardon doesn't know about this sordid incident in his wife's past?"

"Of course not."

"I have to ask, Buck, and I'd appreciate your honesty for once—is there adequate funding in Jennifer's trust to take care of her, and the house she lives in, and Cynthia, and any future care-takers that she might need?"

"I can't say for sure."

"Buck, you know me, and that I'll leave no stone unturned to find out what I want to know. I'll rehire B&B to dig further, I'll go talk to the law firm that Bowles was with, whatever it takes. You might as well save me some time and just spit it out. How much money is left?"

Buck hung his head. "Less than $2 million, give or take."

"So over the past forty years, Jennifer's expenses have drained about one million dollars per year from the trust? That seems excessive to me. Was Sandy administering the funds himself, or did he have an accounting firm or law firm handle the distributions?"

"No, he didn't do it himself. He let the mother be the administrator of Jennifer's trust. She insisted on it."

I leaned forward in my chair. "Are you telling me that Phyllis Reardon has been spending a million bucks a year out of Jennifer's trust for forty years, and no one thought to maybe audit that spending?"

"Sandy stipulated, when his father gave him the money to set up the trust, that Phyllis would be in charge of it. Sandy didn't have much at thirty years old; he was just working for Lowell Petroleum. He had to pay his father back when he became a principal in the company. Sandy trusted Phyllis. He loved her. He knew in his heart of hearts that she would do the right thing by their child."

"I'm curious, Buck. How do you explain to a husband that you have extra money to the tune of ONE MILLION DOLLARS PER YEAR? I mean, Mike Reardon is no fool. He knows how much he makes and he knows what sort of lifestyle they live. Where did he think all the surplus funds came from?"

"Phyllis told him early in their relationship that her favorite rich uncle was a wealthy oil man, and invested well, and left her some money in a trust."

"So you have no idea how much money in the trust was spent on Jennifer, and how much was spent on the Reardon lifestyle?"

"Not a clue. Remember, Sandy insisted that she would administer the trust. Period. No questions asked."

I stood up, feeling like I needed to return home for a shower. "Did Sandy know?"

"Know what?" replied Buck.

"That the trust was down to $2 million? And that it needed to be replenished?"

"Yes. He only discovered it recently, and by accident."

"What happened, Buck?"

"Cynthia called him, told him they needed a new air conditioner, and had asked Phyllis to authorize payment. Phyllis declined, using the excuse that it was a bad time in the market and they would have to wait. Cynthia responded they were sweating in the house, and it needed to be fixed right away. And, according to Cynthia, Phyllis told her that was 'tough shit.' So Cynthia called Sandy.

"As a result, Sandy got his accountants involved, and discovered that while his daughter was being cared for adequately, a lot of money had left the trust in the form of expenses for the Reardon household: trips, foreign cars, jewelry. He called Phyllis on the carpet, read her the riot act, told her he would go to court to have her removed as trustee, and start a new trust for Jennifer with responsible people in charge."

"And did he?"

"No. It was on the table, but the paperwork hadn't been completed. The lawyers were working on it."

"By his lawyers, you mean Hamilton Bowles Sr., the fellow I met here? The now-dead guy?"

"Yes."

"But the new trust was not a part of his will? He was going to create a new trust separate from his estate planning?"

"Yes. He was going to transfer the funds from one of his investment accounts and make good on his commitment rather than put the new trust in his will. He thought he would live a long and healthy life and wanted to create that new trust as soon as possible."

"So what the hell happened?"

"He died."

CHAPTER 13

THE TRUST

The weather was predicted to be lousy on Friday, and golf was only iffy at best. So, I decided to kill two birds with one stone and make the trek to Austin and visit Dr. Robert Warner, plastic surgeon, and the offices of W. Hamilton Bowles, Lowell family attorney.

What did I hope to accomplish? I didn't have a clue, but I was planning to look under every rock, even if it killed me.

I asked Mary Louise to join me on the trek to Austin, and even offered to buy her lunch at her favorite sushi joint. She declined due to a canasta tournament at the club. Being rejected by a double deck of cards was humiliating. I thought about taking Tip, but he was scared to death of thunder. If there was a rainstorm, as predicted, he would be a basket case in the car, jumping and howling, which would threaten to kill us both. I left him at home.

I made an appointment to see Warner at 1 p.m. According to his scheduler, he should be done with patients by then.

Seeing a representative of the Hamilton Bowles law firm was not nearly so easy. Had I been an attorney, perhaps it would have gone smoother, but a doctor trying to make an appointment with a lawyer only subjected you to a series of guilt questions.

"Did you have a DUI, sir? Have you been sued for medical malpractice? Are you intending to file for bankruptcy? Are you getting a divorce?"

"Hell no, to all the above, ma'am. I need to speak to an attorney associated with Hamilton Bowles who would know about the Sandy Lowell estate and the terms of his last will and testament. I have pertinent knowledge about certain aspects of the will. The last time we spoke, he told me his son had joined the firm. Perhaps he would be available?"

"Hmm. Let's see," she said. "Hamilton Jr. will be in the office later this morning, around 11 a.m. After that, he has some pleadings to file with the court. Would that work for you, Doctor?"

"I'll be there. Thank you."

As expected, traffic was abysmal. I followed Highway 71 into the west side of Austin, continued east on Highway 290 onto Interstate 35, and took a downtown exit into lawyerville. The navigation system bypassed the Mopac Freeway, or Highway 1, which was always a source extreme aggravation. I followed the pleasant female voice's directions onto Fifteenth Street and found the firm not far from the Texas capitol. I located a public parking concern near the office building, prepaid, walked a couple of blocks, and arrived fifteen minutes before my scheduled appointment time. The building was a white two-story converted home and resembled an antebellum mansion from the south. A sign on the front porch read Bowles and Associates, so the nav lady had done her job.

There was a living room off to the right, where a couple of customers sat. To my left was a built-in desk, nicely paneled, that matched the plank hardwood flooring. Two young ladies sat there, both blond and impeccably dressed, with headphones, and they sounded like they were sorting clients into categories and referring them to the appropriate legal counsel. The law office version of medical triage, I suppose.

I introduced myself to the first woman who was available.

"Yes, sir, Dr. Brady, Mr. Bowles will be right with you. Please have a seat."

I picked up a magazine entitled *Texas Lawyer* and suffered through a special edition revealing page after page of lawyers for hire, their specialties, and their accomplishments. Many had served in the Texas legislature, and one had even been appointed to the Texas Supreme Court. I put it down, slid down in my comfortable client chair, and closed my eyes.

"Dr. Brady, Mr. Boyles will see you now," said headphone #1 before the snoring process began.

She escorted me into a suite of offices in the rear of the building. She glided in black high heels which clicked on the hardwood floor as she walked.

The nameplate outside his office read W. Hamilton Bowles Jr. That made me ponder—when are you a Jr. and when are you a II? I doubted I should ask the fortysomething-year-old man standing in front of me. He was about my height and completely bald, and he wore pin-striped gray slacks, wing-tip polished shoes, and a white shirt with suspenders.

"Ham Bowles," he said, pumping my hand like a rush chair who desperately wanted me to pledge his fraternity.

"Jim Bob Brady," I said. "Thanks for seeing me."

"My pleasure. Please sit. Beverage?"

"No, thanks. I don't want to take up much of your time. I had a few questions about Sandy Lowell's estate. I had the opportunity to meet your father recently and heard the stories about how close he and Sandy had been. I was invited to a conference to discuss Sandy's bequests, particularly as it involved the Hill

Country Medical Center. I was sorry to hear of your father's pass-ing. I understand he had some sort of uncontrollable arrhythmia?"

"Yes. He was healthy as a horse, never had any heart trouble. He had played a round of golf at Austin Country Club, came into the clubhouse for a beverage, and passed out. EMTs were called, and he arrived at St. David's within a short time, but he could not be resuscitated."

"Again, my condolences. About your dad and Sandy Lowell?"

"Oh, yes, he and Sandy were frat brothers back in the day here at UT. They were good friends, as well as having the client–attorney relationship. Fraternity man, Dr. Brady?"

"Yes. I was an ATO at Baylor, back in the dark ages."

He laughed. "SAE at UT for me. I don't know how it was for you at Jerusalem-on-the-Brazos, but for me, most of my current friends I met and pledged with in college. For us, it's a lifelong relationship. Many of us went on to UT law school, which is on campus, so for three more years, we were able to stay in the midst of all the activity. And many of us stayed on in Austin and practice here, and it's like we never left school. That is the most fun of it all. And then we try and convince our kids to follow us to UT, and the cycle continues ad infinitum."

"Not so much for me. When you leave town and go off to med school for four years, then internship, residency, and fellowship for five or six more years, you've lost touch with most everybody you knew. Nine years is a long time to be separated from your friends from college days."

"I see. Well, what can I do for you, sir?"

I had failed the good-old-frat-boy living-in-the-past test. Good. I got down to business.

"Your father implied that you worked on the Lowell account, that in fact you might have taken over duties from your father over time. He looked to be around retirement age, and I can see how he might gradually turn over business to a son that was well-trained and following in his father's footsteps," I said, sucking up in a more general way.

"Yes, I did work on the Lowell account."

"In that case, would you have any idea, knowing Sandy Lowell's past, why your father would stipulate at that meeting that Sandy and Jennifer Lowell were half-brother and half-sister, as offspring of Lowell II, rather than father–daughter, as DNA testing had proved years ago?"

Young Ham Bowles stared at me for a moment, much like you would stare at some strange insect clinging to the wall of your bathroom.

"And you came by this information how, sir?"

"Doesn't matter, but it's true. Sandy Lowell even paid the mother $50 million in a trust, money he borrowed from his father. And, stupidly, he put the mother in charge of the funds as trustee, funds which have now dwindled down to about $2 million, possibly due to the profligate spending of said trustee. I would have loved to ask your father these questions, but he unfortunately is unable to answer them. We were under the impression that that Lowell II had set up a trust for Jennifer because he was her parent, but we later found out that he was not in fact the father, that his son Sandy was, and that Sandy's father gave him the $50 million to set up the trust with. And at the meeting where your father divulged the proceeds of the will, there was no provision for Jennifer. So, I wonder where Sandy's mind was when he was constructing his will, in neglecting to provide for his daughter?"

"Dr. Brady, these are personal issues between the deceased and his attorneys. Do you have any proof of your authorization to be involved in these matters? Do you have a power of attorney, a court order, anything to establish your legitimate and legal presence involving yourself in Sandy Lowell's last will and testament? I think not. As a result, I'm unable to help you, sir. You have no legal standing."

He stood, my signal to leave. I had one last chance. "I would like you, as a man, and probably a concerned parent, to answer me one question, and then I'll go about my business. In the past month or two, did Sandy attempt to draw up any sort of document, apart from his last will and testament, that would establish a new trust of some sort to care for his daughter?"

He sighed. "Yes, but I tell you in strictest confidence, since there are no more Lowells remaining other than Jennifer, who is mentally disabled and probably unable to comprehend a conversation such as this. He had asked my father to draw up a new trust, with Sandy as the trustee, in the amount of $50 million, for the benefit of Jennifer Lowell."

"Did the trust get funded?"

"No sir, it did not."

"Why, may I ask?"

"Because, Dr. Brady, the documents were not completed, and even if they had been, Mr. Lowell died before he could sign off on the paperwork."

Once back in the car, I programmed Dr. Warner's address into the nav system. He was fortunately at the south campus of St. David's Medical Center. I headed east to Interstate 35, turned south, took the exit to Highway 71/290, and shortly thereafter arrived at an office building adjacent to St. David's on Ben White Boulevard. It was drizzling, and the temperature had dropped at least ten degrees.

Dr. Robert Warner had a beautiful suite of offices on the fourth floor. I was greeted by a lovely receptionist, who stood tall and auburn-haired and was age-indeterminate, possibly due to enhancements and improvements made by her boss. She escorted me back to his private office. I declined a beverage. I stood and looked at his framed diplomas, all from good, respectable schools. His plastic surgery training had been done at Vanderbilt, known to be a mecca for that sort of work. He had numerous awards from the Plastic Surgery Society, as well as commemorations from a number of civic organizations for his work in breast cancer reconstruction.

"Afternoon, Dr. Brady," Dr. Warner said, as he entered. We shook hands, then he sat in his desk chair, and I across from him, at a large desk covered in paperwork. It reminded me of my former desk at University Hospital in Houston. He had a friendly smile, wire-rimmed glasses, receding brown hair, and a short goatee that had retained its brown color.

"I must say, I don't usually meet with another physician about work I've done on patients. My assistant told me you wanted to discuss something to do with Phyllis Reardon and Sandy Lowell?"

"Yes, that's correct. Briefly, I'm an orthopedic surgeon out at Hill Country Medical Center. I'm working part-time, if you call four days a week part-time. I was at University Med Center in Houston for many years. Marble Falls is my stress cure, if you will."

"I know you by name and reputation. One of my friends here trained in your program and was invited to stay, but narrowly escaped back to Austin. You know those UT alums," he said, and we shared a laugh over that.

"I appreciate you meeting with me. I am a close friend of Dr. Buck Owens, chair of the board at HCMC and a longtime close personal friend of Sandy Lowell. Buck initially got me involved in trying to discover what prompted the ventricular fibrillation that cost Sandy his life. I happened to be in the parking lot of the grocery store when his episode began. I performed CPR while waiting on the ambulance. The EMTs resuscitated him briefly, but to no avail. The docs at the hospital couldn't get his heart back into sinus rhythm and he expired.

"An autopsy was performed, as is required by state law when someone dies within twenty-four hours of admission. It was basically clean. No coronary artery disease, no valvular disease, no evidence of what triggered the sudden arrhythmia. The pathologist did note the scarring behind the ears, the classic tell of a facelift. Purely by coincidence, an acquaintance of his who happened to be a patient of yours came to a dinner party at my home."

"That would be Phyllis Reardon?"

"Correct. She mentioned seeing Sandy at your office, which is how I found you. I'm here to see if you would have any clue about what possibly could have caused his demise."

He picked up a chart from the pile in front of him and leafed through it. "I operated on Sandy Lowell five times over the years. He had a blepharoplasty—eyelid lift—first the right, then the left. Then he had a facelift when he was around fifty years old, then a rhinoplasty, and then a repeat facelift about six months ago. He had some healing issues with the second facelift due to scarring and poor blood supply, not uncommon in that age group. Eventually he healed fine. The blephs were done under local anesthesia with IV sedation as an outpatient. The rhino was done under general anesthesia with an overnight stay. No record of any sort of anesthesia problems, and none that I can recall. Both facelifts were done under general, and both times he stayed at few days at St. David's private wing for high rollers. The records don't reflect any problems with his heart on either occasion. Sorry, I wish I could be of more help."

"Not a problem. I didn't think he would have exhibited any prior history of rhythm issues, since his autopsy was clean as a whistle. I just can't understand it."

"Sandy was a great guy, always telling stories, laughing, seemed to not have a care in the world. Maybe that's how life is when you're worth, what, a billion dollars?"

"I wouldn't know. Surely there are some unhappy billionaires; I just don't happen to know any of them. Well, thanks much for your time," I said, rising. "Nice office space. Convenient to the hospital. Living the dream, huh, Doc?"

"Yep, and you know all about that dream of increasing overhead and declining reimbursement, don't you?"

"Been there, done that. Working for HCMC in a salaried position has been an incredibly positive change for me. I do surgeries Monday and Wednesday, see patients Tuesday and Thursday, and reserve my frustrations for the golf course on the weekends. I'm even enjoying the patients and the work again. You'll get there one of these days; you're just not quite old enough."

"I hope so. You didn't have any questions about Phyllis Reardon, did you? I mean, I'm limited in what I can say, due to HIPPA rules. Sandy being deceased, I didn't think it was a problem to share a few minor details with you."

"No questions about Phyllis, just to tell you that's how I came about your name."

"They had appointments on the same days over the years, as I recall. Sandy would mention that to me on occasion. They seemed very friendly together."

"You wouldn't see them together, as patients, would you?"

"Oh, of course not. I remember seeing them together in the coffee shop on the ground floor on occasion, after their office visits, when I would either be heading home or over to the hospital to make post-op rounds. I even saw them holding hands once, leaving the coffee shop together. It occurred to me they might be very good friends, or more, but while Sandy was single, Phyllis is married to a doc. Heart surgeon, right?"

"Right."

"Probably nothing, just for some reason that stuck in my memory."

CHAPTER 14

LAWSUITS

Friday afternoon traffic going west toward Marble Falls and the Highland Lakes was, as usual, a mess. I thanked the traffic gods that I was starting out on the west side of Austin, with ready access to Highway 71. By the time I passed Bee Cave Road, the drizzle had turned to a thunderstorm. My top speed was limited to 50 mph, and the windshield wipers were working overtime. I was also thankful to be fairly high up off the ground in a Tahoe. In spite of the weather, 18-wheelers passed me, thrashing me with buckets of extra water from the road. I screamed and yelled and gestured hand signals at them with no appreciable results.

It had been pretty much a wasted trip. All I had learned from W. Hamilton Bowles Jr. was that Sandy had initiated the formation of a new trust on behalf of his daughter Jennifer, but either the paperwork wasn't completed, or his signature wasn't attached. Sandy was planning to take care of his child but simply had run out of time. He obviously had no clue that he was going to die of a fatal arrhythmia before completing that task. I felt better about him, knowing that. But I still was puzzled by his seemingly irresponsible behavior in not taking a more active role in the management of Jennifer's trust. Allowing his former paramour, the child's mother, Phyllis Reardon, to handle the finances all those years without so much as a second look seemed daft to me. In his defense, however, at least until recently, there had never been a complaint by Cynthia about funds needed for Jennifer or the household, or so I interpreted from my conversation with the caretaker. If there had been problems in the past, she certainly didn't mention it. And what was it that Buck said? Sandy loved Phyllis and trusted her implicitly. Maybe the explanation was as simple as that.

I was curious about the hand-holding episode that Dr. Richard Warner had witnessed, and the seemingly close and friendly relationship between Sandy and Phyllis. Was something going on between them, or was there still a bond from having a shared impaired child that neither wanted? It was a sad situation for all parties concerned.

And so I drove on, anxious to get home to my own lover and my faithful dog. My iPod delivered the perfect song at the perfect time, Stevie Ray Vaughan's "The Sky Is Cryin'." I cranked up the volume, ignored the semis, and sang along with the young man who had died way before his time.

Two and one-half hours of driving in the rain had worn me out. Tip was chomping at the bit for a walk, but as I entered the kitchen through the garage, a loud clap of thunder sent him howling and scurrying to his favorite hiding place, my closet. More than likely, he would relieve himself there, as had happened before. I got the leash, found him under my clothes to be taken to the dry cleaners, and literally dragged him to the back porch. He did his business while shivering, fearing another thunderclap. Thankfully none was forthcoming for the moment, so he ran back into the house and into his favorite place of refuge.

Mary Louise arrived home shortly thereafter and gave me a smooch and a big hug. "I always worry when you're on the road

to and from Austin. Glad you're home safely. Need a drink?"
she asked.

"Yes. Several, in fact."

I related the substance of my meetings with Bowles and
Warner over freshly constructed Tito's vodka dirty martinis, guar-
anteed to cure what ails you, or at least make you forget that you
were ailing. The weather was still stormy, so I hooked up my iPod,
chose the blues genre, and was presented first with Etta James's
"At Last." Having a dirty martini and being with the two women
you love—Etta from afar, of course—caused the frustration of my
relatively crappy day to melt away.

"What do you think about their relationship?"

"Huh? I'm sorry, I had drifted away, like Dobie Gray."

"That's cute. I must remember that. Sandy and Phyllis.
Something current, or reliving past adventures?"

"Not a clue, Mary Louise."

We sat in a pleasant silence for a time, then I became ravenous. "Let's go over to the Lantana Room for dinner. They have a
large portico, and we won't get wet. And it's only a few blocks
away. Sound good?"

"Yes. Let me freshen up."

"You freshen up any more and I'll forget all about dinner."

"Flattery will get you everywhere, darling," she said, as she
danced into the bedroom to the sounds of "Master Card," sung and
played by the late great Albert Collins. When he fired up that Fender
Telecaster, the sound was like a lightning bolt through my chest.

Lantana was relatively empty, due to the storm. We lived
nearby, so the drive wasn't an issue. I tipped the valet an extra
twenty dollars to park my SUV under the covered area. The hostess suggested we choose our table, so we selected one close to the
bar and the multiple television screens. The Friday night specialty

was fried chicken. I opted for that with mushroom gravy and fried okra, and a salad to start to make it a healthy meal. Mary Louise opted for grilled chicken and a vegetable medley.

We also ordered a bottle of Rombauer chardonnay, and while we sipped, Mary Louise related the events of her canasta tournament. At the end of the day, there were two teams remaining, she and another. Over the course of two hands, she picked up the pile and got all the aces and sevens, then followed that with a splash of pairs, and wiped out her and her partner's last opponent to come out victorious.

We were laughing about one of her plays when we heard a "Good evening, Bradys" behind us.

"Hey, Mike, Phyllis, how are you two?" I said as cheerfully as possible as I stood up to greet the Reardons. Mary Louise and Phyllis exchanged air kisses.

"Good night for ducks, Jim Bob," said Mike. "You two eating alone?"

"Yes, just a quick—oh, here's our food now," Mary Louise replied.

"We're meeting another couple," Phyllis responded. "Just thought we'd say hello. Ta."

They wandered off to greet a couple that we didn't recognize, then found their friends at a back table away from the main entry to the dining room.

"She always seems so nice, Jim Bob. I just can't believe these stories you're telling me about her and Sandy Lowell, and an unwanted love child between two first cousins."

"Well, it must be true. I got the information first-hand from Cynthia Stiles, her caretaker, which was confirmed by Buck Owens himself. Sandy was barely thirty, and she was only eighteen or nineteen. What can I say? I started out looking for Sandy's cause of death, and now I've gathered all this extraneous and sordid information that doesn't give me one single clue as to why he died. I don't know what else to look into. Jennifer Lowell is a pitiable creature, and the permanent reminder of a forbidden love turned ugly, but that has seemingly nothing to do with Sandy's death. I think it's time to turn my attentions elsewhere, like to work, or my golf game, or the new Jack Reacher novel. I'd like to sit back, relax, and read about how Lee Child figures out a new mystery for his protagonist to solve."

"You might consider devoting some extra attention to the woman sitting here with you," she said, as she batted those long eyelashes of hers at me. Then she stabbed a baby carrot with her fork, placed it in her mouth, and then withdrew it ever so slowly.

I immediately raised my hand to our server and called out, "Check please."

Mary Louise and I stayed up well past our normal bedtime. I took Tip out for a brief goodnight walk much later than normal as well, so we slept in. I awoke to the inimitable smell of frying bacon. I stretched, and Tip yawned, then rolled onto his back and rolled from side to side, scratching himself, then suddenly catapulted himself onto the floor and ran toward the kitchen.

I made a necessary trip to the bathroom, washed my face and hands, slipped on a pair of shorts and a tee shirt, and joined the family in the kitchen. Mary Louise had fried enough bacon for a small platoon of soldiers and was cooking scrambled eggs with what looked like peppers, onions, and cheese.

"Hungry, my dear?" I asked.

"Ravenous," she said, bending over the bar and kissing me on the cheek. "I think Tip needs to go out."

"I can tell that look, torn between relieving himself or standing by on bacon duty. C'mon, boy," I said, and walked over to the patio door. He followed reluctantly, did his business in record time, and repositioned himself next to Mary Louise, on the alert for crumbs.

"What's on your agenda today, Jim Bob?"

"I'm supposed to play golf, but the weather forecaster predicts more rain. How about you?"

"No definite plans, just thought we might catch a movie and lunch if you were available."

"I'm not sure I can take another drive to Austin. Two days in a row might do me in."

"The owners have remodeled the cinema over in Marble Falls. Want to take a chance?"

"I'm game. Let me take the Tipster for a walk."

I grabbed an umbrella, offsetting the rain possibilities. No umbrella, rain for sure. Tip and I walked around the courtyards of our tiny subdivision, then headed out the gate and down the lane to the dog park. He was pulling so hard, and the ground was so slippery from all the rain, I had trouble keeping my balance. We finally arrived at the flat area, only to find we were the only ones present. Everyone else had either forgone the dog walking or had walked their pets earlier. Probably the latter, since I felt the first hard drop of cold rain, checked my watch, and realized it was already midmorning.

Tip was in the middle of his business when the first thunderclap sounded. He jumped a foot in the air, as though he had been shot. He tore off back up the hill, the leash slipping from my hand. I tried to run, but the muddy ground held onto my shoes like cement. I took them off and ran after Tip, mostly worried one of the four homeowners would exit the gate and not see Tip until it was too late. The rain was pelting so hard I couldn't see, and the wind blowing at a pace that kept me from opening the umbrella.

I heard the screech of tires, thinking shit, shit, shit. I called after Tip as I ran up the hill, saw the neighbor's car, but didn't see my dog. She cracked the window just enough to tell me she had barely missed Tip, and she saw him headed toward our garage. I arrived in time to see Mary Louise trying to dry him off with a beach towel, although he was desperate to get inside and out of the noise.

"That dog is going to be the death of me, Mary Louise. I thought he had been run over."

"No, thank the lord. He's fine. I came out here on the basis of a bad feeling. Thunder, you trying to walk Tip, him freaking out at the first clap, you trying to run up the hill. A recipe for disaster. Glad you're both okay. By the way, Buck just called. I told him you would call him back, that we were trying to avoid a doggie disaster."

Mary Louise had to use the hairdryer to get Tip dry, and I had to shower to get myself clean. After all that commotion, we decided it safer to prepare lunch at home and watch a movie.

"Hey, Buck. I'm returning your call?"

"We have a problem, Brady. Have you by any chance talked to Phyllis Reardon?"

"Not really. We saw her and Mike last night at dinner, but they were eating with another couple."

"How about Ham Jr.?"

"Well, I did go see him yesterday, as well as the plastic surgeon, Richard Warner, that had operated on both Sandy and Phyllis. I can't say that I learned anything, other than the relationship between Phyllis and Sandy might be different than we thought, and that Sandy had told the Bowles firm to draft a new trust with Jennifer the beneficiary, but it had not been completed by the time of his death."

"That is monumental news, Brady. When were you thinking of telling me?"

"Well, maybe during the week, like Monday. It is the weekend, you know. What's the problem?"

"Phyllis has hired an attorney to contest Sandy Lowell's will and has also filed a lawsuit against Hill Country Medical Center to negate his bequest to us as well, that's what."

"I can't say I'm all that surprised. He did leave his daughter out of the will, perhaps inadvertently, but left her out regardless. Phyllis probably wants another $50 million to play with. By the time that runs out, she will either be deceased or won't care. I got the impression from Bowles that the funds for Sandy's new trust would come out of his investment portfolio and not as a codicil to his will, although I'm certainly no lawyer and don't know what all that means, now that he's deceased."

"It means this lawsuit could negate his bequest to HCMC. She is alleging that Sandy was incompetent mentally. It's a damn mess, Brady."

CHAPTER 15

TRUE LIES

When I was younger and didn't want to be disturbed, I simply took the phone off the hook. Modern times dictate that one seeking solace has to turn the cell phone off, along with text messaging, Skype, Facebook, LinkedIn, and whatever other social media programs are active on the computer. And maybe that will give a person a few moments of silence in order to think. I tried that Sunday morning, and after five minutes or so, I heard the landline ring. I almost walked outside and threw the damn thing into the pool, and had it not still been raining, I would have done so posthaste.

"Do you need to answer the phone?" Mary Louise asked.

"Not only no, but hell no. I don't want to speak to anyone other than you and Tip for the rest of the day."

Mary Louise was curled up in a blanket on the sofa next to the great room fireplace, reading the latest Harlan Coben novel. She stared at me for a moment, then went back to her reading.

I promised myself I was not going to get involved in the lawsuit trouble brought on by Sandy Lowell's last will and testament. I had experience with lawyers and lawsuits, and the lawyers always won. I intended, however, to be diligent in pursuing any possible causes of Sandy Lowell's demise. I also wondered if I might be able to sneak a peek at W. Hamilton Bowles Sr.'s medical records, since, according to the grapevine, he had died of the same type of arrhythmia. Being removed, however, from any personal knowledge of his medical issues, I had no dog in the hunt, so to speak. It would require a major effort to obtain his medical history, and his medical records, and I would have to pass through his son, and perhaps a wife if he had one, in order to get permission to snoop around Bowles Sr.'s business. That held a low-percentage chance of success.

I knew the HCMC main phone number by memory, so I went to the landline and dialed and spoke to the operator. She connected me to the pathology lab, where the voicemail system invited me to explore a number of options, none of which was "I want to talk to Jerry Reed!" Despite my frustration with "press 1," "press 2," "press 3," I finally reached a live person in the autopsy room, who simply said: "Speak."

"This is Dr. Jim Bob Brady. I'm looking for—"

"Brady, Jerry Reed here. What's happening? Nothing better to do on a Sunday than to talk to the keeper of the dead?"

"I might have better things to do, but I'm devoting some time to follow up on the causes of Sandy Lowell's death. You called it in your official report an unexplained ventricular arrhythmia, or idiopathic ventricular fibrillation, or something of that nature, right?"

"I'd have to look it up, but that sounds right."

"What in your opinion would potentially cause that, in light of an autopsy showing no cardiac disease of any kind?"

He was silent. "Jerry?"

"Huh? Oh, sorry, I was just looking at this guy's heart. He has all kinds of weird scarring along the ventricles."

"Who are you talking about, Jerry?"

"Oh, this fella I have on the table that I'm doing the autopsy on."

"You're doing an autopsy while you talk to me?"

"Brady, have you not heard of a hands-free dictating system?"

"Of course. I just didn't think about you doing, well, two things at once."

"I may only be a man, Brady, but I can certainly talk to you and complete this autopsy simultaneously, thank you very much. I'm thinking potassium. I would bet that is somehow the key, unless it's a toxin of some sort that couldn't be identified. One of those two."

"You're back to Sandy Lowell? In reference to his arrhythmia?"

"Yes."

"When we last spoke about this issue, you told me Sandy had a very high level of potassium in the post-mortem lab work, but you thought that was most likely due to his cardiac arrest, correct?"

"Correct."

"Did you consider a low potassium level that could have triggered the arrhythmia?"

"I did, but of the causes I can think of that create a low potassium state in the body—for example, alcoholism, kidney disease, diabetes, dehydration—Mr. Lowell didn't have any of those problems. Also, Jim Bob, patients who have low potassium exhibit many signs and symptoms prior to cardiac arrest, like weakness, fatigue, muscle cramps, palpitations, and numbness and tingling. More likely than not, he would have exhibited some of those symptoms prior to having a cardiac arrest and would have gone to see the doctor with some of those problems first. He wouldn't have just died. Besides, most of us know what it's like to feel dehydrated—tired, rapid pulse, extreme thirst—so you down a couple of energy drinks, and all is well again.

"Now that's not necessarily true of high potassium levels. That can cause cardiac arrhythmias and even a cardiac arrest pretty quickly, but again, that's most common in chronic kidney disease, which he didn't have. And besides, patients with kidney disease bad enough to get those high potassium levels are almost always on dialysis, and constantly have their blood monitored for that sort of problem.

"So, my money would be on a sudden low potassium state, perhaps due to extreme dehydration, or an unidentifiable toxin."

"That doesn't give me much to go on. Either he died from dehydration causing low potassium, or a toxin in the blood that cannot be identified. If it can't be identified, how could you possibly find out what it was, Jerry?"

"That's the point, my friend, you can't. It would be the perfect kill drug."

"Are you saying . . ."

"No, I'm not, but on a theoretical basis, if you wanted to do somebody in secretly, that sort of drug would be ideal."

"But no clue what it would be?"

"No. But I'll think about it."

"By the way, Jerry, at a conference a week or so ago, Buck Owens told those present that he had spoken to you about the DNA testing of Sandy and Jennifer Lowell. He told the group that you were of the opinion that the DNA was compatible with the two being sister and brother from the same father. Is that correct?"

"Incorrect. I told him that it was POSSIBLE they were brother and sister, but I also told him that it was much more likely, because of the number of alleles they had in common, that they were father and daughter. Why do you ask?

"Just curious. Thanks."

After talking to Jerry, I had a pounding headache. I took a couple of ibuprofen, washed them down with a cola full of caffeine, and did what I usually did when I am stumped. I made a list. Making a list isn't really doing anything, but by making a list one feels as though something is being accomplished. If the list turns into a task, and the various tasks are accomplished, then one can safely say that one has done something. If the list is, however ignored, shredded, or otherwise destroyed, time has been success-fully wasted by the list maker, which might have been the goal in the first place.

I wanted to know about the health status of Ham Bowles Sr. I could get that from perhaps his son, whom I had met, or perhaps his wife, which might be a stretch, not knowing her at all.

I wanted to see the attending physician's records, or the hos-pital records, of Ham Boyles Sr. at the time of his death. I wanted to check out his lab values, especially his potassium levels, and see for sure what type of cardiac arrhythmia he had succumbed to.

I needed to read about potassium levels and cardiac problems myself and try to understand the electrolyte issues. It had been years since I took biochemistry and physiology in med school, so I would need to brush up on those topics.

I needed to research toxins that caused cardiac problems, and resultant death.

And I needed to eat lunch.

"Mary Louise, are you hungry, and if so, what for?"

"Anything I don't have to cook," she responded.

I called the yacht club, ordered a couple of medium-rare cheeseburgers with curly fries, and a large Caesar salad, and told them I'd pick up the order in an hour or so.

"I'm going to stop by my office and get the schedule for tomorrow, then pick up the food." I leaned over and kissed her, patted Tip on the head, as he was tucked in next to his mistress, and headed out.

The roads were a mess, this part of Texas not accustomed to a continuum of thunderstorms severe enough to cause street flooding. But most of us had large SUVs or pickup trucks, and we sailed along to our respective destinations with undue bother.

I picked up the charts for the next day, along with the mail and letters that needed to be signed or dictated, and placed the stack into a briefcase I kept in the office for just such an occasion. On the way out, I ran into Mike Reardon in the elevator vestibule.

"Hey, Mike. Catching up?"

"Yes. Tomorrow is an operating day. Say, I'm glad I ran into you. Word has come down from reliable sources that you are now aware of the situation that Phyllis got herself into when she was nineteen years old. We've kept that under wraps all these years, but what with Sandy dying and all, and the problems with the will, I worry that information, which would severely damage her, might leak out. I'm hoping that, as my friend, whatever you might hear you would keep to yourself."

"Of course, Mike. I'm not clear on something, though. Since you mentioned Sandy's will and Phyllis's problem from many years ago, you are obviously aware of the true facts, and not the fabrication that a rich uncle left her money years ago?"

"Of course I know the facts, I'm married to the woman. How could she possibly keep something like that from her husband? That was a story I invented a long time ago to cover her tracks and to keep her past separated from Sandy Lowell. People are much more accepting of others with inherited money, rather than hush money to keep a love child secret. That was a good explanation of how we live beyond our means. Listen, I have to run. Good to see you, buddy, and thanks for keeping our business to yourself."

I wondered how hard it would be for everyone I had a relationship with to just tell me the truth about things. I have found over the years that being honest was the easiest way to approach life, because you didn't have to try and remember what the "truth" was the last time you told a story about yourself.

CHAPTER 16

SURGERY

It was fortunate that I had stopped by the office Sunday afternoon. Shelly Wood had scheduled four cases: two hip and two knee replacements, all virgin surgeries. What I wouldn't have known was that I had been on call for the weekend, and Charlotte Stone, nurse practitioner for HCMC, and my part-time surgical assistant, had seen two patients with fractured hips on Saturday, and scheduled them as add-ons for my Monday surgery schedule.

The two broken hips came about as a result of an accident at one of the local nursing/memory care facilities. A married couple was in residence there, both in their late eighties, and had been quietly watching a *Lawrence Welk Show* rerun on television. Apparently, the husband had a memory "spark" and suddenly jumped up from his seat on the couch, grabbed his wife, and started twirling her around to the tune of the "Wabash Cannonball." They danced for a minute or two, then got their legs tangled up in their respective robes, and went down in a heap, resulting in a hip fracture for each.

The man, William Thomas, had an intertrochanteric fracture, which could be repaired easily with a compression screw or flange, and a side plate. Mrs. Thomas unfortunately had a femoral-neck fracture, which most likely would have compromised the blood flow to the "ball" side of the hip joint. Inserting multiple pins might hold it together, but more than likely she would need a ball replacement, or a complete hip replacement, in order to try and minimize further surgeries.

Regardless, this meant six cases for Monday, a tough task even with all the assistants I had at University Hospital in Houston. I called the nursing supervisor at HCMC on call for the weekend, and fortunately spoke to my old friend and fellow board member, Louann Simms. She had been of great help the previous year in assisting me with discoveries in a battered women case I got involved in through a patient. I explained my dilemma to her and requested the use of a second operating room, both for my convenience and the patients' comfort in avoiding making them NPO (without food or water after midnight) for an extended period of time. She heartily agreed to provide that second room and went about calling in additional nursing help for the following day.

I called Charlotte and asked about family members of the two extra patients. She hadn't seen or spoken to anyone the previous day and had not received any calls from a worried son or daughter on Sunday. She assured me she would be assisting me in the operating room. I also called Shelly Wood, my personal nurse, doing double duty as phone answerer and appointment maker, and asked her to be prepared to scrub in and help in the operating room. She was ecstatic, and happy to turn over her temporary duties to the folks whose job that was.

It was like the old days, six cases, two operating rooms, country music in one room, blues in the other, with Charlotte in one O.R. and Shelly in the other. We started at seven in the morning and put the last stitch in at five in the afternoon. Mrs. Thomas ended up getting an artificial ball with a stem, and not a complete hip replacement. She had a concomitant diagnosis of multiple myeloma, and her life expectancy at that age was less than one year. I wondered briefly how Mr. Thomas would handle the passing of his wife, after having lived together in the nursing home, but quickly put that out of my mind.

I went to the waiting room and spoke to all the families in person. I had not had time to do so between cases, working two rooms as I did, but had called each from the operating room. The last person I spoke to was Dr. Bart Thomas, orthodontist and son of Mr. and Mrs. Thomas. I explained the procedures I had performed on his parents. He was in his sixties, had children and grandchildren of his own, and lived in Austin. He was grateful for my prompt response in getting his parents' broken hips repaired, and he mirrored my thought when he wondered aloud how in the world his dad could possibly get along without the wife. Or vice versa.

Shelly had been in the O.R. with me all day, and therefore there wasn't much paperwork to handle on my desk.

"I had a great time today, Doc. That's what I'm trained for, you know, dealing with patients, assisting in the O.R.. I'm not a clerical person. I don't want to answer the phone and make appointments. I want to do what I was trained to do. I took over the other duties because, well, quite frankly, the staff pool whose job that is has not been very efficient lately. Patients are having to wait too long to get in, and they don't get called back promptly."

"Sounds like we need to get a full-time administrative person working in the office. That would free you up for nursing duties."

"Don't get me wrong, I'm happy to help with anything to do with your office, but I don't want to neglect my own duties."

"Totally get it. I'll speak with the administrator."

"By the way, Dr. Owens asked me to dinner."

I had wondered when that might happen. Our dinner party had been a while now, and Mary Louise had positioned them next to each other, thinking about playing matchmaker.

"Where is he taking you?"

"A new restaurant in Austin, near the Galleria on the west side."

"Tonight?"

"Oh, no. Thursday. It's a clinic day for you, and normally you're off on Friday, so I thought I wouldn't have to rush the evening, just in case it became . . . interesting, you know?"

"No, I don't know, and I don't want to know. Thanks much for today, Shelly. You were great in the O.R.."

"See you tomorrow."

I dragged my tired bones into the house and collapsed on the sofa. Tip came over and put his big fat head on my chest, as if to say, "I'm tired too, owner."

Mary Louise fixed me a strong vodka and tonic, and I sat up just enough to sip it without spilling.

"Tough day, I heard."

"Yep. How did you hear?"

"Shelly called me between cases. She was assisting you in the O.R., she said."

"Yes, but I'm surprised to hear she called you about that."

"She called me about her date with Buck, wanted suggestions on what to wear."

"I'm thinking *Fiddler on the Roof.*"

"'Matchmaker, matchmaker'?"

"Exactly."

"You know how I don't like to see a nice smart girl lonely. I'm simply filling in a void. She can do with it what she pleases. But she told me she and Buck each signed the appropriate notifications with HR, for everyone's protection."

"I just don't want to hear any details."

"Don't worry, you won't. Want to shower before dinner?"

I'm always amazed how a hot shower washes away the grime and stress of the day. I stepped out and almost felt human again. Of course, my brain abhors a vacuum, so the first thing that came to mind was undetectable toxins in the blood that could kill, per Dr. Jerry Reed.

Mary Louise prepared a nice dinner of red snapper Pontchartrain, dirty rice, and fried okra. I opened a Ridge chardonnay, which blended with the seafood beautifully. I helped Mary Louise clean up the kitchen, then crawled into bed at eight thirty and, I was told, promptly fell asleep. Something I dreamed must have been unpleasant, because Mary Louise woke me up, as I was yelling something about "No, not that!" I didn't remember any of the details.

All was well on hospital rounds Tuesday morning. No sudden venous thromboses, no pulmonary emboli, no fevers, no bleeding from surgical wounds. All had happy smiling faces punching their pain medication buttons, except Mr. and Mrs. Thomas, who didn't quite have it figured out. Which made me wonder what kind of shape I would be in when my late eighties came. I might not even be alive. These folks had made it a long time and deserved a little extra care and attention when it came to the pain button, or so I informed the staff nurse who made rounds with me.

Clinic went smoothly, although the patient numbers I was seeing were climbing. And most of the folks whom I saw had already been treated with conservative measures for quite some time, either by me or another orthopedic surgeon. Most were there to schedule a knee or hip replacement. I was only one guy, and I took this job in order to slow down and soften the retirement thing. If every day turned out like the day before, I would be inundated beyond my capacity. I strongly felt that HCMC needed to recruit some young, well-trained surgeons to bridge the gap between what all needed to be done and what I and my other two joint-replacement colleagues could handle. I could work at max capacity for a while, but I didn't want to reach that burnout phase again.

"Shelly, would you make an appointment for me to see Dr. Owens, please? Maybe tomorrow, or Thursday afternoon?"

"Yes, sir. It's not about our date, is it? He's too old to need birth control, right?"

"Shelly, please don't make me throw up."

CHAPTER 17

INJECTIONS

I met Buck Thursday afternoon in the conference room, as usual. It was the night of the big date, and I hoped that didn't come up in our conversation.

"I have a driver for my date with Shelly tonight, so you don't have to worry about me drinking and driving with your nurse in the car."

"She's my nurse, not my daughter, Buck. I assume you'll be responsible. I'm here to talk about recruiting new surgeons. I'm already overwhelmed after only a year. I can't go through that burnout phase again. I'll quit altogether."

"We don't want that to happen. The board will start working on it."

"Buck, I'm on the board, and the subject hasn't been mentioned. You can't just hire a surgeon and have them here in a week or a month. It takes time."

"It didn't with you."

"I was an exception. But finding an older established surgeon who is willing to move to a small community with an excellent hospital is an ideal way to increase the staff in a short time. I'm serious, Buck. I'm almost at max. I did six procedures yesterday."

"Great. That's excellent for our bottom line. By the way, I'm going over to Austin tomorrow to see a dermatologist. He does facial injections for wrinkles. If I'm going to start dating, I need to look better."

"Why a dermatologist? Why not a plastic surgeon?"

"Those guys want to do surgery. I've asked around, and the injections are usually done by a nurse working for a plastic surgeon, or by a dermatologist."

"I went over to see Robert Warner Friday. He's the plastic surgeon that worked on Sandy, as well as Phyllis. He didn't mention anything about injections."

"I called his office. They don't do them. They referred me to a dermatologist colleague in Austin."

"I know nothing about injections. Injections of what?"

"Where have you been, Brady? You've got filler, like Juvéderm and Voluma. And paralytics, like Botox."

"How would I know about injections? Mary Louise hasn't had those, I'm sure."

Buck looked at me like I was crazy. "Are you kidding? As good as she looks? That isn't genetics, son, that's successful injections. Trust me. Now get out of here. I've got to get a haircut and get ready for my date."

I called Mary Louise on the car phone and told her I was on my way home, and I'd like to ask her some questions about facial injections. I told her that Buck Owens had brought it up and said that he was going to be seen by a dermatologist in Austin, and that I was totally ignorant on the subject. That was met with a short silence, then a "See you soon."

She met me at the door, gave me a tight hug, then took my hand and led me into the kitchen, where all the lights were on.

"Look at my face. Tell me what you see."

"I see a beautiful piece of work there, a natural beauty. You have a few laugh lines around your mouth and eyes, and a few worry lines on your forehead, but far less than I would expect for a woman married to a guy like me," I said, trying to keep the moment as light as possible.

"I look good because I take care of myself, and periodically, I have a little touch-up here and there with facial injections, and have for years."

"How could I not know? I mean, wouldn't you have some side effects, like bruising? Surely I would notice that."

"You're always very interested in my anatomy, but you concentrate on other parts, shall we say."

"I feel like an idiot. I know nothing about these injections. Can you enlighten me?"

"Let's start with Juvéderm. It's a hyaluronic acid dermal filler that is injected into problem areas. It can provide six months, sometimes longer, of improvement of facial wrinkles and folds, like nasolabial folds—those would be lines from the nose to the corner of the mouth. Hyaluronic acid is a naturally-occurring sugar in the body, so it's completely compatible with body chemistry and non-allergenic. It's also good for maintaining lip volume."

And at that point she puckered her lips and turned her head from side to side. I had no idea what I was supposed to be looking at, except those pouting lips made me think of other anatomical parts.

"See, I know that look of yours. You're already considering other physical features of mine, and that's the point! Injections keep me looking younger, and you interested."

"I'll try and control myself. Please tell me more."

"Okay. Juvéderm is designed for wrinkles that are present when your face is at rest. It's a filler, see, so it makes wrinkles disappear because they are filled in. This is opposite of Botox. Botox is used for wrinkles that appear on movement, such a laugh lines around the mouth, crow's feet, frown lines, and those nasty furrows we get on our foreheads."

"Are there side effects to the injections of filler?"

"There can be, and that's why selection of the physician or nurse is so important. Overfilling of the cheeks results in overly puffy cheeks which look unnatural and inappropriate for women my age. Also, lip overfilling can result in some bizarre and scary-looking side effects. Didn't you notice women, especially, in Houston, with big giant lips?"

"Uh, maybe."

"I know you, you'd go from looking at big lips to looking at big boobs very quickly. Sometimes excessive filler can be injected into the chin, which leaves a sharp, pointy chin. Again, a result of bad technique. There is much written about fillers, and just so you know, they are very expensive. One syringe of dermal filler, depending on the brand, costs about $1,000 for one cc."

"What?! Is that covered by insurance?"

"Are you kidding? Of course not."

"I should be doing injections for a living, sounds like."

"A lot of docs have gone into that field, qualified or not, for just that reason. Do you want to hear about Botox?"

"Of course, but at least I've heard something about that. It's botulinum toxin, and it has some clinical uses, like lazy eye, hyperhidrosis, cervical dystonia, which means neck spasms, and migraine headaches. I don't know anything about its use for wrinkle reduction."

"It's used to reduce wrinkles in the forehead and around the eyes by stopping, or paralyzing, the muscle movement in those areas. It's not quite as expensive as a dermal filler, but it costs $10 to $15 per unit, and it would take twenty units to take care of forehead wrinkles, so $200 to $300. It lasts for three to six months, and then muscle action gradually returns, and the lines and wrinkles begin to appear again, so the process has to be repeated."

"I'm totally astounded at how knowledgeable you are about this stuff."

"Well, I've done a lot of research over the years, and have experience with all the various modalities used to keep me young-looking and desirable."

"What about Botox side effects?"

"I've had friends who have developed short-term side effects, like trouble swallowing, shortness of breath, and muscle weakness, but they went away within hours. I had one friend back in Houston who developed severe breathing problems and had to be hospitalized and intubated, but apparently that is very rare. She recovered completely, but that ended her Botox treatments for good."

"Interesting. From what you've told me, injecting a filler could have local side effects—swelling, bruising, nodule formation—but probably not systemic side effects. But, injecting Botox could. In order for that to happen, though, it would have to get into the blood stream and effect other organ systems."

"I don't know about all those details, Jim Bob. You'd have to research that."

"I think I'm hungry now. Are we eating in?"

"Yes. I've got baked potatoes, fresh broccoli, and a couple of rib eye steaks if you don't mind firing up the grill."

"Sounds good. I'll do that, have another drink, and walk Tip. A favorite form of multitasking."

I worked hard to get the steaks medium rare, perhaps easier for a professional cook than a part-time novice on the grill. If

Tip's slobbering all over himself was any indication, the steaks were ready.

I shared my day with Mary Louise, and we laughed over Buck and Shelly having a date. She wondered how serious it could get on a first date, and I wondered if Buck remembered what to do if it did.

"I'm sorry to keep things from you, but I haven't discussed the injections with you because . . . well, I don't know exactly why. I think perhaps I would like what few mysteries I have about myself to be kept to myself. You know everything about me, and you are very familiar with my anatomy, and maybe I wanted to keep looking young for you and not have to explain it."

"I get it, and don't worry about it. I was just embarrassed Buck mentioned your having injections, and I have been either so self-centered or unobservant that I had no idea about it. Never even crossed my mind. Does that make me a bad husband?"

"Of course not, silly. You attributed my continued good looks into middle age to outstanding genetics, right?"

"I guess so. Really, I always have appreciated how good you look, and never even thought about what it takes to maintain that. Feel free to discuss the subject in the future, or not, as the case may be."

"You look beat, Jim. Let me clean up while you shower and get ready for bed."

I must have been tired after the long week, because the last thing I remember after my shower was climbing into bed. About two in the morning, I woke up with a start, got out of bed, and went into the kitchen for water. As I stood there in a daze, my mind wandered to all the information Mary Louise had given me that evening. Her knowledge about the injection subject was impressive. All sorts of ideas rolled around in my head, but then my mind became stuck on one concept. If Botox could get into the bloodstream and affect other internal organs, and cause breathing problems, could it cause a cardiac arrhythmia? And if so, was that what had killed Sandy Lowell?

CHAPTER 18

BOTOX

I went in early on Friday to make rounds because of the number of patients I had in the hospital. The four joint replacements were comfortable and would be moved to the rehab section of the hospital over the weekend. The two Thomas dancing lovebirds from the nursing home would go to rehab as well. The staff had put them together in a semi-private room. They seemed to have their own language, babbling at each other constantly, most of which was unintelligible to me. They both seemed to be comfortable and were getting up to sit at the bedside with the assistance of the physical therapists.

I stopped by my office, filled out a few forms on my desk, signed a couple of letters, and started out when Shelly came around the corner.

"Morning," I said. "I made rounds. Everyone is in pretty good shape, and I think all six will go over to rehab either today or tomorrow."

"Good. Sorry I'm late."

"It's only 9 a.m."

"I'm usually here by 8. The date with Dr. Owens dragged on for a while."

"Please, Shelly, minimal details."

"Oh, nothing bad, just that the driver he had hired had a little accident on the way back from Austin, ran over a nail or something and had a flat. He and Buck spent an hour changing the tire to one of those temporary jobs, which had just enough air to get me to my place. I'm not sure what they did after that, but I went in and went to bed. It was pretty funny, seeing the chair of HCMC on his knees, changing a flat tire. I offered to help them, but to no avail. When I left for work, the SUV was gone, so they must have figured it out somehow."

"I'm surprised to hear that Buck didn't call a service, like Triple A."

"I suggested that, but the air was pretty thick with testosterone."

"That's almost funny, were it not so tragic. Listen, I've got to run, tee time and all. Have a great day, Shelly."

"You too, Doc."

I happened to be paired with Mike Reardon again in my golf foursome and took the opportunity to quiz him about plastic surgery procedures, specifically in relation to injections of filler and Botox.

"Sure, Phyllis has been doing those for years. Warner hasn't been doing those procedures, although with all the revenue he's missing out on, he's thinking of starting. He doesn't want to do them himself, but rather hire a qualified nurse practitioner to handle those patients."

"Buck Owens told me that he had called Warner's office about Botox, and they had referred him to a dermatologist in Austin for injections."

"Phyllis uses Larry Goldfarb. I don't know if that's who Buck was referred to or not, but he's done a great job for Phyllis. Is Mary Louise thinking of getting some injections?"

"I'm embarrassed to say she's been doing it for years, and I just found out about it yesterday."

"You're a piece of work, Brady. A cross between a choir boy and an ostrich. You always seem to be the last guy that knows what's going on in the planet."

"That's because I keep my head down, and work, and mind my own business."

"Maybe you keep your head down, but you don't mind your own business. You're always digging into other people's issues, like Phyllis and Sandy's child, and god knows how many other people's private business. And yet, you don't recognize your own wife has been getting a face full of filler and Botox for years. I mean, really? What's up with that, man?" he said, as he grabbed a few clubs and walked toward the driving range. I caught up to him fairly quickly.

"I have to ask, Mike, you must be under some stress, Phyllis having filed a lawsuit to contest Sandy's will. According to Buck, she filed suit against HCMC as well, although I'm not sure that one will hold up. After all, HCMC didn't write the will; it is simply a beneficiary."

He stopped and took a deep breath. "You see, Brady, that's what I'm talking about. I'm out here to play some golf, put my personal troubles on the back burner for a few hours, and what do you do? Throw all that shit in my face that I'm trying to forget about. I am not party to these lawsuits. Phyllis did that on her own, much to my dismay. Her lawyer has filed a lawsuit against the hospital I work at every day. Can you even begin to put yourself in my shoes? Probably not, because as the town's most notable busybody, you're primarily interested in finding dirt about your so-called friends, while you strut around acting like you're better than the rest of us. I'm not playing golf with you today, so switch with one of the other guys."

I hated to hear he thought I was a busybody. Maybe that was true, although I held myself to a higher ideal and preferred to call it something else, something kinder and more professional. Part-time detective? Medical investigator? Righter of wrongs? Anything but busybody. That word reminded me of my dear departed mother, always in other people's business, trying to fix everybody's problems but never her own. I certainly hoped that wasn't me. Looking back, I had solved some pretty devious crimes, and had helped folks along the way, and not with any self-interest other than seeing justice done when appropriate. I was definitely not a busybody. Neither was I self-righteous, as Mike had implied.

When I arrived home after an absolutely crappy round of golf due to distractions of my own doing, I asked Mary Louise if she thought I would be labeled as a self-righteous busybody. She was quiet for a moment, then said, "Well, your interest in a subject may start out that way, but ultimately you're a solver of mysteries, a diligent delver into those things hidden from others for a good reason, usually, and you uncover malevolence in unlikely people and places. You're no superhero with special powers; you're just a man who won't leave any stone unturned to get to the truth of the matter. I don't know what to call what you do, but you do it well and have for some time. Look at all you did for the women at Mourning Doves last year."

"I didn't cure the problem of battered women, though, but maybe I made a difference in some lives. Who knows?"

"Don't start beating yourself up, Jim Bob. You have helped patients with their orthopedic problems for many years, and now, in addition, you're helping folks in a somewhat different way, a way which, to me, is much more difficult than operating on patients. You've discovered problems some folks were trying desperately to hide. At least with your patients, they come in and say,

'I hurt here, please fix me.' In this series of unwanted investigations you've been involved with, you've been beaten up, you've been given a concussion, you've been shot at. What better proof of a job well done than someone shooting at you to prevent the truth from coming out? You're no busybody. Forget what Mike said to you. He's under a great deal of stress right now, I'm sure, with a wife that's gone off like a loose cannon. You're a saint, and I mean that with the utmost respect."

She gave me a big hug, then had to hurry off to a meeting, or a canasta game, or maybe even more injections. I didn't ask. Mr. Busybody didn't want to know.

Tip and I went for a stroll down the hill, into the dog park, and beyond. It was a long walk to the shore of Lake LBJ, but we were there before I realized how far we had walked downhill. An engineered beach had been created, and Tip frolicked in the sand unabashedly for a time. I took off my sneakers and enjoyed the wet sand on my bare feet, thinking about Botox and breathing problems. I had yet to research the internet but felt I should do that prior to calling Dr. Goldfarb. I wanted to sound somewhat knowledgeable. But then, maybe if I sounded totally ignorant on the subject, he would be more forthcoming.

I leashed Tip, put my walking shoes back on, and slowly started back up the hill. About halfway there, we stopped for a breather. Just in the nick of time, a golf cart appeared from below and the neighborhood security guard offered us a ride back home. I'm sure he wondered what we were doing walking all the way down the hill and back, but he was too polite to ask.

After I recovered from my aerobic exercise and fed myself and Tip lunch, I called Dr. Larry Goldfarb's office in Austin. I introduced myself to the receptionist as an orthopedic surgeon in Granite Falls, and I was seeking some information about Botox.

She apparently thought I wanted patient-type information, and I didn't discourage her from that perception. She suggested a 4 p.m. phone consultation, which I gladly accepted.

I had a brief postprandial nap and called Dr. Goldfarb's office promptly at 4 p.m. I was patched through immediately.

"This is Larry Goldfarb. Is this Dr. Jim Brady?"

"Yes, sir, thanks for taking my call. I got your name from several sources, including Dr. Robert Warner there in Austin, and Dr. Mike Reardon, a colleague here at Hill Country Medical Center."

"It's good to hear that my fellow physicians are referring me patients. There is no greater compliment. So, Dr. Brady, what kind of injections are you looking to have?"

"Oh, I didn't mean to misrepresent myself to your telephone receptionist," I lied smoothly. "I'm seeking information about the potential complications of Botox that might possibly be severe enough to cause a cardiac arrhythmia and subsequent death."

The phone was silent. "Tell me you're not a lawyer looking for information in a possible medical malpractice case."

"Of course not. I'm an orthopedic surgeon here at HCMC. Look me up in the Texas Medical Association directory, if that would ease your mind."

"Wait, please," he said. I heard movement and a shuffling of papers over the phone. "Ah, there you are. Dr. James Robert Brady, orthopedic surgeon, with a hip and knee specialization. Okay, you're legit. Now what can I do for you?"

"Truth of the matter is that I'm looking into the death of Sandy Lowell, who may have been one of your patients. He was a patient of Dr. Robert Warner and had undergone several plastic surgery procedures over the years—eyelid lifts, nose job, and a couple of facelifts. Dr. Reardon's wife has also been a patient of Warner's, and your name came up in a conversation about fillers and Botox. As I understand from talking to colleagues, a filler is composed of hyaluronic acid, a chemical that naturally occurs in the body, and which would be highly unlikely to cause the cardiac complications that resulted in the demise of Sandy Lowell. But from what I've read, Botox is an entirely different chemical which, on rare occasions, has caused breathing issues and swallowing problems due to leakage of Botox into the bloodstream. I would appreciate your expertise on the subject."

"I'm curious as to what your relationship is, or was, to Sandy Lowell."

I anticipated he was too smart not to ask that question. "In truth, we barely knew each other, but I'm on the board of HCMC and have been informed by the estate law firm of Bowles and Associates that the hospital has been bequeathed a large sum of money in his last will and testament. I was put in charge of legitimizing that donation, if you will, making sure that portion of his will was aboveboard and that his bequest was without reproach. I'm no lawyer, but simply doing what Dr. Buck Owens, chair of the board, asked me to do on his behalf." Wow, what a crock of shit that was, but it sounded reasonable, I thought.

He was silent for a moment or two. "I don't know what the HIPPA laws dictate about divulging information on deceased individuals, so let's just have a conversation about Botox in general, its benefits and potential hazards.

"Botox is an injectable drug made from botulinum toxin type A. This toxin is produced by the bacterium Clostridium botulinum. As you probably know, this is the same toxin that causes botulism, a life-threatening form of food poisoning. Its effects vary, however, relative to the amount and type of exposure. It is termed a paralytic agent because, when injected, Botox blocks signals from the nerves to the muscles innervated by those nerves.

This prevents the targeted muscles from contracting, which can ease certain muscular conditions like torticollis, hyperhidrosis, and spasms from cerebral palsy, but at the same time can improve the appearance of fine lines around the eyes called crow's feet, frown lines between the eyebrows, and forehead creases.

"Although botulinum toxin is life-threatening, small doses such as those used in the application of Botox are considered safe. Some scientists speculate that the cosmetic applications are safer than the therapeutic applications because the doses are so small.

"Minor side effects after Botox injections include pain and bruising at the injection site, headaches, low-grade fever, and chills. These are usually temporary and fade in a day or two. Occasionally, patients will develop drooping of the eyelids and drooling, which are unintentional effects of the toxin on muscles around the target area of the drug, which may take weeks to improve as the toxin gradually wears off.

"In rare cases, botulism-like symptoms can occur, with difficulty speaking, swallowing, or breathing, and heart palpitations, all of which would require immediate medical attention. Statistically, those patients who have had regular injections of Botox over time, and therefore had the most exposure to the toxin, are at the highest risk for the more severe complications."

"So, in essence, a patient who comes in to see you every few months for injections of Botox over a long period of time is more susceptible to the more severe complications of the injections, including what you mentioned as heart palpitations. Essentially that would be an arrhythmia, correct?"

"Yes, I believe so."

"And would Sandy Lowell, without sharing a confidence, qualify as that sort of patient? A regular over a long period of time?"

"Yes, most definitely."

"Can you share with me the last time in was in for Botox injections?"

I heard the rustling of paper and envisioned him opening a chart sitting in front of him and thumbing through the pages. "There is a notation in the chart of the date of his demise, so looking back, it was six days prior to his death."

"I'm curious how you would know the date of his death. You're not next of kin, or his primary physician. That seems odd to me."

"I believe we were notified by Phyllis Reardon, a good friend of Sandy's, and a patient of mine, as you have learned from Dr. Michael Reardon."

I thought about that for a moment, then thought of one more question. "Without violating another confidence, could you tell me if Ham Bowles Sr. was a regular customer? He succumbed recently to some sort of arrhythmia as well, which, through secondhand information, I was told was under similar circumstances as Sandy Lowell."

He was silent for a moment, then said, "I can tell you he was a patient of mine, Dr. Brady, that's about it. Any other information that you need should come from his family. Now if you will excuse me, I need to get back to work."

And with that, he hung up.

CHAPTER 19

BOTULISM

I had a later tee time Saturday morning, so I set about searching for Dr. Jerry Reed. I knew he would have answers for me, and if he didn't, he would find them soon enough. The operator located him after half an hour or so, and I posed a question to him.

"Jerry, can you find out if there is some sort of blood test, or tissue test, for Botox?"

"Brady, there is a blood test for botulism, which would identify the Clostridium toxin. I don't know of any test for the presence of Botox in the bloodstream. Off the top of my head, I would say there is not, since rarely would Botox be absorbed into the system in sufficient quantities to register on a blood screening test."

"When you tested Sandy's blood, you checked for toxins, correct?"

"Yes, but the usual search would be for drugs, such as opiates, amphetamines, marijuana, alcohol, and barbiturates. Also, the basic tox screen uses an immunoassay, which looks for drugs in the blood using specific antibodies that detect various classes of drugs. And if something shows up, a more sophisticated test such as mass spectrometry is done.

"Mr. Lowell's initial tox screen was negative, but final interpretation usually takes four to six weeks. I'll have to check, but I don't think I have the final tox screen report. But I think you're going to be disappointed if you're looking for botulism caused by Botox injections. Botulism is hard enough to diagnose, and that's usually done by finding the toxin in consumed food, or in urine or feces. It tends to be a clinical diagnosis, you know, with symptoms of muscle weakness, difficulty breathing, that sort of thing.

"After our last conversation, I did a literature search, and there are cases reported of botulism occurring after Botox injections. I read a study done in Beijing where a number of patients were diagnosed due to signs and symptoms of botulism combined with the history of Botox injection and confirmed by laboratory testing. The patients were all treated with supportive measures, as well as the botulism antitoxin. The clinical symptoms occurred from 0–36 days after Botox injection, but especially from day 2 to day 6. All the patients survived. The article did say that paralysis of the respiratory muscles is the main cause of death in botulism patients, even though there were no fatalities in their study. The study almost read like a clinical trial, as though the patients had Botox injected in such a quantity that they all developed botulism, and then the treatment protocol was initiated. The article didn't specifically say that, but then it came from China, where the truth is not often forthcoming.

"So, Brady, your suspicions are correct. Botox injections can lead to botulism in rare cases, and it's just possible Sandy Lowell succumbed to an idiopathic arrhythmia that started as a result of respiratory muscle paralysis. I don't think it can be proved unless we find botulinum toxin in his bloodwork."

"Jerry, are you telling me that you still have samples of Sandy's blood?"

"I do."

"Jerry, you are an amazing dude."

"Don't forget that."

I had the information I wanted about Sandy Lowell's death, even though I couldn't prove it to be the cause of his demise unless his blood test showed the presence of botulinum toxin. I had given up on a test specifically for Botox, since Botox is botulinum toxin in a diluted state. And I still couldn't prove that Sandy's ventricular fibrillation came as a result of breathing difficulties secondary to botulinum toxin, but I thought it was a natural sequitur. If Jerry could find a toxin level in the residual blood that remained, that would be the end of my quest.

There was nothing criminal about choosing to inject one's face with Botox, and there was nothing criminal about the complications thereof. I was sure when a patient signed up for a Botox injection, or an injection of filler for that matter, there were forms to fill out absolving the injector of liability, not that those releases would stand up in court. But still, all procedures have risks, and those risks must be accepted when a patient agrees to those risks. I doubted death would be at the top of the complication list for a Botox injection, but it was probably in the fine print. Poor Sandy. One day he's at the top of the world, wealthy, driving one of his five vintage Rolls, and later that day he's a dead man due to facial injections he received to make him look younger and more attractive. That certainly reminded me of the fragility of life as we know it.

I tried to speak to Mike Reardon after our golf groups were all done and the players were settling up our accounts over beer. He avoided me, unfortunately. I would hate to lose Mike as a friend, but I probably had gone too far in delving into his wife's affairs. None of her business was my business, and I meant no harm, but discovering facts about her secret life was just a by-product of my insatiable curiosity for the truth.

I called Mary Louise from the car and asked about dinner plans. She informed me that Buck Owens was having us over for dinner, and that Shelly Wood would be in attendance. Grand, I thought, just grand. I mentioned my findings about Botox and botulism and told her that I had been shunned by Mike Reardon.

I went straight home, showered, and dressed in my evening uniform, which was jeans, a long-sleeved white western shirt, and boots of the day. That day I chose ostrich boots of a burnt-orange color, which I wore on occasion in deference to my colleagues who were UT alums. Buck loved it when I wore those boots, and he always said it made me seem more loyal to the cause, whatever the hell that meant.

I poured myself a stiff single malt Macallan scotch and await-ed my bride's exit from her dressing room. We had always main-tained separate baths and closets but shared, of course, the bed-room. Having separate side-rooms was my idea originally, in order to keep the mysteries of marriage intact, and not share every tiny detail about each other. She had gradually supported my idea, and probably would find it almost impossible to share a bath and clos-et with me after all these years.

She emerged looking like a runway model with a full figure. She wore tight black pants, black and white heels, and a white silk blouse accented by a black and white pashmina. Her blond mane was done in an "up" style, with strands of thick hair carefully posi-tioned on either side of her youthful face.

"Wow," I said. "You must have a hot date for a special occasion."

"Whatever do you mean? I have the hottest date in town, love."

"Maybe a few years back, but not so much now. Drink?"

"Do you have any wine open?"

"Of course. Rombauer chardonnay is available for a small finder's fee."

"No price is too great to have a glass of wine with you, my darling."

"You're being terribly nice to me. You must have sensed my somewhat fragile nature."

"I know you well, Jim Bob Brady, and I can feel your pain, more than you realize. You've worked hard trying to decipher the circumstances around Sandy Lowell's demise, and in the course of that you have stepped on some toes, as usual. You and Mike will patch things up between you in time. It sounded to me when you called as though your search for facts is almost done. You're just waiting on a lab report from Dr. Reed?"

"Yes, the test would show whether or not Sandy had evidence of botulinum toxin in his blood at the time of death. If he did, that would solidify that he died of an extremely rare complication of a Botox injection. I think I could actually put my investigation to bed if the bloodwork turns out positive."

"Better to put me to bed, don't you think?"

"Do we have time?"

"No, but hold that thought until after dinner."

Buck lived in Horseshoe Bay, on the waters of Lake LBJ. He had built his home on a pie-shaped lot at the end of his street, such that the house seemed very small from the front but expanded into a grand view space as the house broadened upon entering. He had the requisite great room and walk-in bar, with an open kitchen and dining room. It was a pleasant evening, so he had the patio doors open to a screened-in porch, designed to keep out the "no-see-ums": tiny bugs. The lake water lapped at the edge of his patio, which was several feet above lake level, but the lake would actually become part of the great room in case of a storm surge. Sorta risky, but his choice, apparently.

Shelly had not arrived yet, so Buck took the opportunity to give Mary Louise a hug and ask if I had completed my tasks that seemed so important to me in solving Sandy Lowell's cause of death.

"Almost, Buck. I'm waiting on one more lab test. Turns out Jerry Reed saved some blood from the autopsy."

"What kind of test?"

"Botulinum toxin."

"What?!"

"I think he died of botulism as a result of repeated Botox injections. It's reported in the literature, you know."

"I didn't know, and quite frankly, I'm not sure I care. What difference could it possibly make at this late date?"

"I don't know that it makes any difference. Sandy is still dead. It's just closing the book, for me."

"I'm worried, Brady, about losing our bequest. Phyllis Reardon has sued to contest the will, as you know, so the distribution of the proceeds of Sandy's estate are on hold until the matter is resolved."

"What about HCMC? You told me that she was filing a lawsuit against the hospital and the board members."

"She is trying to sue us under some sort of undue influence clause, probably in relation to my dealings with Sandy and his donations to HCMC over the years. Our lawyer is trying to get that squelched."

"Who's representing her?"

"Ham Bowles Jr."

"What? Isn't he Sandy Lowell's lawyer, now that his father is dead?"

"Well, apparently he's represented Phyllis in the past, so he has a history with her. And because his father was the primary attorney for the Lowell family, not him, he managed to dodge a conflict of interest situation."

"Man, that doesn't set well with me. I was hoping to get more information about his father's death. I'm sure he'll be inaccessible to my questions now that he's representing Phyllis."

The doorbell rang and Shelly entered, so that conversation ended.

We had a pleasant evening, the highlight of which was Buck and Shelly cooking dinner. He grilled New York strip steaks, and she cooked baked potatoes with chives, sour cream, real butter, and cheese. She and Mary Louise concocted a huge salad with butter lettuce, hothouse tomatoes, shallots, radishes, and peppers, topped with grated Parmesan cheese and a creamy Italian dressing.

"This food is amazing. Thanks to all the chefs," I said.

"You're welcome," said all three other attendees in unison.

Buck served a Ridge chardonnay with the salad, and a Tor cabernet sauvignon with the entrée. Both wines were delicious and complimented the meal perfectly.

Coffee was offered, but Mary Louise and I declined. We saw no reason to diffuse a nice buzz. We thanked our host and hostess and departed around 10:30 p.m., both of us remembering our preprandial commitment to put each other to bed. Tip got a very quick walk, and when I re-entered the hacienda, I merely followed the trail of clothing, picking up her pants, her blouse, her pashmina, and lastly, undies. There were no shoes noted during my traverse to our bedroom so I knew what awaited in bed . . . a beautiful naked woman with high heels.

Oh boy.

CHAPTER 20

EMERGENCY SURGERY

I woke up during the night to empty my bladder, a not uncommon occurrence. I felt bone tired, as some would say, which was probably a combination of working almost full time, playing weekend golf, and mental strain associated with my compulsive desire to find the cause of Sandy Lowell's death. I popped a couple of ibuprofens, drank a Gatorade, and returned to bed. It took me a while to get back to sleep, but I eventually entered a REM cycle, only to be disturbed by a distant ringing. It was my cell phone.

"Hello?"

"Dr. Brady, I'm so sorry to bother you. This is Charlotte Stone from the hospital. I have some bad news, sir."

"What is it?"

"A little while ago, Mrs. Thomas, the fractured hip from Monday, threw off a massive pulmonary embolism, confirmed by MRI scan. She's intubated and on a ventilator in ICU. The prognosis is poor, especially at her age. The blood clot must have been huge. Her entire left lung is out of commission.

"This is compounded by an injury her husband sustained in an attempt to get out of bed and help his wife but fell onto the floor as a result. The nurses on duty think he woke to his wife having breathing problems. He has fractured his other hip. The one we repaired is intact, thankfully. I've made him NPO so we can repair that hip this morning."

"What time is it, Charlotte?"

"It's 4:30 a.m., sir. Again, I'm so sorry—"

"Forget it. How long will it take to get an operating room crew ready to go?"

"I spoke to the nursing supervisor. They can be ready by 7 a.m."

"Okay. I'll be there. Thanks much. Good job."

I sat on the side of the bed for a minute, debating on whether I could get back to sleep or not, and whether I should set the alarm.

"I'll make coffee if you want," Mary Louise said.

"That's okay, I can do it. I don't know whether to try and get some more sleep or not."

"Set the alarm for five thirty, then lay back down and see what happens. If you can't get back to sleep, we'll get up and make coffee and breakfast."

I did just that, and next thing I knew, the alarm was signaling my wake-up time.

I showered and dressed and walked into a kitchen with coffee, eggs, bacon, and toast ready, and a very sleepy wife standing by the stove.

"You heard the conversation when Charlotte called, I guess."

"Yes. Will Mrs. Thomas make it?"

"Doubtful, sorry to say. Now I have to fix her husband's other hip, and that puts *his* survival into question."

"What a sad situation, Jim Bob."

I ate ravenously while checking for phone messages. There was one from the prior evening which I hadn't bothered to review when we returned home from Buck's. I had more pressing issues on my mind. The voice was unmistakably Dr. Jerry Reed.

"I know it's late, Brady, and I figure you're out having fun or staying home and having fun with that wife of yours, or some combination of the two, but I thought you would want to know that Mr. Lowell's blood sample showed POSITIVE for botulinum toxin. You were right all along, you persistent devil. I can finally sign off on the death certificate. Dr. Owens has been bugging me about that, so he can get on with the program, like cremating Lowell and scattering his ashes, and cashing that big ol' fat check for the hospital. The cause of death will be ventricular fibrillation secondary to pulmonary failure due to botulism as a result of Botox injections. You should be very happy with yourself."

The nursing staff had called the Thomases' son, Bart, and he was in the waiting room outside the operating room.

We shook hands. "Mr. Thomas, I must say this is not how I envisioned my Sunday morning. I'm sure you feel the same."

"Yes, sir, I would agree. The nurses in ICU let me see my mother. They tried to talk around the issue, but I get the impression that the prognosis is poor."

"Unfortunately, sir, that's true. I looked at the scan. The clot had to be huge. It blocked off the main bronchial vessel to the left lung. I don't see how she can survive that."

"She wouldn't want any unnecessary measures taken, Doctor. My mother has a DNR order on file. As far as Dad, what's your take on him now?"

"In his age group, the odds of some type of cataclysmic medical event causing death after breaking one hip is over 90%. With a second break a week later, I think his survival chances would be minimal. I'm sorry to be blunt, but you should prepare yourself."

"Dad has a DNR order as well, so please keep that in mind. Having both of them in the memory care section of the nursing home, sharing a room, was a godsend. Now this. I just can't imagine . . ."

His voice broke, and he walked away.

Charlotte had the hip X-rays on the viewing screen in the O.R.. Mr. Thomas had shattered his opposite hip. The fracture extended down into his upper femur, a combination of an intertrochanteric and subtrochanteric fracture.

"My god, Charlotte, I'm not even sure I can fix that."

"Well, Doc, if anyone can, you can. When I saw the films, I had the staff call the rep from the orthopedic equipment company. They have some special screws and long plates designed for this type of fracture. He'll be here by 7 a.m."

"Smart thinking. That may bail us out."

I fixed the hip by inserting a large flange nail up into the head of the femur and screwing on a long side plate. I then added a second plate to try and secure the fractures. The construction was stable but the hip wouldn't survive another fall. Neither would Mr. Thomas, although he did well during the surgery, with no apparent problems.

I talked to Bart Thomas, told him what I had done, and assured him that his dad was getting the best care possible. I got his cell number and promised to call him with any change in the condition of either parent. He said he needed to drive back to Austin, talk to his family, and make arrangements to be out of the office for the next few days, just in case.

I returned home and shared with Mary Louise the saga of the Thomas family, and then the message from Jerry Reed.

"So, this means you're done?"

"Seems like it. All I wanted to prove was a cause for Sandy Lowell's death. I had a secondary goal of trying to somehow relate his deceased lawyer Ham Bowles's demise to a Botox reaction, but all I could get from Dr. Goldfarb was to confirm that Bowles was in fact his patient. I guess I could place a call back to Dr. Warner, the plastic surgeon who had performed work on both Sandy and Phyllis, and ask if Ham Bowles had been his patient as well."

"But what good would that do if Dr. Warner doesn't do the injections himself? He could only tell you he referred the lawyer to another doctor who performs injections, who would probably decline providing you more information due to privacy laws and the like. It sounds to me that you accomplished your goal, and that you should be proud of yourself."

"There is still the issue of Jennifer Lowell's trust having been depleted, and Phyllis Reardon's lawsuit contesting the will. But those are legal issues, not medical issues, and I don't really have a role in those."

"No, young man, you do not. So why don't you change into golf clothes, and let's go over to the Summit, have lunch, and play a few holes of golf?"

We both had the Cobb salad, after which we warmed up, hit a few drivers and 8-irons, putted a bit, and went to the tee. Each hole on Summit takes you higher in elevation, peaking at the ninth, tenth, and eleventh holes. We planned to play just the front nine, but we were both feeling good and playing good, so we continued. We stopped at the comfort station just past the thirteenth green, got hydrating beverages and a snack, and ventured on.

I was about to tee off on the tricky little par 3 hole 15, taking care to aim to the right side of the green to avoid pulling the ball down into the trash left and short of the green. As I was about to swing, I asked Mary Louise, "Are you going to tell me who did your facial injections?"

"Certainly, if you want to know."

"I do."

"Dr. Goldfarb in Austin."

"Huh. So he had to know that I was your husband when we had our phone conversation."

"Yes, I told him in advance."

"You did? How did you know—"

"You tell me everything, Jim Bob. Remember, I'm your partner, not your adversary. You mentioned you were talking to the man who did the injections, so I called him the day before and asked him to be as forthcoming as possible, it being in our best interests if you concluded this investigation soon. And I assume he was?"

"Yes, very. He gave me most of the information I requested on Sandy Lowell. The only item he wouldn't talk about was Ham Bowles's care, other than to say he was a patient."

"You're not a relative, nor a law enforcement officer, nor did you have a subpoena, correct?"

I laughed. "Yes, correct. I had no standing with respect to Bowles."

"Do you think he does good work?"

"If you mean Goldfarb, yes. Excellent in fact. Your face is beautiful."

We played the last three holes in thirty minutes. I didn't talk much, as I was preoccupied with the missed opportunity to glean more information about Ham Bowles from Dr. Goldfarb. If I had only known Mary Louise had called him, that could have been my calling card, and I might have been able to use that to further my knowledge about the lawyer. Maybe it wouldn't have worked, but maybe it would have.

At any rate, maybe the doctor would want to know that his patient Sandy Lowell had died of botulism, not really good publicity for doctors performing Botox injections. And would he want to know if a second patient of his, Ham Bowles Sr., had probably died of the same disease? Maybe between Mary Louise being his patient and losing a second patient to botulism, I could get the information I wanted about the lawyer.

"What are you up to? Scheming? Was my impression that you were done with this Botox business short-lived?"

"Mary Louise, are you talking to me?"

"Yes, and I know that look. I have a feeling that you're not satisfied with your level of knowledge and want to pester poor Dr. Goldfarb about the other possible botulism case."

"Possibly," I said. "You know my theory—it ain't over till it's over."

CHAPTER 21

SUSAN BEESON

Mary Louise asked if there was anything she could do to help, somewhat absolving me of guilt over continuing to research the botulinum toxin business. I asked her to call Susan Beeson, our friend and now assistant special agent in charge of the Austin FBI office. Mary Louise had a handle on the issues and could ferret out from Susan if the feds could get involved in a death case regarding Botox injections. If Sandy were the only one, that would be different, but with Ham Bowles's demise, presumably from the same cause, might there be more?

At the least, Susan could get information on Ham Bowles's treatment history that was not available to me. And once that door was opened, other doors might open as well. I considered calling J.J. and asking B&B to research Ham Bowles for me. The firm could get all sorts of information about him and his family, as it had done with Sandy Lowell, but I was primarily interested in specific medical aspects of his life, issues probably unattainable by B&B.

I didn't have anything against Dr. Goldfarb specifically, considering the work he had done on not only Mary Louise, but other friends as well, but he needed to know if there was some sort of pattern present among his patients who had adverse side effects from Botox injections. And I would think that if there were, he would know about it, because the ever-present plaintiff's attorneys were always looking for a new tort case to handle, and I believed their theory to be sue the doctor first, then go from there.

Monday was another busy day, with four joint replacements. Charlotte and Shelly had already secured a second operating room for the team to use, so the day went remarkably smoothly. I enjoyed working with the two nurse practitioners, and they certainly knew how to maximize my efficiency in surgery. This process could be a new beginning for all of us, or a deal breaker for me and my attempts to slow down my practice.

Mr. and Mrs. Thomas were still with us, although she was still on a ventilator and had no response to external stimuli. Essentially, she was brain dead, according to the neurologist who I saw on rounds Monday afternoon. Bart Thomas was present and reminded both of us of her DNR—do not resuscitate—order. Bart had called a family meeting when he returned home, and their decision was to discontinue life-sustaining measures at the earliest reasonable time. This made sense to me, and to the neurologist, and it was decided to give it another twenty-four hours, and if her condition had not changed, her life support system would be discontinued.

Mr. Thomas, on the other hand, was sitting up in bed, mumbling but having some broth, and seemed to be reasonably comfortable. Whatever fate had in store for him, I did not know, but his options were limited. There was no happy ending for him, regardless of the outcome.

When I arrived at home Monday evening, loud music was playing through the speaker system, and I heard laughter from the terrace. I made myself a Talisker single-malt scotch and wandered outside to find Mary Louise and Susan Beeson enjoying each other's company.

"Jim Bob!" Susan yelled, as she stood up to give me a Texas-sized hug. "My third favorite man on the planet!"

"What a surprise to find you here. Welcome," I said.

"I'm half in the tank already. Your wife and I started drinking wine around three thirty, catching up on our lives."

"And Susan's been regaling me with stories of miscreants and their misdeeds. I'm just amazed how stupid people can sometimes be," said Mary Louise.

"How's the family, Susan?"

"Gene Sr. is enjoying his new accounting job in Austin. And Gene Jr. is getting ready to go off to college in the fall."

"And where did he decide to go?"

"You'll be happy to know he's going to be a Baylor Bear!"

"Yea!" I said. "We stole another one from UT!"

"He loved the Baylor campus, and the new stadium, and they have a top-ranked B-school. As for me, he's only a couple of hours from home, and that makes me very happy."

We sat down and visited for a bit.

"I decided to come over after speaking with your wife this morning. She gave me the details on this acquaintance of yours who died of an arrhythmia, and who you doggedly persisted on behalf of to determine that he was a chronic Botox user who developed botulism and went into respiratory failure. That was a nice piece of investigative work, my friend. And then she told me there might be another? A lawyer out of Austin named Hamilton Bowles?"

"All I know is Mr. Bowles is said to have died of a similar arrhythmia that Sandy Lowell died of. I spoke to Dr. Larry Goldfarb, the cosmetic dermatologist, on the phone about Sandy, but he wouldn't give me any information about Bowles other than to confirm he was a patient. I was hoping you could find out more."

"Jim, they don't call us the Federal Bureau of Investigation for nothing."

She reached into a purse, or satchel, or briefcase, and pulled out a thick sheaf of papers and handed it to me.

"You can review these documents at your leisure, but I'll give you the abbreviated version. He's lived a pretty clean and low-key life. Went to UT undergrad, then UT law school. He opened an office in Austin after graduation and gradually built up the firm to an average of ten lawyers. That's small potatoes for Houston, but in Austin, the legal people tend to cluster in smaller, more intimate groups. Eventually his son joined the practice, and while he assisted his dad on some cases, he basically built his own oil-and-gas law practice. His dad was more into traditional law—wills, estates, contracts—business law, if you will.

"A few years back, Ham Bowles's life was turned upside down by an unsuspected divorce: his own. His wife of thirty years found solace and greener pastures in the company of her personal train-er, a man twenty years younger, and they ran off into the sunset together. She had her own money from a wealthy father, so Mr. Bowles didn't get wiped out by the divorce financially, but he did not fare so well emotionally. He went into a deep depression, had to go on medication, and was unable to function as a lawyer for six months.

"He eventually rebounded, discovered the magic of fillers and Botox, and improved his looks substantially with plastic surgery. He used the same plastic surgeon your buddy Sandy Lowell used, Dr. Robert Warner, and, as you know, began to visit Dr. Goldfarb for injections every few months. He started dating and seemed to be back on track to enjoy his life when he had a cardio-pulmonary event of some sort after playing golf and was unable to be resusci-tated at St. David's.

"I paid an unannounced visit to Dr. Goldfarb this morning with a subpoena, and I reviewed Mr. Bowles's records. There was nothing out of the ordinary, just visits every three months for fillers and Botox. He had no history of allergies or adverse reactions after any of the injections. He was fine one day, and the next he was dead."

"I'm sure the docs at St. David's didn't realize the implications of the injections and so didn't order a botulinum toxin blood test," I said. "They probably got a standard tox screen, not having any clue as to the cause of his demise."

"That's correct, but I spoke to the chief of pathology there after my visit with Dr. Goldfarb, and it turns out that it's customary to save blood samples in certain death cases with no discernible cause. After our conversation, they decided to run a botulism test today, and the results should be known by tomorrow."

"Wow. Don't mess with the FBI and Susan Beeson. The power of the badge."

"And the full force of the federal government, my friend."

"Susan, you've got to tell him the story of the Botox party. I have to put the finishing touches on dinner. We're having chicken Parmesan with rigatoni pasta, and Caesar salad."

"Yum," I said. "A Botox party?"

"Yes. Botox costs a fortune, so these women, sometimes men, get together for these parties where they inject themselves with Botox. The source of Botox is the problem. Botox is regulated and approved by the FDA like any other drug. Sometimes you'll get these quack doctors who have no certification whatsoever to inject filler or Botox. And sometimes the source of the Botox is sketchy. It's illegal to import Botox from another country for injection use here in the US. It is designed to be administered by a physician, or a nurse that has been trained and certified in the procedure, in a physician's office, in case there are complications.

"So, EMTs were called to a fashionable home in Westlake this past weekend, where someone had allegedly quit breathing. They arrived, and there was a well-dressed woman on the floor, passed out, having trouble breathing, whose lips were the size of small saucers. She had received the injections, felt faint, then passed out. The EMTs intubated her and took her to the closest hospital, which was St. David's. The techs called the Austin police, who responded to the home and found all sorts of drug paraphernalia there. Turns out they were drinking, snorting crushed opioid tablets, and injecting Botox and filler, and not a single attendee was sober.

"The so-called doctor was some sort of naturopath, without a valid medical license, and no clear reliable source for the Botox. When the officers ran his name through their computers, it turns out that he had two priors, both for illegal pharmaceuticals distribution. He was arrested and charged with illegal Botox possession, impersonating a physician, illegal possession and distribution of a controlled substance, and a bunch of other charges appropriate for the moment."

"What happened to the lady with the lip and breathing problem?"

"I checked on her before I drove over. She's still in the hospital, but extubated and breathing fine. Her lips are a problem, because the so-called doctor injected the lips with Botox, not filler. Some women like that full-lip look, and to achieve that, filler has to be injected, and re-injected periodically to maintain that look. Filler doesn't affect the nerves or muscles. However, Botox is a paralytic agent, so when the idiot injected the lips with Botox, that caused all the lip muscles and other muscles in the area to quit working."

"So, she couldn't smile, or open her mouth."

"Correct, although she is better today. The doc told me it would take a while for those effects to wear off, but she could have some residual paralysis. Think of the amount of Botox you would have to inject to puff up those lips. She probably had an overdose of Botox, which explains the breathing issue. I think he said they gave her the antitoxin as well to prevent full-blown botulism."

"Wow. What a story. She's lucky she survived."

"Just goes to show you how toxic that stuff can be in large doses. And speaking of your two fellows with the death-producing arrhythmia, I don't see that we have a criminal case in either situation. It's not against the law to get Botox injections, and Dr. Goldfarb is a board-certified dermatologist and has all the necessary credentials to treat patients with Botox, as do his staff nurses. His Botox source is direct from the manufacturer, and he willingly opened up his medical records to me. There is no evidence of a crime in either the death of Lowell or Bowles, except to confirm what you suspected, that both deaths are Botox-related. I think Goldfarb is running a good office and treating his clientele well. I thought he was going to pass out when we discussed the deaths of his two patients. It was a sobering occurrence for him, I could tell.

CHAPTER 22

PASSING

After Tuesday clinic was done, I met Bart Thomas in the ICU at his mother's bedside. He introduced me to his wife and two of his grown children. The neurologist, Dr. Barnes, was present, along with the ICU head nurse.

"Dr. Barnes here is going to disconnect Mrs. Thomas's life support systems," I said. "Feel free to change your mind, or say something meaningful if you like," I said.

We were in a large semi-private room, with Mr. Thomas on the entry side of his wife's bed. He was muttering incoherently and seemed agitated. Bart walked over to him, told him everything was going to be fine, not to worry, and patted his arm.

Dr. Barnes waited for another moment, until it was apparent nothing was going to be said by the family. He then went about his business of disconnecting the respirator, then the cardiac monitor, then the two IVs that contained hydration and nourishment. Both the monitor and the respirator began their programmed beeping, then were quiet as they were unplugged from the wall socket. All was silent for a moment. Mrs. Thomas made no sound and showed no reaction to being separated from her life support. After a couple of minutes or so, Dr. Barnes pulled her eyelids back, checked for pupil dilation, then listened to her heart with his stethoscope. He shook his head.

"I'm afraid she's gone, folks," he said.

I escorted the family into the hallway, offered my condolences, and returned to my office to complete the requisite paperwork of the day.

"How did it go, Doc?" asked Shelly.

"Somber. I went into the field of orthopedics to avoid the dead and the dying. Seems there is too much of that surrounding me lately."

I completed my dictation and signed some documents. "Anything else, Shelly?"

"No, sir. I did interview a couple of administrative staff prospects. I'll let you know when I'm down to the final two choices, so you can talk to them yourself. You have the final say so."

"Okay. Let me know. I'm going home. Have a nice evening."

"You too, sir."

Tip's jubilance in seeing me warmed my heart and dulled the sorrow of witnessing Mrs. Thomas's demise. I poured myself a drink and walked outside so Tip could do his business. It was cloudy, with a great deal of moisture in the air. I smelled a tinge of ozone, like before or after a lightning storm. My faithful canine apparently did as well, because just as he completed his obligatories, he lifted his head, sniffed deeply a few times, and ran back inside.

I saw a note on the kitchen counter from Mary Louise that said she had accompanied Susan back to Austin in order to do some shopping, and probably wouldn't be home until seven. And that there was a casserole in the fridge, with instructions on heating, and a salad already made as well, that just needed dressing added. I followed her directions, poured myself a glass of Ridge chardonnay left over from last night's dinner, and ate at the bar counter. Rain started to fall, and lightning struck. I walked into my bedroom closet and as usual found Tip on the floor, huddled underneath the sack that housed my dry cleaning.

"You hungry, buddy?" I asked, but got no response. I walked back into the kitchen, poured his kibble, and finished my meal.

I was worried about Mary Louise driving in this weather, so when my cell phone rang, I figured it would be her. But it was the hospital operator, asking me to please call the ICU.

"Hello, this is Dr. Brady. Someone call me?"

"Yes, sir, this is Charlotte. I wanted to inform you that Mr. Thomas coded about thirty minutes ago. I called the team in, and they worked on him for a few minutes before the head nurse came into the room and told us there was a DNR in place. So, our revival activity was stopped immediately. I'm afraid he's gone, Dr. Brady."

"Charlotte, you do know that Dr. Barnes pulled the plug on Mrs. Thomas late this afternoon, after which she expired? And now you're telling me that Mr. Thomas coded, and has expired, not more than two hours since his wife died?"

"Yes, sir. I think he must have been desperate to be with her, Dr. Brady."

I poured myself an eighteen-year-old Macallan single-malt scotch, added one ice cube, walked through the house and out into the garage, and raised the garage door in order to get some fresh air. I wasn't religious by nature, although I had grown up in a very conservative and religious household. I felt myself to be spiritual, however, and was open to any reasonable sign that a Higher Power had some interest in our insignificant human lives. Well, that evening, with the thunder and lightning, and the news that the Thomas couple were once again reunited, I felt the glimmer of some modicum of understanding of the universe. Of course, it could have been purely coincidence, two older souls, one having the life support system disconnected, the other watching helplessly as his soulmate withdrew from his presence, into the Great Unknown. And then he followed, a few hours later. I'm a romantic, and if I want to think that our Maker influenced that near-simultaneous departure of two of his children who loved each other deeply, then I'm entitled. I officially left my prior certainty in Cosmic Coincidence behind.

Mary Louise thankfully pulled into the driveway just as the skies blackened further. I embraced her as she exited the car and held her tight. I was happy to see her, and apparently allergies had affected my tear ducts to the point of uncontrolled watering . . . that would be my story in the future, should anyone ask.

The remainder of the week was uneventful, thankfully. I wondered how Jennifer Lowell was faring without frequent visits from her dad. I decided to pay them a visit and see for myself. I also wanted to share with Cynthia Stiles the details of Sandy's demise. Friday morning after hospital rounds seemed like an appropriate time, since I had a couple of extra hours prior to my standing golf game.

I rang the doorbell and heard, as was the case last visit, Jennifer screaming something unintelligible. The door opened, and I noticed she was dressed in another track suit, same as last time, hair not in pigtails but hanging loosely about her face.

"Morning, Jennifer. Remember me? I'm Dr. Brady."

"Yes," she said, staring at me. "Have you seen my dad?" she said, in a loud but somewhat inarticulate voice.

"No, sweetie, I haven't."

"Cindy said he went on a trip, but I miss him. I want him to come home."

With that, she ran off, shrieking something about her show.

"Morning, Doc, please come in," said Cynthia, as she arrived at the door.

"Jennifer thinks he's on a trip?"

"Yes. She keeps asking me where he is. She seems to have forgotten about the hospital stay, and her reaction to his passing away. Either she doesn't remember or doesn't understand. Coffee?"

"Love some. Same as last visit if it's available."

"Of course, it's my go-to brand."

We walked into the kitchen and she started coffee prep, while I sat at the counter and stared at the lake.

"Things are going okay for you two, Cynthia?"

"Yes, except money is tight, according to Phyllis. She said that Sandy didn't leave us any money in his will, and she's contested it to try and provide for Jennifer and me. But I'm worried. She said we might have to get out of the house."

"What?"

"She told me upkeep is a problem—insurance, taxes, maintenance. She said we might have to move to an apartment. Can you image what that would be like, Jennifer the way she is? This big ol' house is the only reason we're able to survive together."

"I hope I'm not talking out of turn here, but there is plenty of money in Sandy's estate to take care of you and Jennifer for the rest of your lives. I'm appalled that Phyllis is trying to dislodge you and Jennifer from your home. Here's the story about the money. Sandy put $50 million into a trust after Jennifer was born. He put Phyllis in charge of that trust, which was probably a mistake, but nonetheless, that's what happened. Over the years, that trust has depleted itself down to a little less than $2 million. Yes, Phyllis has provided for your and Jennifer's needs, but she's also taken care of her own needs. Sandy recently discovered, after your call about not having air conditioning, that Phyllis had used a great deal of the money for herself. At that point, he instructed his lawyers to draft a new trust agreement, leaving Phyllis out as trustee, but providing another $50 million for your support. The problem is that he died before it could be signed and executed. That's why you're in limbo."

"What's going to happen?"

"I don't have a clue. Sandy left $50 million each to five favorite charities of his, plus a whopping $150 million to Hill Country Medical Center. There is plenty of money in the estate. Unfortunately, it's between lawyers and judges now to decide what to do with the unsigned trust agreement. Originally, the money going into the trust should have come directly out of his investments, but now that he's passed, it will have to come out of the will proceeds. If I was king, I would simply take an even amount of money out of each bequest and apply it to the new trust for you and Jennifer. The $50 million deficit problem would be solved."

"But you're not king, Dr. Brady."

"You're right, Cynthia, but I can tell you one thing for sure."

"What's that?"

"If there's any way I can help persuade the players to do the right thing, I'll do it."

After finishing and thanking Cynthia for the absolutely excellent coffee, I went on to make my tee time. I played spectacular golf at the Summit Rock course in spite of my anger and frustration over the Sandy Lowell estate. I regretted involving myself at all in Sandy's business. To me, the amounts of money involved were beyond the comprehension of most folks. And from my vantage point, the solution was so incredibly simple. As I had told Cynthia, shave a little off from the beneficiaries and come up with a more than adequate settlement for Jennifer and for her current and future caretakers. And to my way of thinking, Phyllis Reardon should not be trusted with trust management. She had squandered a large portion of the original trust for her own gain. She had failed in her fiduciary responsibilities once; why would she be expected not to fail a second time? Sandy had called it right in the draft of his new trust. Leave her out of it.

I ran into Mike Reardon at the bar after golf. "Hey, bud," I said, and patted him on the back. "Did you play well today?"

He stiffened for a moment, then relaxed. "Sure did, Jim Bob. Shot a 78. Best in a long time."

"Wow. Way to go. What was your secret?"

"Keeping my head down through the shot. No chunking, no skiving, no hitting the top half of the ball, except for a couple of times. I don't get why I can't do that every time I play."

"Human frailties, my friend. We're all flawed. Golf brings that out more than any sport I know. Hell, football, baseball, basketball, you name it, you can make a little mistake and still complete a pass, get a hit, make a basket. You miss-hit a golf ball by less than a quarter of an inch and your day is ruined. That's what make the pros so special."

"True, that, Brady. Buy you a beer?"

"Sure. Listen, sorry about getting sideways with you the other day. I was sticking my nose where it didn't belong, which is a fault I'm trying to correct, but I'm not doing a very good job at it."

"Listen, that was on me. If I may speak frankly, Phyllis is driving me up the wall with this business of contesting Sandy's will. I mean, I make a good living as a heart surgeon. We can live very well without that extra money she's been managing since Jennifer was born. Phyllis has become used to controlling the funds, and the ability to spend portions of it that she thinks she is due because of her and Sandy's . . . relationship. I have to live with that shit every day of my life, and sometimes it gets to me."

"Man, I wouldn't want to be in your shoes. As you know, I became involved in all this mess simply by being at the wrong place at the wrong time. Ten or fifteen minutes earlier or later in time and I never would have known who Sandy Lowell was. Weird, huh?"

"That's true, like that old movie *Sliding Doors*. Anyway, I'm sorry I lashed out at you. I'd like it to be over. That's all Phyllis talks about, how Sandy made a provision for a new trust of $50 million for Jennifer's benefit, but it never got signed. And the worst is that she is barred from having any control over the funds, at least according to the lawyer in Austin she hired. Bowles?"

"Yep, son of the father who was Sandy's friend. I'm still confused how she was able to hire him to contest the will, considering his father is the one who drew up the old will as well as the new unsigned document. Someone told me—and I think it was Buck Owens—that she had prior dealings with him, so it wasn't a conflict of interest."

"Phyllis has had some legal issues in the past, nothing serious, but when she called Bowles's office the first time, some years ago, apparently the problem was too small for Bowles Sr. to handle, so she was pawned off on the son, who had just joined the practice. She knew the Bowles name from back when she had Jennifer. Bowles Sr. handled the original settlement, being an old friend of Sandy's from the UT days. So, over the years, when an issue came up, she would call Bowles Jr. He's been handling our legal issues for a while now."

"I see. Anyway, it's not my business any longer. I don't know if you heard through the grapevine, but I was able to prove that Sandy died from an overdose of Botox, resulting in botulism, which caused his respiratory failure and subsequent ventricular fib. And through a friend of ours at the FBI, there is a high index of suspicion that Bowles Sr. died from the same thing. I'm expecting a phone call from her today regarding his blood tests for botulinum toxin."

"Botulinum toxin? The source for botulism? I thought that came from poorly preserved food. What am I missing?"

"Mike, Botox is botulinum toxin. Diluted and in small doses it rarely causes a problem, but patients can develop a buildup in the body over time, depending how frequently they have injections, which can lead to botulism. I've learned a lot, having read up on the subject lately."

Mike had a funny look on his face, not funny ha-ha, but weird.

"Everything okay?"

"Uh, yeah. Say, I have to run. See you later."

CHAPTER 23

DINNER

There was a voicemail message on my phone from Susan Beeson, which I picked up while driving home.

"Jim Bob Brady, you old dog detective. You missed your calling, friend. You were spot on. G. Hamilton Bowles Sr. had a large titer of botulinum toxin in his blood, high enough for the pathologist in Austin to decide his cause of death was complications from botulism. Way to go, old friend. Now maybe you can get back to concentrating on your day job, your wife, and your golf game. Enjoyed seeing you two. Don't be a stranger."

And that was it. I had solved the mystery. I should have felt elated about that, but I was still a little melancholy. Part of discovering secretive items is the rush of the hunt. Like when you go out on an ordinary day without expectations and shoot a golf score in the 70s. During the round, when the impossible is being accomplished, you get into a zone. And when it's done, there is a let-down, a sudden precipitous drop in the adrenaline levels in the bloodstream. I felt that way because the solving was done, and my life was going back to normal. I should have been ecstatic. Maybe there was some lingering sadness about Mr. and Mrs. Thomas, although the newly enlightened Jim Bob thought they might well be happy, tiptoeing through the tulips together in a better place.

Or, as the former cynical Jim Bob might put it, rotting away in the cold, dark ground.

I put negative thoughts about the Thomas family aside and put on a happy face. I called Mary Louise and told her the news from Susan, and that we should go out and have a celebratory dinner, place of her choice. She opted for the Waterfront Grill, at an upstairs table in the back where it was reasonably quiet. I called and made the rez, sped home, and showered and shaved and put on one of my dressier Tommy Bahama shirts, black slacks, and black ostrich boots with a matching belt.

"You're looking mighty spiffy," Mary Louise noted, when I emerged from my dressing room. She was decked out in black slacks as well, with black heels, a red sweater, and a red and black pashmina wrapped around her neck and shoulders in a fashion that only she could decipher. Her hair was down and fell around her shoulders. I felt the familiar stirrings deep in my gut, and apparently got "the look."

"Down, boy. Drinks and dinner first."

"I didn't say a word."

"Words coming from you are unnecessary, my dear. Your expressions say it all."

"That's not fair. I usually have no idea what you're thinking from the expression on your face. You've always been able to read me like a book."

"And thus the difference between a man and a woman, between testosterone and estrogen. Why do you think so many psychics are female?"

"Are a lot of psychics female? I've never noticed."

"Think of every movie you've ever seen, or any storefront in a big city that advertises for Madame See-All, Tell-All. Women."

"Well, I certainly can't prove you wrong."

"Don't waste your time, big fella. Estrogen reigns. Now how about that dinner?"

We greeted a few couples we knew in the downstairs section. We opted to take the elevator since the steps were way too steep for boots and high heels. I sneaked a smooch on the ride to the second floor. Her lips parted just enough to get the message of good things to come later. I disengaged as the elevator door opened onto the second floor, and as we were stepping out, we ran right into Phyllis and Mike Reardon.

Hugs were exchanged, although Phyllis hugged me in a perfunctory fashion and didn't look me in the eye.

"You guys already ate?" Mary Louise asked.

"Yes," replied Phyllis. "We had an early dinner. Our nephew has a baseball game tonight, and we didn't want to miss it. He pitches for Marble Falls High School, and they are undefeated. Good to see you," she said, stepping into the elevator.

"Okay, good luck at the game," Mary Louise responded.

The hostess seated us, and our waiter brought us Tito's vodka dirty martinis in a timely fashion. We toasted and watched the sun slowly set over Lake LBJ.

"Did you get an odd vibe from Phyllis?" Mary Louise asked.

"No more than usual."

She laughed. "You're always so suspicious."

"Yes, and now that I've come to know her better through researching her life, she deserves my suspicion."

"She was very young and impressionable when she had the affair with Sandy Lowell. She had a child out of wedlock and to everyone's dismay, the child was mentally challenged. Sandy set up a generous trust for her and the child. The families wanted her to terminate the pregnancy, but neither she nor Sandy would hear of it. I guess that if had they known the child would be profoundly affected, they might have made a different decision. But this was their love child."

"How in the world do you know all these details? Did we have a discussion I don't recall?"

"Some of it I heard from you. Some I heard from Phyllis over coffee this week."

"Phyllis called you and asked you to coffee? Why didn't you tell me?"

"Jim, I have coffee with a lot of people."

"I wonder if she knows that I've been involved in this, this quest to discover Sandy's Lowell's cause of death."

"Oh yes, she knew. I think one of the reasons she wanted me to have coffee is so that I could in some way keep you from thinking she's a bad person."

"Let me think about that, Mary Louise. She has an affair with her first cousin who is twenty years older. They have a child together who is significantly intellectually challenged, and Phyllis has power of attorney over the generous trust Sandy set up for that child, and she goes through a significant amount of the money for personal gain. Now she's contesting Sandy's will, probably not because her daughter is left out of it, but because she's not going to have control over the funds this time. What am I missing? How is she not a bad person?"

"I admit, she's made some mistakes."

"Mistakes? I think it goes a lot further than that."

Fortunately, our dinner arrived, and we ate in comfortable silence for a time. I had soft-shell crabs, and Mary Louise the king-crab legs with drawn butter. I ordered a bottle of Santa Margherita pinot grigio, which was cold and the perfect complement to the meal.

We took the rest of our wine and strolled outside after dinner, found a quiet table, and watched the boats traverse the lake, heading home as twilight fell.

"Sorry if I was too militant about Phyllis," I said. "I have only seen the negative side. And quite frankly, I liked her before I started researching this Sandy Lowell business. Mike is a very good friend of mine, and I would hate to lose that friendship."

"You know, after she had Jennifer, her uterus was damaged, and she could not have children. Mike wanted kids, so they tried all available infertility options, but to no avail. They thought about adopting, but it just never happened. I think there is some resentment on her part about that, but she is the one who chose to have sex with Sandy as an eighteen-year-old, and she is the one that insisted on keeping the child. I feel somewhat sorry for her, I admit."

"You're a kind and loving person Mary Louise, and I admire that about you. And sometimes I can get on board with you, and sometimes I just can't. This is one of those times. I'm sorry."

She patted my hand. "We can't agree on everything, but we agree on most issues, so I'm okay with your position on the subject."

She started running the toe of her high heel along my calf, slowly, up and down.

"Think it's time to pay the bill and head for the hacienda?" I said.

"Thought you'd never ask."

CHAPTER 24

BOARD MEETING

Without having something to investigate, I was a little lost over the weekend. I played golf with my buds Saturday and with Mary Louise Sunday, and caught up on my reading with a Stuart Woods novel featuring the escapades of his recurring protagonist, Stone Barrington. I decided to grill steaks Saturday night, which ended up in a small disaster. I had intended to char them at high heat about three minutes per side. Tip was frolicking in the back yard as I grilled, chasing butterflies but never quite catching up to their incongruous flying patterns. My cell phone rang, and I stepped away from the smoke in order to answer it. It was Buck Owens.

"Can you and Mary Louise attend a meeting of the board Monday late afternoon?"

"I haven't seen my schedule yet, but probably. I'd need to check with Mary Louise. Why?"

"This lawyer representing Phyllis Reardon has a proposal he wants us to hear regarding Sandy's last will and testament. I've booked Darrell Bledsoe, and I need as many of the board members as possible to be there."

"I'm sure I can make it, so count me in, and I'll let you know about Mary Louise. Want to tell me what's going on?"

"No. You'll find out Monday. Thanks."

I realized the error of my ways when I turned back to the grill and saw black smoke billowing from the hood. I lifted the handle, only to see my two beautiful ribeye steaks on fire. I grabbed each with tongs and put them on the upper rack for a moment until the fire was extinguished by the lack of steak juices feeding it.

The previously nice-sized steaks looked like oversized hockey pucks. I cut into one, and instead of the expected medium-rare center, nice and pink, I cut into well-done steak.

I turned off the grill and closed the hood after placing the steaks on a platter.

"Little problem with the grill, Jim?"

"You might say that. What are you doing?"

"Frying up a couple of pork chops on the stove."

"How did you know?"

"It looked like the grill was on fire, and I saw you on the phone, so I put two and two together and made an executive decision."

"Thanks. Look at these pitiful little things."

She couldn't help laughing, and neither could I, at the sight of the smoldering black pieces of char.

"Who kept your attention to the extent that the steaks burned up?"

"Buck. He's called a HCMC board meeting for Monday afternoon. Something about Phyllis Reardon and her contesting the will. Mandatory attendance for both of us. Can you make it?"

"Yes, no problem. Did he give you any details?"

"No. He said wait until Monday. How about I open a bottle of Kosta Browne pinot noir? That will lessen the pain of my burning the steaks."

"Yum. That's nectar of the gods and goes with anything."

I popped the cork on an excellent vintage, let it breathe for a moment, then poured us a glass.

"Ah-h-h," said Mary Louise. "You can burn the steaks any-time, lover."

The HCMC board meeting began promptly at 5 p.m. All members who were able to attend were present, including the chair, Dr. Buck Owens; Bill Porter, hospital CEO; Dr. Jackson Morse, chief of surgery; Dr. Dan Burns, chief of anesthesia; Lynn Abbott, head of HR; Del Anderson, publisher of the local newspaper, the *Highlander*; Sister Madeline O'Rourke, director of Mourning Doves; Louann Simms, nursing supervisor, HCMC; Mary Louise Brady, retired retail executive and head or member of various charitable organizations; and me, as well as Darrell Bledsoe, chief counsel. The staff had booked five operations for me, and I barely was on time for the meeting.

"For those of you who don't know him, this is G. Hamilton Bowles Jr., attorney of record for Phyllis Reardon. Ham's father was present the last time we met to discuss the distribution of Sandy Lowell's will. We are sorry to hear of his passing."

"Thanks, Dr. Owens. He will be greatly missed by his family and his many friends. He was a fine father, a consummate attorney, and a great spokesman for the state of Texas.

"If I may, let me summarize the reason for our meeting today. Sandy Lowell's will was prepared by my father and reviewed on an annual basis. At the time of his last review, about nine months ago, there were no changes to his will. As you all know from the meeting with my father, he had bequests listed as follows: $50 million to Pet Rescue, $50 million to the University of Texas Athletic Fund, $50 million to the First Baptist Church of Austin, $50 million to the Mental Health Research Fund at Dell Medical School, and $50 million to Child Advocates. The remainder of the estate,

$150 million, was earmarked to Hill County Medical Center. I feel comfortable sharing this information with you all, since Dad shared it with you when he was alive.

"Since the last discussion you had with my father, other developments have come about, primarily centering on Sandy's daughter, Jennifer. Sandy was under the impression for years that the trust fund he established for Jennifer, in the amount of $50 million, was still intact, or at least a large portion of it was. It was his understanding that the mother of the child had upheld her fiduciary duties and had spent the income from the trust for the care of Jennifer and her caretaker, and that most of the principal of the original trust was intact. I obviously had nothing to do with the original trust set up by Mr. Lowell and my father. I don't see how it would be possible for neither Sandy nor my father to check on the trust spending at some point over the last forty years, but all I can tell you is that it apparently didn't happen until recently. The mother was the sole trustee, and she never, to my knowledge, invited any scrutiny.

"As it turns out, the original trust has been depleted down to a little less than $2 million. At one time, the identity of Jennifer's mother was not discussed, but that was the worst-kept secret. I don't doubt that everyone in this area now knows who she is. So, I have made no attempt to hide her identity. The mother, Mrs. Phyllis Reardon, wife of Dr. Michael Reardon, asserts that there have been many financial swings in the trust over the past forty years, and that the income from the fund was never enough to take care of all of Jennifer's and her caretaker's needs. She also asserts that Sandy intended for her to spend some of the money on herself. He loved her intensely and trusted her to take care of their daughter, but at the same time felt she should enrich herself to some degree, to be able to travel and afford some of the nicer luxuries of life, such as a comfortable home and automobiles.

"As a matter of fact, I made copies of Sandy Lowell's original trust, a lot of which is legal boilerplate, but if you refer to the highlighted areas, you can read that Mrs. Reardon is entirely correct in her interpretation of the terms of the trust."

We all read along in silence, and I must say Sandy had given Phyllis broad powers to handle the trust. She had control over investments made by the fund, and control over distributions as needed, both to herself and Jennifer. I had no training in the law, but as a layperson, the document read as though Phyllis could do any damn thing she pleased with the money, both income and principal.

Darrell Bledsoe spoke up. "Ham, I understand that you now represent Mrs. Reardon in a lawsuit filed against the estate of Sandy Lowell in an attempt to contest the will. Since Mrs. Reardon is not mentioned in the will, how do you propose to give her 'standing,' a necessary prerequisite for contesting the will?"

"As you know, counselor, a person with standing can be someone who is not a beneficiary, but who would inherit under the will if the will is deemed invalid. Mrs. Reardon certainly qualifies under this rule."

"I also seem to remember that you have filed a lawsuit against your own firm, Bowles and Associates, which I don't think is legally possible. Can you tell me where you stand on this issue?"

"Certainly. I have resigned from the firm my father started and have formed my own new law firm with some of the associates from the old firm, as well as a few paralegals and administrative staff. Since I have done legal work for Mrs. Reardon in the past, she is my client, and I am within my rights to continue to provide legal representation for her. The same applies to other clients of mine who are joining me and leaving my father's firm, as well as the clients of the associates forming the new firm with me. The new firm will be called Law Offices of Hamilton Bowles Jr.

"I have been considering forming my own firm for quite some time now. The son of the founder is always, in my opinion, trying to fill the father's shoes, and I felt I needed to stand on my own two feet at this point in my life. The timing turned out to be advantageous, with Mrs. Reardon needing representation right away. So, I am perfectly within my rights to file a lawsuit against Bowles and Associates on behalf of Mrs. Reardon in order to recover documents pertinent to her case.

"Before you mention it, Darrell, there is the issue of our lawsuit against the hospital for undue influence regarding Sandy's will. I need access to the reams of paperwork from years past, including correspondence and telephone records between Sandy Lowell, Phyllis Reardon, my father, and Dr. Buck Owens, all of which I am entitled to review on the basis that it represents work product relating to my client, Phyllis Reardon."

"I think a judge might disagree, Mr. Bowles," opined Darrell Bledsoe.

"My former law firm felt that same way because of the potentially murky waters relating to our joint clients, so there is a hearing scheduled for tomorrow afternoon to address that issue. You are welcome to attend, or I can send over the judge's ruling after the hearing is complete. I have no doubt I am within my legal rights to take possession of copies of the many documents in question, or so the legal experts I consulted have told me.

"Before I go, here's what I am proposing. This is an easy solution to a very complex problem, and all parties come out ahead, without the nasty business of depositions and embarrassing trials. First, Sandy's draft establishment of a new trust for Jennifer in the amount of $50 million would be honored, even though he hadn't signed it. It was clearly his intent to honor that verbal agreement, and I believe a judge will approve that. Second, Phyllis Reardon would be named executor of the new trust, and would continue to serve as executor of the existing trust until those funds are exhausted. Third, Hill Country Medical Center will forfeit a portion of their bequest, in the amount of $50 million, in order to fund the new trust. This would allow HCMC to retain a $100 million bequest, enough to maintain the highest level of care possible and not deprive Sandy Lowell's other favorite charities of the much-needed funds he so generously left them."

The room was deathly quiet.

Darrell spoke first. "As I understand it, Sandy Lowell was adamant that Mrs. Reardon NOT be allowed to act as trustee in the new trust. Changing that provision would go against his wishes and also put Mrs. Reardon in a position to abuse the terms of the new trust, as she did in the original trust."

"Counselor," Ham responded, "if you read the terms of the original trust, you will see that in fact Mrs. Reardon did NOT violate those provisions. She functioned within the latitude offered her by the creators of that document, which was Sandy Lowell and my father. And, if you review the documents that had been drafted thus far regarding the establishment of a new trust, there is no mention whatsoever of disallowing Mrs. Reardon to perform the duties of trustee.

"Gentlemen and ladies, the three proposals are quite fair and put each party in a win-win situation. Jennifer is taken care of. Phyllis Reardon, the mother, is taken care of. HCMC is taken care of, without the necessity of besmirching the reputations of any of the parties involved. I'll await your decision prior to taking any further action."

Ham Bowles Jr. stood, nodded, and left the room.

There was quite a bit of chatter once he left, then quiet as Darrell Bledsoe spoke. "Buck, are there elements of your past dealings with Sandy Lowell and Ham Bowles Sr. that perhaps you wouldn't want to come to light?"

Buck was very slow to answer. "Possibly, although I'm not sure what that asshole was referring to with that phrase of 'undue influence.'"

"I think it concerns your cultivating the friendship of Sandy Lowell over the years, having him become your angel donor to the tune of a million dollars a year, and influencing him to leave the majority of his estate to HCMC. Perhaps a case could be made for undue influence, but in making that case, a lot of laundry would have to be aired. From where I sit, if you sign off on his proposal, the hospital gains $100 million. And Jennifer Lowell has a new trust that should last until well after her death. The only fly in the ointment is allowing Phyllis Reardon to control the trust, but remember, she would be spending money earned by the Lowell family, and not by any of you or the hospital."

"Except for giving away the additional $50 million bequest that she would then have control over," said Buck. "And I don't believe what Ham Jr. said, about there being nothing in the paperwork excluding Phyllis Reardon from managing the new trust. I think Sandy told Ham Sr. she was not to have any control over a subsequent trust, and somehow, now that it's in Ham Jr.'s hands, that stipulation has disappeared."

"The additional $50 million was never the hospital's money to begin with, Buck. This agreement would be a win–win for the hospital, and for you personally. There would be a hearing before a judge, and with all parties in agreement, Sandy's last will and testament, and the establishment of the new trust, would be rubber-stamped and the issue closed. As the attorney of record for HCMC, my advice is to take the deal and thank your lucky stars that Ham Jr. is a reasonable man."

CHAPTER 25

THE NEW HOUSE

"**W**hat was your take on the meeting?" I asked Mary Louise over dinner at the yacht club bar.

"I have mixed feelings. First and foremost, I want to see Jennifer, the daughter, be well taken care of. Under this agreement, that should happen. Also, I want HCMC to get the bequest, because the hospital does wonderful work for the community, and that sum would put us in great stead for a very long time. And lastly, part of me wants Phyllis Reardon to be happy."

"I totally agree with your first two points, but I'm not so concerned about Phyllis's happiness. And the lawyer, Bowles, was very bullish on the issue of whether she could function as trustee of the new trust."

"Apparently, restricting her is no longer part of the deal."

"But—"

"According to her attorney's presentation, Phyllis will not excluded from the trustee position. That she would be excluded was mentioned somewhere along the way by Buck, or by Sandy second hand, which would be third hand for me, but perhaps there was nothing written about that when Bowles Jr. drafted the new documents. The story in my mind is that Sandy, in a fit of anger after discovering the residual amount left in the original

trust, insisted that Bowles Sr. draft a new trust with $50 million
and exclude Phyllis from managing the funds. However, Bowles
Sr. turned it over to Bowles Jr., and he supposedly drafted the
documents and perhaps elected to exclude that clause, seeing as
how he was planning to leave his father's firm and start a new firm
of his own. And maybe he thought, if he played his cards carefully,
he might end up with a nice piece of business for the new firm,
Phyllis Reardon and her two trusts, the old one and the new one."

"You're thinking perhaps some collusion went on between
Bowles Jr. and Phyllis? That the decision to start his new firm
might have been prompted by an omission on his part of Sandy's
wishes to exclude Phyllis from the new trust, with an agreement
from Phyllis that she would take her business to the new firm
in exchange for assuming the managerial role in the new trust?
That's devious. And if you feel that way, why in the world would
you care about Phyllis's happiness?"

"You probably can't fathom the depth of her despair over the
child she created with her first cousin. She feels the obligation that
a mother would have to see that the child is well taken care of, but
she cannot lay eyes upon the child. She has extreme guilt over the
decision to have an affair with her cousin, over the decision not to
terminate the fetus, and about the fact that all of Jennifer's issues
are likely a direct result of those decisions. That's why she has
been unable to see the child for years. It's too painful for her. She
knows Jennifer is deserving of all the love and care and support
that Phyllis has never provided to her, and that compounds the
guilt. And that guilt is excruciating. There is no amount of money
that can make that go away."

"I'm sorry, Mary Louise, but I just don't see it. I can't help
feeling there is darkness in her heart. I don't know why, just a

gut-level response to all that has gone on. Maybe in time I'll change my mind. But for now, I'm exhausted and can barely stay awake."

"Then let's get you home, sweetie."

The rest of the work week was a blur, as was the golf weekend. Surgery on Wednesday consisted of seven cases, and had it not been for the two operating rooms I was granted, and my two nurse practitioner assistants, I would still be in there. I also had to add on two broken hips for surgery on Friday morning, which supplanted my Friday golf game. The only other highlight I clearly recalled from that busy week was a phone call from Buck, confirming that the judge had ruled in favor of Ham Bowles's petition, giving him access to ALL legal records and communications from his father's firm that had anything whatsoever to do with his new client, Phyllis Reardon, period, end of sentence. That included years of records involving the interactions between Bowles Sr., Sandy Lowell, and Buck Owens, and encompassed phone calls as well. Those pesky lawyers had to justify their billable hours, such that each and every call between Bowles Sr., Sandy Lowell, and Dr. Buck Owens was summarized in painful detail, and soon was going to be in Bowles Jr.'s possession. Buck sounded like his stroke was imminent. I really could not fathom what the underlying issues were, other than perhaps those records made a case for "undue influence" on the part of Buck Owens in relation to Sandy Lowell's donations to the hospital, past, present, and future.

Buck sounded anxious now to agree to the settlement. He did not confide in me about any possible previous misdeeds he was involved in, and in Buck's defense, his goal of seeing to it the hospital was taken care of in the long term was admirable. He wasn't in the business for personal gain. He had plenty of money. The hospital was his baby, and come hell or high water, he wanted to make sure it was financially set for the future.

The purpose of the call was to take a vote of each of the board members regarding Ham Bowles Jr.'s proposal. Mine was a yes, even though I knew that Phyllis Reardon would end up being the trustee of the new trust, the same position she was in before. I tried to take the high road—Mary Louise's words, not mine—and give my colleague's wife the benefit of the doubt. I had decided to leave my suspicions behind and do the right thing for all concerned. The hospital would get the needed cash infusion of $100 million and would be competitive with all institutions of similar size, and Jennifer Lowell would have a $50 million trust that would hopefully ensure she and any subsequent caretakers she might have would be well taken care of for the foreseeable future.

A month or so passed, our lives becoming routine. I had given up my Friday golf twice a month in order to get the work done. There were two surgeons looking at the job position at HCMC, one just out of fellowship looking to start a practice, and one gentleman who had been in practice for twenty years in a large group in Dallas, looking to change his environment. I had interviewed both, and both looked good on paper and in person. The older man, who was fifty, was a little jaded, but then what doctor wouldn't be after twenty years of orthopedic surgery practice?

I had two other associates in the HCMC orthopedic group essentially doing the same work I did at that time, and we were all busier than we wanted. Patients seemed to keep coming to HCMC in droves, from even further locales. Granted, it was a state-of-the-art facility, with a friendly and competent staff, and with a nearby hotel of 500 beds—the Hill Country Resort—there was plenty of opportunity for overnight stays for family members. The planners of this burgeoning medical complex had done their homework.

The place was destined to be a star in the crown of one of the largest not-for-profit healthcare systems in the United States.

Mike Reardon and I had put our differences aside and resumed our friendly ways. He and Phyllis had scheduled a party on Saturday night for their nearest and dearest friends and close relatives. They lived on Applehead Island in a beautiful home on the water. The address on the Evite, however, was in the Trails of Horseshoe Bay, on a tributary of Lake LBJ called Sandy Creek. We arrived at the address to find a long circular driveway and many liveried valet parkers. The home was an ultra-modern structure, somewhat unusual for this area of traditional homes built with Texas limestone. It was all on one level and done in stucco painted gray. When one entered the home, it seemed the entire place was open to the air, an effect made possible by electronically controlled sliding doors that disappeared into the walls as if by magic. Mary Louise estimated the interior space under roof to be 10,000 square feet, with another 2–3,000 feet of covered outdoor space.

There were interior walls in the bedrooms constructed to create private spaces, but the rest of the place was open, including the kitchen, the two dining areas, and the three sitting areas. The furniture was a combination of gray, black, and white, and accent pieces of sculptured glass were scattered about in custom cases throughout the house. It was a showpiece, and I was duly impressed.

"Makes me feel like I live over in the slums. How about you?" I asked Mary Louise.

"We have a beautiful home, just not as ostentatious as this."

As we were about to make further comments about the Reardon property, Phyllis came up from behind us and squeezed us both. "What do you think?"

"About the house? Incredible. It looks brand new," said Mary Louise. "I assume it's yours?"

"It is. We just finished it recently."

"How long have you been building it?"

"Two years. It was completed a couple of months ago, but we wanted to wait to inhabit the place until after the party."

"How in the world did you keep that a secret in our little town?"

"Believe it or not, neither Michael nor I told a soul. The contractor and architect were sworn to secrecy. We wanted it to be a surprise. It helped that we kept our other house and the furnishings intact, since we continued to live there during the building process. I so wanted to move in here, but we waited the two months that we agreed upon. Last night was the first time we slept here."

"Well, it certainly is beyond spectacular, if you know what I mean," responded Mary Louise.

"I knew you would love it. I'll give you a private tour later. Sorry to run, but I have to meet and greet. Thanks for coming, and Jim Bob, I'm so glad that ugliness between us is over, and we're back to being friends," she said, rushing off to greet more admirers.

Once she was out of earshot, I commented to Mary Louise, "No wonder she wanted to settle that business with Sandy's will quickly. She had a house to finish building."

"Try and be nice."

"I'm nice, just stating the facts, ma'am. And I'm sure glad we helped Phyllis get another $50 million under her belt. This place with the land and the furnishings had to cost close to $10 million, don't you think?"

"I think $7–8 million, but let's not dwell on the past, Jim Bob. Walk with me and peruse the property, and get me a cocktail, please. I have suddenly developed an intense thirst."

We accepted glasses of chardonnay from a server behind a handsome circular bar adjacent to the kitchen and walked outside to one end of an enormous patio, with large ceiling fans spaced evenly throughout the covered space. In contrast, there were fire pits scattered about as well, the yin and yang of decor, I presumed. We stopped and made small talk with acquaintances, oohing and aahing together over the magnificence of the place. We ran into Buck Owens and Shelly Wood at the opposite end of the patio, although "terrace" was probably the more appropriate description. Greetings were exchanged between the four of us.

"Some place, huh, Brady?" said Buck.

"Yep. Bet it takes a lot of money to run a place like this."

"I'm sure glad we facilitated that transaction a month ago. She's been building the house for two years, she told me, without any shame whatsoever."

"Same story I got, Buck."

"Boys," said Mary Louise, "let's save that conversation for another time and place, please."

"Fine," I said. "I need to find the head. Can you keep Mary Louise company, Shelly?"

"Of course. My pleasure. Buck, are you joining Jim Bob on a trip to the facilities?"

"Sure am, but if I get lost, I'm using the nearest bush I can find, inside or outside."

With that said, I detected some urgency in Buck's tone, so we set about on our mission. We wandered here and there and finally spotted Mike Reardon from a distance. Figuring he would know about bathroom locations, we headed toward him. Just as we were behind him, we noticed another person nearby, who appeared to be pressed up against a wall in front of Mike. She was young, and apparently a server, seeing as how she had on a short black skirt, black hose, black high heels, a white blouse with puffed sleeves, and a tray of canapés she was balancing carefully with one hand, and fending off her potential suitor with the other.

"Hey, Mike. We're looking for the bathroom."

He turned his glassy eyes toward me, had a look of non-recognition for a moment, then broke into a wide smile. "Hey Jim, Buck. How're y'all doin'?"

"Good, friend. Looking for the head."

The server slipped around Mike, mouthed a "thank you" to me, and left.

"Oh, man, this place has seven or eight bathrooms. There's a couple back here for sure, that's our bedroom. Go on in," he said. "We have his and hers, so each of you can have one." He cackled loudly, thinking that what he said was funny, but I didn't get the humor.

Buck and I entered a lavishly appointed main bedroom with high ceilings, a large ceiling fan, and more of those disappearing doors. We wandered into the first bathroom suite, which had a higher-than-normal vanity table, a mechanical chair that resembled one from a salon, a small built-in refrigerator, Hollywood lights, an enormous tub, a walk-in shower, a tiled rather than carpeted floor, and a separate water closet. Buck ducked into the water closet, while I entered the next bathroom through a door adjacent to the water closet. I stepped into a smaller and less opulent bathroom with a large sink and mirror, a walk-in shower with side sprays and overhead nozzles, and another water closet. I made use of the facilities there, then stepped over to the sink to wash my hands. There were no towels left out by the host and hostess, probably because they assumed there would be no guests invading their private space. I opened a couple of drawers, found a hand towel, washed up, then pondered what should I do with the towel.

It was barely damp. I could neatly fold it and reinsert it into its rightful place in the drawer or leave it on the counter for future use. I heard Buck call me before I could decide.

"Brady, get in here."

"What?" I said, walking back into what I assumed was Phyllis's bathroom.

"Look at this."

"What? I don't see—"

And then I did. Buck apparently had to search for a towel as well, and at the bottom of the drawer there were small thin packaged syringes, each with a small-gauge needle. There were dozens in the drawer. I picked one up and looked to see the label and the contents.

"What is it?" Buck asked.

"They appear to be empty."

I thought for a minute, then said to Buck, "Let's look in the fridge."

Buck crouched down and opened the fridge. We noted several bottles of water. He moved those aside and found a number of vials. He handed me one, and I held it up to the vanity lights, which were bright enough to power Times Square. It looked like . . .

"It's Botox."

"What the hell is she doing with Botox?" Buck asked.

"Nothing good."

CHAPTER 26

SUNDAY

I didn't want to discuss our findings in the Reardon bathroom at that time with Mary Louise, so Buck and I got four vodka tonics in plastic glasses and found our companions.

"What's this?" asked Shelly.

"Tito's and tonic," answered Buck.

"I don't drink hard liquor."

"Good. More for me."

Mary Louise accepted hers gratefully, and we downed them rather quickly.

A bell rang, and Phyllis stepped up to the bar with a small microphone in hand.

"Thanks to all of you, our dear friends and relatives, for attending our open house today. We are so privileged to live in this beautiful community, and I love each and every one of you. Dinner is served on the patio. Help yourself and seat yourself."

I would have left but I was starving, and they were serving barbecue catered from Opie's in Spicewood, one of my favorite places, so we stayed. Fortunately, the mariachi band cranked up the music toward the end of dinner, and by the time we were done, there was enough dancing and singing for us to slip out without seeing our host and hostess.

"Call me tomorrow, Brady," Buck said.

"Will do. I want to discuss our findings with Mary Louise before I do anything else. Goodnight Shelly."

"Goodnight, Doc. See you Monday."

Mary Louise gave Shelly a hug, and we were out of there.

I couldn't wait to tell Mary Louise what Buck and I had seen in that bathroom drawer, but I held off until we arrived home and had a calming drink in hand. We opted for Kosta Browne pinot noir again and sipped while we supervised Tip in his search for the perfect spot to do his business.

We sat in the outdoor recliner chairs once Tip was relieved, and I relayed what Buck and I had seen in the Reardon bathroom.

"What do you think is going on?" she asked.

"I don't have a clue. What's the deal with storage of Botox? Does it have to be refrigerated?"

"Yes, as I understand it. You keep it in the fridge until you're ready to use it, then mix it with saline, and inject the desired areas. I've obviously never kept any around the house. I buy it directly from Dr. Goldfarb and get the injections at his office. I can't imagine why Phyllis would keep that much Botox on hand, unless she was planning on having Botox parties, or was doing self-injections, or maybe had plans to inject her husband. What's confusing to me is that she said they had just moved in and had slept in the house last night for the first time. Why would her bathroom be stocked with Botox and syringes if she had only been there one night?"

"Another Phyllis mystery, Mary Louise. Don't you have to have some sort of qualifications to buy it, store it, and inject it?"

"Jim Bob, I have no clue. That's not something I have an interest in."

"I'll call Susan Beeson tomorrow morning. She seems to have a handle on the sale and distribution of Botox."

We slept in, although I dreamed of being attacked by small glass vials of liquid that would coalesce into macabre shapes and then descend on my poor defenseless self. We made a large breakfast of tacos with eggs, sausage, and pepper jack cheese. Once the time was appropriate, per Mary Louise, I called Susan's cell and put her on speakerphone.

"Morning. How's the great orthopedic surgeon and his bride?"

"Fair."

"Hello, Susan," interjected Mary Louise.

"Hello, friend."

"How's the FBI ASAC?"

"Much better than fair. What's got your panties in a wad, Jim Bob Brady?"

"Why do you say that?"

"I've known you for a long time, and I can tell from your tone of voice that you are upset about something. What is it?"

I gave her the story of my discovery the previous evening of syringes hidden in a drawer and Botox vials in the fridge of Phyllis Reardon's bathroom.

"I don't guess you happened to pocket one of the vials, did you?"

I hesitated. "Yes, I did. Is that a crime?"

"Let's see. Breaking and entering, stealing prescription drugs. I believe so. On the other hand, I might be able to track a vial of Botox using information on the label, so I could consider you aided and abetted the federal government, if there happens to be some sort of crime involved."

"I prefer the latter scenario, if you please."

"You know, we had a conversation about this Botox business not too long ago, Jim."

"I realize that, but this seems to be a different conversation, more about how a large amount of Botox would get into the hands of a private citizen?"

"Botox requires a prescription, and by law the prescriber should be a doctor, dentist, nurse, or pharmacist. There are 100 units in every vial, and physicians pay around $400 per vial. The recommended dosage is four units in each of five sites on the forehead, totaling twenty units, so one vial would be good for four or five treatments. It's expensive, so there is always a black market for Botox and Botox substitutes.

"A counterfeit product can be identified by one of three ways. One, the vial is missing the lot number. Two, the outer carton does not have any entries next to the LOT: MFG: EXP. And third, the outer carton and vial both display the active ingredient as "Botulinum Toxin Type A" instead of "Onabotulinumtoxina." Do you have a carton or just the vial?"

"Just the vial. I didn't see any cartons."

"Look for the lot number and the active ingredient on the vial. Do you see both?"

"Yes."

"Okay, it's real Botox, not counterfeit. The question now is how did she get all that Botox? Is she a nurse, doctor, dentist, or pharmacist?"

"Not that I know of, although I do remember her telling me once that her father was a pharmacist. He probably wouldn't still be alive, though."

"There are programs available to become a 'cosmetic injector,' which require some sort of nursing degree one must qualify for, but I don't know how tightly the certification is controlled. If you get a certificate, an individual can purchase Botox, and inject Botox, so your friend may be qualified in some way. That's about all I can tell you without more information. I'll get one of the fellows at the office to check into that lot number, but that has a low percentage of return unless by chance the entire lot was stolen, which would be unlikely. Sorry."

"Well, you've been very helpful, Susan. Sorry to disturb your Sunday. My best to Gene."

"Now what are you going to do, Jim?"

"I don't know. Discuss the situation with Mary Louise and go from there. I'm trying to stay out of harm's way—you know, conduct my doctor business, play some golf, be attentive to the lovely and charming Mrs. Brady, and leave investigations to the professionals."

"That would be wise, but an unlikely occurrence in my experience. Goodbye."

"Did you mean that part, about being attentive to the lovely and charming Mrs. Brady?"

"Of course. Do you need attending to this morning?"

"Absolutely. Are you available?" she asked, as she undid the drawstring of her robe, revealing herself in all her splendor.

"I am at the ready for you, madame."

"I can see that clearly, monsieur."

We spent the rest of Sunday morning in repose and woke up famished.

Mary Louise, still in bed, stretched like a cat. "What are you preparing me for lunch?"

"That's a frightening thought. I can order something and bring it home if you like."

"That would take too long. How about I throw on some jeans and a tee shirt, and we'll go on a search-and-rescue mission?"

"What would we be rescuing?"

"Ourselves from hunger."

We dressed quickly, put Tip in the rear of my SUV, and drove out our small cul-de-sac and down the hill to Bay West Boulevard, then down to FM 2147. Instinctively, we drove east, looking for places to stop for lunch, and stumbled upon Julie's Cantina, a Mexican restaurant and bar in Cottonwood Shores. We sat at the bar and had Bloody Marys, chicken enchiladas with tomatillo sauce, crispy ground beef tacos, black beans, and fresh tortillas. It resembled our breakfast, but it was Sunday, and the perfect day for spicy south-of-the-border food.

In the midst of a bite of enchilada, I heard a voice behind me say, "You have anything you'd like to tell me, Jim Bob Brady?"

It was Phyllis Reardon, with a sheepish Mike standing behind her.

"Lovely party last night, right, Mary Louise?"

"Yes, Phyllis, lovely. Thanks for inviting us."

"That's not what I'm talking about. He knows quite well what I mean, just as this worthless husband of mine does."

"I'm sorry, but I'm confused. I have no idea—"

"You stole some of my private property from me, and I want it returned. Today!"

"Phyllis, I—"

"I'm going to give you twenty-four hours, then I'm calling the police."

She turned on her heel and walked out of Julie's. Mike trailed behind her like a lost puppy.

"How could she know?" I asked Mary Louise.

"She counted? Or has a bathroom camera?"

"No idea. Looks like I'm in trouble."

"Not the first time, won't be the last."

CHAPTER 27

BUSTED

After another nap, I decided to do some online research on the procurement of Botox. I discovered that it didn't appear to be that difficult to acquire. While the marketers will say that only doctors, dentists, nurses, and pharmacists can prescribe the drug, there are loopholes. There is a prescribing course, which nurses, midwives, pharmacists, and even paramedical professionals can take online in order to become prescribers without the requisite training and background. One can even take online courses and become certified in something called aesthetic medicine, which allows the certificate holder to prescribe and inject. Some advertisers asserted there was a 300–400% markup on Botox injections, so whatever the costs were to become a prescriber would be well worth it financially.

The more I read, the easier I realized it would be for just about anyone, including Phyllis Reardon, to obtain Botox for personal use. Maybe she was involved in what Susan had described to me as "Botox parties," either as a hostess, or possibly an injector, if she somehow had the requisite training and certification. I really knew nothing about Phyllis's background, other than she had Jennifer Lowell when she was nineteen years old, and that she was married to Dr. Mike Reardon, and what she told me briefly at lunch that day at the Bluebonnet. She said she grew up the daughter of a pharmacist and had gone to SMU on loans and scholarships. I had no idea if she had ever worked for a living. There was no chance of her divulging any of that missing information to me now that she knew about my pilfering of one tiny vial of Botox.

And that brought up the critical question of how she knew I had stolen that vial. Did she count the vials daily? Had she just put them in the fridge, having moved in the day before? Was there a bathroom camera, and if so, why? And then it dawned on me. Injecting fillers and Botox was on the messy side. Sticking a needle into someone's face caused bleeding, and a room that supported that would preferably be tiled, with a chair that could be rotated, and would be brightly lit in order to provide the injector with good visibility. That was it. Phyllis was planning on performing injections in her bathroom, either on herself and/or Mike, or perhaps customers outside her immediate family, and she had designed the room during the building process so that injections could be done once she moved in.

She might have kept an accurate mental count of vials of Botox in the small fridge, but a better idea was that she had installed cameras in the "injection room" in case of a medical problem or a complication of some sort, or for liability reasons. Had she been doing any injections in that room? That was doubtful since, according to Phyllis, she and Mike had only occupied the house for a couple of days.

And that brought me full circle, back to the reason I had meddled in all this business to start with. Sandy Lowell. Dr. Robert Warner had performed a number of plastic surgery procedures on Sandy over the years. And Dr. Larry Goldfarb had admitted that Sandy was a regular patient for injections of various fillers and Botox. To me it was clear that Sandy was somewhat obsessed with his appearance and had procedures frequently to keep him looking young. Would that include, by any chance, having his former paramour and mother of his child perform injections on him? I remember reading somewhere on the internet that there was a maximum allowable dose of Botox in order to minimize complications. What if he chose to ignore those dose maximums? Phyllis wouldn't necessarily be fully informed about his previous injections and their doses unless Sandy told her, and would she, at his request, inject him with whatever he wanted, whenever he wanted? How close were they still, after all these years?

A picture was emerging. Excessive doses of Botox over time was fraught with complications, including muscle paralysis, speech impediments, difficulty swallowing, and respiratory distress. What if Sandy was having Dr. Goldfarb inject his face at the appropriate intervals and with the recommended doses, and then unbeknownst to the doctor, came to Phyllis for further injections in between the Goldfarb injections? Over time, he could have developed problems but continued on with the treatments due to his extraordinary vanity, until he got to the acute breaking point in the parking lot of the HEB the day I first saw him. The respiratory paralysis that ensued then created a build-up of potassium in his bloodstream, which prompted his cardiac rhythm into ventricular fibrillation, from which he was unable to recover.

It all made sense to me then, except for one thing. Were Phyllis's interim injections a sign of good will and camaraderie between two old friends and lovers, or an excuse for her to literally do him in and manipulate the will in order to enrich herself? That would necessitate the demise of Hamilton Bowles Sr. in the relatively same time frame as Sandy Lowell. The tacit cooperation of Hamilton Bowles Jr. would also be necessary, giving him an impetus to leave his law firm and take with him Phyllis Reardon and all her legal records into his client base. And he would gain oversight on two trusts, the combined value of which would be $52 million. That kind of money could generate some hefty legal fees.

Or was Sandy's demise just an accident? Phyllis could have been giving Sandy injections at his request, without knowledge of his previous injections and doses, and he just happened to die of complications brought on by a case of botulism. And maybe Ham Bowles Sr. was undergoing similar treatments, and he just happened to die of complications about the same time as his friend and client. And to complete a series of coincidences, Bowles Jr. decided to leave his father's firm after his father had passed and just happened to take Phyllis and her soon-to-be $50 million plus with him as a client, and happened to be successful in contesting the will. Many coincidences would have to be in play for that innocent scenario to have happened, and although unlikely, it was certainly possible.

For me, though, skeptic that I am, I opted to get behind the theory that Phyllis knew what she was doing and planned the whole thing out, poisoned both Sandy and Ham Bowles Sr. with overdoses of Botox, enlisted the aid of Bowles Jr., got the trust and will changed, and set herself up for life. Yep, that sounded right to me.

Not that Mary Louise and I needed another cocktail, but I thought it best to provide us both with a libation while I described to her the two scenarios, a tale of two different Phyllis Reardons. She listened attentively and completed consumption of her glass of wine in record time.

"Wow. Do you really think she could be that devious? Enough to essentially commit murder, not once but twice?"

"I don't know her all that well, Mary Louise. I would say that anything is possible under almost any circumstance."

"What would be your next step?"

"Well, the first thing that comes to mind is to talk it over with Susan Beeson. She is the assistant special agent in charge of the FBI in Austin, and a close friend, so I wouldn't feel silly discussing it with her."

"I'm just reeling, Jim Bob, thinking of one of our friends, a doctor's wife, involved in murder. It just doesn't seem possible."

"I hope I'm wrong, Mary Louise, but we have to notify Susan. If there is in fact a bathroom camera in that new house, I don't want to take a chance on any video being removed or erased."

"But Jim, she said they had only moved in the day before. That wouldn't give her time to do any injections, or anything else, so I would expect any recording to be blank, provided there is even a camera in that bathroom."

"If you believe her about the move-in date. If someone has the skills and planning ability to carry out two murders, what's a little lie about a moving date?"

"I see your point. Let's get Susan on speaker phone."

We bothered Susan for the second time that day, and I went through my spiel with her.

"Jim Bob, you've taken a quantum leap from this morning's conversation. You've taken this to a whole new level, leaping from your friend possessing a vial of Botox to her planning a double murder. I'm impressed with your imagination."

"Don't you feel the need to investigate, Susan?"

"Let me think about it. There would have to be probable cause to try and obtain a search warrant to a bathroom that might have a camera overlooking a small fridge that might have what, twenty or thirty vials of Botox? A judge might laugh me right out of the courtroom. Is there any other possible evidence of a crime?"

"I don't know what it would be. I saw the Botox vials at the party and stole one. She accosted me at lunch this afternoon, saying she knows what I did. That I stole private property, and that she's going to call the police if I don't hand it over. She gave me twenty-four hours. Unless she keeps a running count of her Botox vials, she has to have a camera in there somewhere."

"Hm. Then let her show her hand. Don't return the vial. Let her call the police. That will give me an in."

"You want me to go to jail?"

"You won't go to jail for stealing $500 vials of Botox, Jim Bob. If she calls the police, you can turn it over to them, tell them you forgot you had it and pocketed the vial by accident or something. Or tell the officers you had too much to drink. Just make up some story. That's what you're best at. I've got your back."

Monday was another full day in surgery with my two new favorite assistants, one in each of the two operating rooms which had become a standard almost overnight. As we worked together, we developed a rhythm and became even more efficient. We completed the six cases around 4 p.m., and after speaking to all the families, I headed up to my office.

"There are two police officers to see you, Dr. Brady. Shall I put them in your office?" Shelly Wood said, having arrived a half hour before me.

"Sure. Wonder what that's about?" I asked no one in particular.

She escorted the two burly fellows dressed in street clothes into my small space. I sat behind the desk, and they each took a chair in front of me.

"I'm Detective Myers, this is Detective De La Garza. We're with the Horseshoe Bay Police Department. Sorry to bother you, sir, but we're here to determine if a crime has been committed. You are accused of stealing an item from a home Saturday night, a home in which you were a guest at a party. The accusers are Dr. Michael Reardon and Mrs. Phyllis Reardon. She filed the complaint and said you broke into her bathroom and stole a vial of Botox." He had sort of a half-smile when he said it, perhaps thinking that with all the miscreants out there, this particular misdeed was fairly minor.

I reached around behind my desk, opened the mini-fridge I kept there, and pulled out the vial of Botox.

"Here you go, gentlemen."

Det. Myers reached for the vial and studied the label. "How did you come by this, sir?"

"My friend, Dr. Owens, chair of the board of the hospital, and I were seeking a bathroom in the house, which has around 10,000 square feet. We spotted Dr. Reardon, a friend of ours and the homeowner, and asked him to direct us to the closest bathroom. There was some urgency on the part of Dr. Owens, you see."

Myers looked at his partner, and they nodded, indicating perhaps they understood urgency in a man seeking out a bathroom.

"Dr. Reardon told us to go into his bedroom, which was nearby, and use the master bath, which we did. They have separate facilities, so Dr. Owens went to the first water closet, and I went into the second."

"Water closet, sir?"

"Fancy name for a toilet that has a door on it."

There was more nodding.

"Anyway, I did my business, then walked back into the first bathroom, where Dr. Owens was staring at a drawer. He was looking for a towel to dry his hands, and under the stack of hand towels there were dozens of syringes. They were each in a sealed package. Then Dr. Owens said he was dying of thirst and opened a small fridge next to the vanity table, where we found several bottles of water and a whole lot of vials. I picked one up and was studying the label it when we heard a knock at the door. Out of reflex, I guess, I stuck it in my pocket, closed the fridge door, and left the room."

"Who was knocking at the door?" asked Detective De La Garza.

"A woman I didn't know, in desperate need of the facility. We headed to the bar, picked up some vodka tonics, and found our better halves."

"And that's it?" asked Det. Myers.

"Yes, until lunch yesterday at Julie's. Phyllis Reardon accosted me at the bar and accused me of stealing her private property, said she was going to call the police if I hadn't returned it within twenty-four hours. And here you are, as promised."

"Why didn't you return it yesterday?"

"First of all, I forgot about it. I had on a blazer at the party, which I'm not used to wearing in the first place, stuck it in a pocket, and didn't remember the incident until she waylaid me at Julie's. When I got home, I found the vial in my jacket, put it in the fridge, and brought it to work with me this morning in case you fellows came calling."

They looked at each other, nodded, and stood.

"All right, Doctor, thank you for your time and cooperation. I'm of the opinion that the situation is one of no harm, no foul. I'll return the vial to Mrs. Reardon."

"That's fine. I just have been wondering about her need for all those vials of botulinum toxin and the syringes. You fellows know about that drug, that it's toxic, and used in diluted quantities to create Botox, which is injected into people's faces to reduce wrinkles, don't you? But one of the side effects is botulism, a bacterial disease which can be fatal. Do you think she has a license to possess, or use, or distribute a drug like that? And what's with all those syringes? I wonder what else she might have in that fridge. It's a potentially dangerous situation, if you ask me."

"Thank you for the information, sir. We'll speak to our chief."

CHAPTER 28

SEARCH WARRANT

Susan called me that evening. She was laughing when I answered.

"You laid it on pretty thick, Jim Bob. I got the case in record time."

"Whatever do you mean?"

"I don't know what you told those officers from the local PD, but they made a beeline to their chief, who made a call to the DEA in Austin. When the agent got the call, and discovered it was not about narcotics but possible illegal possession and distribution of a potentially toxic drug used for cosmetic treatments, he punted it to the FBI. The DEA didn't want to handle that. And voilà, it was on my desk. Good job."

"I've been trained to lie well. What's going to happen next?"

"The FBI is going to pay a visit tomorrow to the Reardons' new home. I will be undertaking that duty myself. Maybe we can get together for dinner?"

"Absolutely. What happened to the Botox vial I returned?"

"Evidence. The HSB police department has it refrigerated."

"Man, would I love to be there for that encounter at the Reardon home, but I'll be in clinic all day. I can't wait to hear what happens. Are you just going to show up unannounced?"

"I'll put an agent on her vehicle, and we'll track her move-
ments during the day in case she does something evasive or suspicious. My plan is to enter the house around 4 p.m. I don't know
what we'll find, but at least you've provided us with enough information to have a legitimate reason to get a search warrant for the
house. I plan to head straight to the master bathroom, open the
refrigerator, then look for a camera. I'm hoping it will still be oper-
ational, but I'm worried that you may have aroused her suspicions
by stealing that Botox vial. Since the incident was Saturday night,
she would have had time to erase any video she might have accu-
mulated since—wait, when did she move in?"

"The house has been completed for a couple of months.
Allegedly they slept there for the first time the night before the
party. But with the bathroom setup I saw, she could have been
using it for a while to inject Botox and fillers, if in fact that's what
she's been up to."

"I'm getting a search warrant for the other house as well. Mary
Louise told me they have a beautiful home on Applehead Island
that is on the market. If she's been injecting friends and clients for
a while, she had to be using the other home before she moved into
the new digs. Or she might still be using it. Never know what we
might find there, either."

"Man, how stupid of me. I never even thought about the other house. How can you get a search warrant for a house that you
haven't proven has any sort of contraband?"

"Fruit from the potentially poisonous tree."

"Okay, Susan, good luck. See you at our house after work."

Tuesday rounds and clinic passed so slowly, I thought perhaps
Father Time had slowed down our planetary rotation. I finished
up a little early, called Mary Louise, and told her I was on the
way. She responded that she had prepared a dinner of meat loaf,

mashed potatoes and brown gravy, fresh baby lima beans, and a shrimp salad for starters. She had already mixed the Titos dirty martinis, and they were in the freezer. Susan had called recently and said she would be arriving around 6 p.m. and looked forward to seeing us.

The other interesting call was that J.J. was going to be in town on Thursday, and he and Kathryn would like to see us for dinner. Mary Louise was ecstatic about that visit. I had my suspicions as to the reason for the drop-in but thought it best not to spill the beans in case there was exceptional good news.

Susan's car was already parked in front when I arrived home. As I entered the house, I heard the girls talking out on the patio.

"Man alert," I yelled.

Mary Louise yelled back, "Get a martini and join us."

I took the martinis out of the freezer, gave each woman a hug, sat down in a recliner, and waited to hear the story of Susan's exploits of the day.

"I'm all ears, Susan. Did you just arrive?"

"Yes, I walked in not five minutes before you."

"I can't wait to hear what happened."

"So, my team arrived at the new house a little before 4 p.m. I had an agent tracking Mrs. Reardon's movement during the day so we would know where she had been and where she might likely be at the time we had planned to arrive. Lucky for us, she made a grocery stop around 3 p.m., so we figured she had to be headed home after. As soon as she pulled into her driveway and opened the garage door, we showed up. She slammed on her brakes before she made it to the garage, jumped out of the car, and headed for our lead car. She was yelling something about being followed onto her private property when agents from both vehicles stepped out of the cars and showed her their badges. I walked up to her from my personal vehicle, introduced myself, and produced the search warrant.

"She started yelling something about that fucking Jim Bob Brady, then walked away and pulled out her cell phone. We didn't wait for her to escort us, we just walked into the open garage door, then entered the home through a side door that was unlocked. The house was enormous, and I didn't have a clue where to start, so after we passed through a mudroom and the kitchen, I sent two agents to the left, and the other agent and I took a right turn. I found the master bath at the opposite end of the house, located the refrigerator you removed the Botox vial from, opened it, and found it chock full of vials.

"I asked the agent with me to go back out to the garage and find a ladder. By then the other two agents had joined us. A ladder was produced, and I climbed up about three steps or so and looked into the nearest light fixture, which resembled a small chandelier, one of four evenly spaced in the bathroom ceiling. I saw an extraneous wire exiting the top of the chandelier into the ceiling, climbed up one more step, and there it was. A small video camera was nestled between the individual light bulbs.

"By then, the owner had joined us and stood with her arms folded, staring at me. Our conversation went something like this:

"'Where's the feed?' I asked her. She just shook her head. I explained to her that we had a search warrant that included all her personal devices including her cell phone, and that she was just delaying the inevitable.

"She finally said, 'It links directly into my smart phone.'

"'Show me, please,'" I said.

"And she responded, 'Not without my lawyer present.'

"Then I responded that her lawyer could speak for her if she chose, but they could not prevent my searching through her cell phone. So, she handed it to me and walked away.

"I'm no tech expert, but one of my guys is. He tried to find the video feed from the camera, but apparently it had some sort of lock on it requiring a password, and he was unable to open the app. I instructed him to take it back to the office after we were finished and get one of the young techies on it.

"I walked into the master bedroom and saw her sitting on the side of the bed, crying. 'Am I under arrest for something?' she asked.

"'Not yet, ma'am,' I said.

"'You know, I have a license to purchase Botox and other medications, and a license to inject them as well. That is not against the law,' she asserted.

"'Ma'am, I don't know what's legal and what's not in whatever business you're in, but I will find out, and you will suffer the consequences if whatever you're doing is illegal. Remember, this search and seizure came about because of the vials of Botox found in your bathroom by Dr. Brady the night of your party. And it might have ended with that, except you accosted Dr. Brady at lunch on Sunday and accused him of theft. And the only way you would know he accidentally took the vial was if there was a camera in the bathroom. And that raises the question of why there would be a camera in a bathroom of a private residence, aimed at a refrigerator containing, among other items, botulinum toxin, a poison. Then add into the mix the deaths of two individuals, Sandy Lowell, father of your child, and Hamilton Bowles Sr., your former attorney, both of whom died of botulism after overdoses of Botox. If there is any evidence on that smart phone that you were somehow involved in those deaths, your goose will be cooked. Is there anything you want to tell me?' I asked.

"At that point, she pulled back the covers, got into the bed, and wept.

"My people searched the house and found nothing more of interest in the way of cameras or surveillance equipment. I sent two of the agents to search their other home. They will call me this evening with their findings.

"On the way out, her attorney showed up. He introduced himself to me and asked what was going on, although I couldn't imagine him not knowing what was happening. I told him the essence of the problem, and that most importantly we would be going through her cell phone to look for any video evidence that would incriminate his client. He asked to see the search warrant, then confirmed that we had permission to confiscate her cell phone and search it.

"He gave me his business card and told me I was to have no further communication with his client unless he was present. He did ask me if she said anything that could incriminate herself before he arrived, and I told him no. I did tell him Mrs. Reardon said she had a license to own and inject the meds we found, and asked me if she was under arrest, but that was all the communication between me and his client. Wait, she did tell me she wouldn't release the codes to open her phone without her attorney present, but since we had the warrant, we didn't need her permission anyway."

"What was his name?" I asked.

"I must say he looked a bit like a fish out of water," Susan said, as she rummaged through her purse looking for the attorney's card. "His card reads 'W. Hamilton Bowles Jr.'

"You know, Jim, that I went out on a limb on this case. She is probably telling the truth about having a license to purchase and inject Botox, and that means more than likely she can legally store the medications as well. If there is nothing usable on that video, we may not have a case connecting her to those two deaths you've been looking into."

"What happens if the video doesn't show anything incriminating?"

"I'll have to research current laws regarding the Botox injection business, but if she's in the clear regarding the purchase, use, or sale of the meds, and the video has nothing, then we apologize and walk away."

"What?! How could you let that happen, when we know damn well she overdosed Sandy Lowell and Bowles Sr. and gave them botulism in order to enrich herself in a new will? She wouldn't have installed a camera in the bathroom in the first place if she wasn't up to something nefarious."

"Jim Bob, we do NOT know she overdosed those two people, and we have no idea why she installed the camera at this point in time. You have suspicions. I have suspicions. But we need something critical and it's called e-v-i-d-e-n-c-e. You don't put folks in jail because you suspect them of a crime. You need proof. And without proof, the suspicions all go away, she goes back to her life, and you'll probably end up with a cease-and-desist order from the judge."

Lovely, I thought. Whoever said "no good deed goes unpunished" knew what they were talking about.

During dinner, Susan received two calls from her office. The first was from the two agents she had deployed to the Reardons' unsold home. The search didn't turn up anything of value. The agents did note that the furniture was covered, and there were multiple sealed packing boxes throughout the house. The other was from the young techie in her office telling her he had deciphered the password and broken the code, had retrieved the data from the video camera app, and had found absolutely nothing. The SAVED VIDEO folder was empty.

"She erased it, Susan," I said. "Maybe Phyllis saw Buck and me talking to Mike at the party and she became suspicious. Or maybe Mike got nervous about letting us into their personal bathroom, and he told Phyllis what he'd done. Either way, I would bet that after the party was over, whatever was recorded on her phone was deleted. I'm no expert, but can't you retrieve erased data somehow?"

"Jim, it doesn't make any sense to me that she would leave incriminating video on that phone in the first place. What could she have possibly recorded? Videos of her injecting her friends? Or videos of Sandy Lowell and the lawyer getting Botox shots in her bathroom? And to answer your question, I think you can opt for a permanent deletion of recorded data, such that it's gone forever into that celestial trash can. Trust me, if my guy in Austin says the data is gone, then you have to believe me, it's gone. Not that we can prove there was any data in that file to begin with. It's possible the camera had not been used, and there was never any video data in the file."

Mary Louise had been very quiet during the discussion, hadn't asked any questions, hadn't made any comments. "The one thing that stands out in my mind is that Phyllis laid down on the bed and cried. That to me says that she is feeling remorse about something. Perhaps, Susan, you can use that to your advantage. Maybe it all happened like Jim Bob said. Maybe she was injecting Sandy and the lawyer on a regular basis, in addition to their regular treatments from Dr. Goldfarb, and purposely exceeded the limit, which resulted in both developing botulism and dying. Or maybe it was an accident. Maybe Phyllis was injecting both as a favor, without any desire to create a medical problem for them or to manipulate the will. Regardless, she showed extreme remorse in your presence. Maybe she's scared to death of being found out. Or maybe she's just an emotional wreck. I'm just saying, maybe that could help you bond with her, woman to woman, and she'll end up telling you what happened. I can tell you, as a woman, that you don't lay down on your bed, crawl under the covers, and cry without a damn good reason."

CHAPTER 29

SEX, LIES, AND VIDEOTAPE

As my military father would have said, put your nose to the grindstone and you won't have time to worry about matters that aren't your business. So it was that I went after my orthopedic surgery job with abandon. Could you add on a case, Dr. Brady? Sure. Could we work in a couple of extra patients with emergent problems? Sure. At least with patients, you know where you stand. They have a problem, and they want it fixed by you. That's why they are in your office. So, I told myself, oblige them, wear your sorry self out, and quit thinking about Phyllis Reardon, Sandy Lowell, Ham Bowles, and botulism.

Susan told Mary Louise and I over a subsequent dinner that Phyllis Reardon had been interviewed by the FBI on several occasions, with Susan leading the charge. Ham Bowles Jr. was with her on each occasion, prompting her responses. Phyllis had indeed completed nursing school after she graduated from SMU, at her pharmacist father's suggestion. She had worked in Dallas at Parkland Hospital, made famous by a well-known shooting victim, John Fitzgerald Kennedy. She had met Mike there when he was in residency, and they later married. Once he completed his cardiovascular surgery training, he joined a large group of cardiologists and surgeons at the Heart Hospital in Dallas. Phyllis eventually quit working as Mike's income rose, but she had the availability of the backup funds from the settlement that occurred after she birthed Jennifer at age 19.

The Reardons had moved out to the Hill Country after ten years of Mike's hard work in Dallas. He established for himself a stellar reputation as a heart surgeon with his own clinic and team of physicians at HCMC. Phyllis had never let her nursing license lapse, got interested in the Botox craze, and had gone back to school and obtained a certificate in order to treat her friends. There was nothing malevolent about injecting fillers and Botox, she had told the agents. Her excuse for having the small camera in the bathroom focused on the refrigerator was to identify thieves. Botox was expensive, she stated, and there was always an underground market for it.

No amount of tech savvy would reveal any data from the video camera or Phyllis's cell phone. The FBI had gone over both Reardon residences with a fine-toothed comb and found nothing incriminating in either home. Lawyer Bowles produced all the paperwork necessary to prove that Phyllis was on the up and up with respect to Botox purchase, resale, storage, and treatments. She was legit. There was no evidence of any foul play whatsoever. There were no charges the FBI could file on her.

Susan emphatically pointed out that it was time for me to leave my amateurish investigation behind and work my real job. And that's what I did. I concentrated on the work I was trained to do and did the best job I knew how to do. I immersed myself in golf when I wasn't working, and I devoted as much time to Mary Louise as possible. And I tried, really tried, to forget about Phyllis, the two deaths, and the Botox business. Those were all suggestions made to me by my FBI friend, Susan Beeson. They were good

suggestions, and I appreciated them, and I tried really, really hard
to adhere to my good intentions.

But on occasion, I would wake up during the night, walk into
the kitchen for a cold glass of water, and think about what Mary
Louise said about a woman who climbs into bed, crawls under the
covers, and weeps. Sobs. She is emotionally distraught. And why?
Because she killed two people? Because she spent her daughter's trust fund on material things for herself? Because a man she
loved is dead?

And on one of those mornings, I sat straight up in bed, wak-
ened by a strange dream, and remembered what Dr. Robert Warner
had told me. He had seen Phyllis and Sandy holding hands. How
could I have forgotten about that? Had they been lovers, even
after all the traumatic events of their lives, and after all that time?
Mike was a heart surgeon and worked 24/7, constantly at the hospital in the middle of the night, saving lives. He was gone all the
time. Phyllis had plenty of alone time, and plenty of opportunity
to have an affair.

And then it came to me. What had happened to Sandy's
house? Had it been sold? And how would I get that information? Who was handling his estate now that Ham Bowles Sr. was
deceased? Had one of the other partners in the law firm taken
over that business, and would they divulge any facts to me? I had
no legal standing in the case, as I had been told repeatedly.

Should I go off on my own, call a real estate friend of mine,
and find out the status of Sandy's house? Ours was a small town,
so the sale of a house like Sandy's would be common knowledge
amongst the real estate folk.

And what about the disposition of Sandy's estate? If I called
the Bowles and Associates firm, would someone tell me who was
the attorney of record now?

Or should I just call Susan and see if she would run interference and gather what I now felt was important information? She had dismissed my ideas enough times that I felt certain she would no longer entertain my suspicions.

"What are you doing up, Jim Bob Brady?" asked a sleepy Mary Louise. "It's three o'clock in the morning."

"I couldn't sleep. I have things on my mind."

"Still flustered about Phyllis?"

"Truth be known, yes."

"You can't let it go, huh?"

"No, I'm sorry to say."

She padded over to my side of the bed and nestled up against me. "What can I do to help?"

"You won't like it, and neither will Susan."

"We've been expecting this, and thought it was just a matter of time before you awoke with an idea that might solve a lot of unanswered questions."

"So, I'm not in the doghouse, with either you or Susan?"

"Never. We know your intentions are good; it's just the execution that lacks finesse sometimes."

"What you're implying is that I should list my concerns, that you'll share them with Susan and discuss them with her during business hours, and I should try and get a little extra sleep and be prepared for work in a few hours."

"Exactly, young man."

Thursday happened to be a clinic day, and though I struggled through the day due to lack of sleep, my alert level was high enough to see my patients and dispense them proper care and advice. At the end of clinic, I ambled up to my office and sat at my desk.

"Dr. Brady, you have a phone call to make, if you please," said Maya Stern, the new hire for our administrative assistant position.

She was mid-forties, with excellent credentials. She was a single mother of two high school daughters and had moved to our area after an unpleasant divorce in San Antonio. She was intelligent, efficient, caring, and polite, and the patients had nothing but good things to say about her.

"I may fall asleep during the call, Maya, but you can get whoever wants to speak to me on the phone."

A minute passed, then my office line buzzed.

"Is this the famous Doc Brady, investigator to the stars?" asked Susan Beeson.

"Hey. I hope you're still speaking to me."

"Always. I'll get right to the point. I spoke to the law firm of Bowles and Associates, the firm of the deceased Hamilton Bowles Sr. Trustee of Sandy Lowell's estate fell to the son, Hamilton Bowles Jr., because he had worked on the estate from time to time when his father was alive, and because he was named the trustee in Sandy Lowell's last will and testament in case his father became unable to handle it. He was the logical and legal successor. Not long after his father's death, however, as you know, he formed his own firm, the Law Offices of Hamilton Bowles Jr. He is now the trustee of Sandy's estate and operating independently of his old firm. The executor of the estate, however, was Dr. Buck Owens.

"Secondly, Sandy Lowell's home has not sold. A couple of contracts have fallen through, and it's on the active market. Mary Louise shared your notes with me first thing this morning, and reading between the lines, you think we should take a look at that house, don't you?"

"Yes. I'm suspicious of an affair between Sandy and Phyllis for reasons I can discuss with you later, and wonder if their trysts, if they existed, occurred at Sandy's house."

"I called the real estate agent of record, name of Chuck Strauss, who gives you his regards, and told him we needed to see the house. And he said anything for Jim Bob Brady, and of course, the FBI. I realize the home is uninhabited, but I got a search warrant in case we have to tear any structure up looking for cameras or recorders. That's what you're getting at, right? That maybe their affairs took place at Sandy's, he being the unmarried one, and that the sessions were possibly recorded?"

"Exactly. Maybe there will be scenes of them in bed together, or videos of her injecting him with Botox, or whatever fancied them at the time. And maybe I'm completely wrong about their relationship and my suspicions are totally unfounded. At least we'll know for sure, and I can finally put my mind to rest."

My suspicions were not unfounded.

I met Susan, one of her minions, and Mary Louise at Sandy's house. Chuck had kindly arrived early and opened the house, turned down the air conditioner, and turned on the lights, as though this were a real estate showing.

Sandy's home was on a point just off Lighthouse Drive in Horseshoe Bay. He was near the Ferguson power plant and had an unobstructed view of the lighthouse. His house sat about three feet above the waters of Lake LBJ. The sprawling one-story home featured an electronic wrought-iron gate at the entry, which led to a long driveway which branched at the house, the right wing leading to a set of garages, the left a circular drive which passed under a covered portico.

The house was constructed of white Texas limestone, with a red tiled roof.

We entered a foyer, greeted Chuck, and I introduced him to Susan Beeson. He had been the broker for our home and was an avid golfer, so we knew Chuck well. He shook Susan's hand and bussed Mary Louise on the cheek.

"Excuse the heat. We keep the A/C up normally, trying to cut expenses. This place costs a fortune to maintain."

"Who are you dealing with regarding the house sale and maintenance issues?" I asked.

"The executor for the estate is Dr. Buck Owens. I've mostly dealt with him. The estate lawyer, name of Bowles, came here once with a real estate appraiser. That's been my only contact with him."

We took a tour of the home. The furnishings were dated from possibly twenty years ago. The foyer connected to a living room without the high ceilings, so after having been in the Reardon's new home, Sandy's place felt a little claustrophobic. There was a wet bar in the kitchen. The appliances were dated as well. We saw the dining room, in the center of which was a pool table. Chuck showed us the five bedrooms, all off a corridor on the side of the house opposite the kitchen. The house was large, and the rooms huge, but it did not have an expansive view of the water.

"May I use a ladder?" Susan asked Chuck.

"Of course. There's a sturdy one in the garage," he said, and went off to get it.

"So, I'm the federal agent, Jim Bob, and my capable assistant here and I are going to search the light fixtures in each room first, then go through the place carefully. Let us do our job and let Mary Louise keep you company. I'll let you know if we find something relevant."

Mary Louise and I walked outside, found a reasonably clean couch to sit on, and admired the view of Lake LBJ.

"The house is all right," I said, "but not what I expected, after the Reardon's place. Seems old, and sad."

"I agree. You holding up okay? You didn't get much sleep last night."

"I'll be fine. I've mentally worn myself out this time. I could use a vacation. Where would you take me?"

"Oh, let me think. It's almost summer, so someplace cool. Vail, Colorado? Sun Valley, Idaho? Whitefish, Montana?"

"Yes to all." I laid my head back and fell right to sleep.

Next thing I knew, Mary Louise was tapping me. "Jim, wake up." Susan was standing in front of me. "Come look," she said.

We followed Susan into a hallway, then down to the last bedroom on the right, which looked out onto Lake LBJ. The ladder was standing beneath an overhead light fixture which had been dismantled. Hanging from the ceiling were wires, which were attached to a large embedded out-of-date VHS camera. The fixture was directly over the bed, and Susan had had to remove the surrounding sheetrock to get at the camera.

"Chuck assured us this is Sandy's bedroom, especially considering his clothes are in the closet and manly toilet articles are present in the bathroom. I mean, how many women use Stetson aftershave and Nike deodorant?" Susan asked. "And check out the chair."

I stepped into Sandy's bathroom, and there sat an old-fashioned barber's swivel chair, with a foot crank to adjust the height of the seat. A row of vanity lights was installed above the mirror, the center of which had been dismantled, and another oversized VHS camera hung from detached wires.

"Well, we have two old-school VHS cameras hidden in the wall and the ceiling. There must be VHS tapes somewhere," commented Susan.

She stared at Chuck for a moment, then said, "Chuck? Can you help us out?"

Chuck sighed deeply. "I'm most interested in preserving the legacy and reputation of Sandy Lowell. He was a good man for the most part, but he had his demons, and his addictions. I guess there is no way to keep this hidden, considering the circumstances."

He reached into his pocket, produced a keyring, and entered the master closet. "Agent Beeson, if you'll assist me, please?" he said.

Susan joined him, and we crowded in front of the entry door.

Chuck stood before a long rack full of leather jackets, both western and traditional. He reached into the rack and, with his arm, moved half the jackets to the left, and had Susan move the other half to the right. This exposed what to me looked like a blank wall, but at the top of the wall was a small built-in lock. Chuck entered the key and twisted, and the wall became a door, which he gently moved inward.

Chuck stepped out of the space and allowed Susan, Mary Louise, and I to enter the hidden space, which was basically a second walk-in closet measuring roughly six feet wide by six feet deep by eight feet high. Sturdy shelves had been built, and each contained an array of VHS videotapes, the old plastic kind designed for use in a VCR, with labels containing dates and other notations.

"Videotapes in VHS for a VCR?" I commented. "That is such ancient technology. I told Mary Louise when we arrived that the place had an old feel to it. That recording system confirms it, as does the barber chair. This goes along with that ancient Rolls Royce he was driving the day we met. He was a retro kind of guy."

"I think we have a bigger issue than Sandy being a retro kind of guy, Jim Bob. Chuck," Susan said, "do you know what's on these tapes?"

"Yes, ma'am. Recordings of his . . . escapades, if you will."

"Sex tapes?"

"Yes, ma'am."

"Have you seen any of these?"

"Yes, ma'am. On occasion, Mr. Lowell would share a new video when he returned from a trip."

"Trip? You mean he would travel the country and create sex tapes? With whom?"

"Oh, you know, ladies he met in bars, or in restaurants, or in clothing stores."

"And he would record their . . . activities?"

"Yes, ma'am."

"I'd like to view a couple of tapes, Chuck."

"Help yourself, Agent Beeson."

Susan looked through the stacks briefly, determined they were in order of dates filmed, pulled out a couple, and went back into the master bedroom.

The VCR was sitting on a dresser adjacent to a large-screen television on a stand, which itself was a throwback to older technology. Susan inserted one of the tapes into the VCR.

"This first tape is dated two days before he died."

She clicked on the bulky remote, and a somewhat grainy picture appeared on the TV. She hit PLAY, and the image of a nude Sandy Lowell appeared, lying on his back in his bed, being serviced by an equally nude Phyllis Reardon. We watched for a moment, long enough to make sure we were certain about who and what we were seeing.

Susan paused the tape, ejected it, and inserted the other. "This tape is dated four days before he died." She hit PLAY on the new tape and, after a moment, said, "Notice the brightness of the vanity lights. They're almost blinding."

In that video, Sandy was also nude, but sitting in the barber chair. Phyllis had on what looked like a teddy, and was bent over him provocatively, injecting Sandy's forehead with substance from a tiny needle and syringe. He had his left hand on her buttocks and was massaging her as she plied her trade. When she finished the process, she put the syringe on the vanity, climbed onto the chair, kissed him full on the mouth, and mounted him. Susan turned down the volume to try and mute the sounds of ecstasy, but left the tape running. After only a few minutes, Phyllis dismounted him, reached over and grabbed the syringe, and started injecting Sandy's forehead again. They were both laughing.

"There are hundreds of tapes, maybe thousands. This has been going on a long time, I presume," Susan said, in Chuck's direction.

"Yes, ma'am."

"Were all these women willing participants in the filming of their liaisons?"

"I don't really know, Agent Beeson. Considering the two cameras were hidden, I would assume not."

"My people will have to go through each tape and catalog all the activities of Sandy Lowell. I can only guess as to how many partners we'll find. These tapes are standard size, seven inches wide, four inches deep, and one inch thick. In a room this size, accounting for lost space from building shelves, I would estimate there are 900 tapes per wall, which would be about 2,700 tapes."

"His family doc that I spoke to, Billy Stevens, said Sandy was a cocksman, a hound-dog type of guy of the nth degree. He said he was surprised he hadn't died of an STD, sort of jokingly, but I could tell he was serious. This would confirm that, provided these tapes all represent the same sort of . . . activity," I said.

Susan and her agent carefully went through the rest of the house but didn't find evidence of other cameras or tape collections. "It will take my agents weeks to sort through all this."

"Where does this leave Phyllis?" asked Mary Louise.

"Well, we have her dead to rights on being unfaithful to her husband, but that's about all."

"What?!" I exclaimed. "She was clearly seen injecting his forehead with Botox."

"Did you see that? Because I didn't," responded Susan. "How do you know that was Botox? Could have been one of those fillers, or even saline. Where are the medications that prove she was injecting Botox? There were no meds in this bathroom. I checked the kitchen fridge and found nothing of interest there."

"She probably brought her supplies with her," I pointed out.

"Listen, we have a lot of tapes to review. Maybe we'll find some consistent pattern of injection, perhaps some evidence that she possibly overdosed Sandy Lowell, but none of this proves an INTENT to murder him. I'll reserve my judgment, though, until after all these tapes have been reviewed and catalogued. And that will be a while."

"I think there is a problem," I said. "Wouldn't Phyllis know about all these tapes, in which she is a seemingly willing participant? Wouldn't she make every effort to get hold of them after Sandy died to avoid incriminating herself? And because of their intimate relationship, wouldn't she have access to the house, like a door key, or a garage door opener, or a keypad entry code for an entry door?"

"You do have a point there," said Susan.

"I might shed some light on that," interjected Chuck. "Mr. Lowell and I go way back and have been friends for years. I sold the big house for him after the '87 crash and found this one for him. He didn't like handling house staff, or cleaning crews, or gardeners, or pest control people, or repair people, all those services necessary to maintain a large home. So, he put me in charge of handling those folks for him. I was his house manager, and he paid me a salary for performing those services. He still traveled quite a bit and didn't want the responsibility of caring for the home himself but wanted to make sure it was always in tip-top shape in case he needed to sell or became incapacitated.

"Some time ago, he gave me explicit instructions in case of his sudden demise. I have those in writing in my safe, and they are notarized, so if you need to see those documents, let me know. He wanted the house to be sold, and the proceeds added to his estate. But he very specifically wanted the locks and the garage door keypad code changed immediately after his death, such that no one would have access to the property except me."

"After Mr. Lowell died, did you have anyone requesting admittance to the property for any reason?" asked Susan.

"Yes. Mrs. Reardon. She started calling the day after he passed and has called at least once daily since. The last time I spoke to her, she implied that she had a court order to enter the premises, but I've yet to see that paperwork. Now that the FBI is involved, and in charge, may I assume that I am within my legal rights to stand my ground?"

"Chuck, you have it directly from me, Susan Beeson, ASAC of the Austin FBI, that you are to stand your ground. And sorry about the damage to the walls and ceiling. Get it repaired and send me a bill. I have two more agents driving over from Austin with a U-Haul to gather all this evidence, so I'll need you to wait for them. Also, I'm going to confiscate that VCR to make sure we can see the videos. It would be a shame to take all those VHS tapes as evidence with us and find we have no hardware to view them on."

"Of course. Happy to be of help," said Chuck. "I don't think Mr. Lowell will be needing that VCR."

CHAPTER 30

NO BILL

Had it just been Susan, her associate, Mary Louise, Chuck, and me involved in the video tape discovery, the outcome probably would have been different. However, once the truckload of sex tapes arrived in the FBI office in Austin, the news leaked out. Two days after their discovery, the local Austin paper ran an article on the scandalous behavior of the deceased oil tycoon G. Sanford Lowell III, and named one of his sex partners as Phyllis Reardon, wife of cardiac surgeon Michael Reardon of Marble Falls. The remainder of the article was more innuendo and assumption than anything else, but blood was in the water and the sharks were after it.

What started out as a local news story quickly spread to readers up and down the I-35 corridor, from Laredo and San Antonio to the south, to Waco, Dallas, Ft. Worth, and Oklahoma City to the north. And that spread to New York, Los Angeles, Chicago, and all the other major markets and beyond. The legend of Sandy Lowell and his sexual conquests became the fodder of magazines and television talk shows. Suddenly everyone knew who Sandy Lowell was, and lists of his identifiable paramours were published indiscriminately. The possibility of him being murdered by a current lover took a backseat to the absolute horror of him having literally hundreds of sexual partners over the years. Many sociologists, psychologists, and psychiatrists were interviewed, both in print and television media, about what sort of sick individual would engage in such illicit activity over a twenty-year or thirty-year period. And the pundits went on, and on, and on.

A number of women who were local residents were identified as Sandy's video sex partners, so that reduced the limelight on Phyllis Reardon considerably. Still, she was incommunicado and had not been seen in public. Mike continued to be buried in his work and had no comment for any reporter who dared try and talk to him.

Interestingly, G. Hamilton Bowles Sr. was not seen in any video that came from Sandy's collection. If he had Botox injections by Phyllis Reardon, it was not documented. I had been certain his picture would show up somewhere in the mix, but I was mistaken.

Sandy's conquests extended to women throughout the state of Texas, and into various cities across the country to which he had traveled for business and/or pleasure. Questions came up as to how he had managed to set up a camera in the many hotel rooms he had stayed in and had continued the recording processes when he wasn't at home. Would he bring small portable cameras on his trips in order to film his escapades? For the most part, most questions went unanswered because Sandy was no longer with us. And the reporters found neither a concierge nor other representative in any hotel that would volunteer any information about Sandy Lowell. Most of the hotels that Sandy used for his activities were identified on-screen purposely by some identifying object—such as a matchbook cover, a logo on a bath towel, a room service menu.

An industrious reporter in New York claimed to have found an employee at an upscale hotel on the Upper West Side who knew Mr. Lowell well. When interviewed, he talked about the "special suitcase" that Mr. Lowell always brought with him, and how he never let anyone handle that piece of luggage other than himself. When another reporter tried to contact the employee and corroborate the story, he was told that the man no longer worked at the hotel.

After a couple of months, the furor died down, mainly because not one single woman of those hundreds seen on the videotapes came forward to complain of rape or forced sexual conduct of any kind. The news media begged and pleaded unabashedly for women to come forward and complain about Sandy Lowell, but none did.

The media, out of boredom and frustration, went about discovering a new tragedy to report on, and Susan and her agents were able to get back to the business of trying to determine if Sandy had been poisoned, whether accidentally, or on purpose for financial gain. His most recent and repetitive sexual partner had been Phyllis Reardon, either out of love or convenience, and she was the only person identified out of all those tapes who was seen injecting him with any kind of substance. Susan again obtained search warrants for both Reardon houses and searched them thoroughly with multiple agents, but found nothing incriminating other than those original vials of Botox and the packaged syringes in the new home. She again searched Sandy's home, took it apart, and could find no evidence there either. There was no smoking gun. There was no direct link between Phyllis and Sandy other than a few tapes confirming sexual relations between the two, and those same tapes showing her injecting his face.

At some point in the midst of the negative publicity surrounding Sandy, I started to wonder about Jennifer Lowell, and how she was holding up with the television full of stories about her father and her mother. One afternoon, after a light clinic, I stopped by her home. I called first, spoke to Cynthia the caretaker, and received the okay to visit. When I rang the doorbell, as usual, Jennifer ran screaming through the house, opened the front door, and stared at me.

"My daddy on TV. My mama too. All day," she yelled, and ran from the door.

"Come on in, Doc," Cynthia yelled from what sounded like the kitchen. This was a house of yellers, which would drive me up a wall in a short time.

"I smelled the coffee from the front porch. How are you holding up?" I asked.

"She's had that TV on 24/7 since all the troubles began. I've tried to get her to watch her shows, but she keeps flippin' back and forth from one news channel to another. It's just horrible."

"She greeted me by saying that her mama and daddy are on TV. How much do you think she understands?"

"I have no idea. Every so often she'll yell 'Daddy on TV,' or 'Mama on TV.' Then she comes and gets me, grabs my hand, drags me into the TV room, and makes me sit down and watch it with her. After a bit, she'll settle down, and I leave the room and try and tend to my chores, then she yells, and the process starts all over again."

"I guess there is no way to stop her from watching all the . . . trash talk?"

"Lord, Doc, if I didn't have that TV, I don't know what we'd do. We would kill each other. That's my only salvation. Normally, she watches her game shows, *Law and Order*, or *Blue Bloods*, and it keeps her occupied. Seeing Sandy and her mother on the TV, though, I know it upsets her, but there isn't much I can do."

"Great coffee, by the way, Cynthia. New flavor?"

"Sumatra. Thick, dark, rich African coffee bean. Loaded with caffeine. Two cups of this, the house cleans itself without me knowing."

We laughed at that, and I reflected that Cynthia probably had few light moments. We sipped our coffee in silence for a few minutes, then I asked, "Have you had any trouble with repairs on the house getting done, or cash flow problems of any kind?"

"Nope. Everything is smooth right now. Phyllis even paid us a visit."

"What?!"

"Yes, showed up one day unannounced. We sat right here, had a cup of coffee. She apologized for her past neglect of Jennifer, and her holding back on repairs and such. I wasn't sure Jennifer would remember who Phyllis was, but she stood in the corner of the room, stared at her mother for a while, then ran back to the TV room."

"When did this happen?"

"Right before the news stories about Sandy's recordings started. She told me that there might be some negative publicity about her and Sandy, that most of it wasn't true, and for me to try and keep Jennifer from watching too much of it on TV. She didn't want the stories to interfere with her and Jennifer's relationship. Well, hell, she hadn't laid eyes on her daughter in years, so what relationship could she have been talking about? Anyway, I assured her I would do my best. She laid an envelope full of cash on the table here, then she left. Now that I've seen all that mess on TV, I can see what she was talking about."

"Did Jennifer seem to know Phyllis was her mother?"

"Who knows. She didn't call her Mama, if that's what you mean. But here lately, like I told you, she's been talking about Mama and Daddy on TV, so maybe she made the connection."

The only highlight of that tragic time was the dinner Mary Louise and I had with J.J. and Kathryn, where they announced they were expecting. It was too early to determine the sex of my soon-to-be grandchild, but I didn't care about that. We just wanted a healthy child. It was a joyous occasion in the midst of a local tragedy. The due date was around Christmas time. We were all pumped with emotion. A new Brady bun was in the oven. That added new meaning to the phrase "Happy Holidays."

Susan called Mary Louise, told her she was coming down on business, and asked if we could have dinner. Mary Louise planned the meal at home, such that if Susan was overserved, she could sleep over. It was a Thursday night after a long work week for me, and no emergencies had come in that had to be taken care of Friday, so Tip and I were having our second eighteen-year-old Macallan scotch on the patio, awaiting Susan's arrival. Both the surgeons I had interviewed accepted the new positions as orthopedic hip and knee surgeons at HCMC. They agreed to share the E.R. call for a while, until they were established, which took a great burden off me. I would be back to a Monday through Thursday schedule except for rare occasions. I was a happy man.

Mary Louise brought me a beautiful shrimp cocktail with just enough horseradish to make my eyes water. Tip looked longingly at the martini glass which housed my appetizer, but I assured him it was way too spicy for his sensitive stomach. He seemed to sense that and laid down.

Susan arrived, and she shared stories of her agents viewing and cataloging the videotapes from Sandy's abode. It had taken them weeks to get through years of tape. After a while, the agents were able to fast forward through much of the material. And while there were many faces, the names of his partners were never seen, at least on the screen. Some were recognized, such as Phyllis and other local women, and a few national personalities, but for the most part, they were anonymous participants. Whether or not they were willingly filmed, Susan said the FBI would never know. Most of the known personalities in Sandy's films that had been identified had lawyered up upon being questioned. After all, there had been no crime committed, as far as the FBI could determine, and this being a free country, one could sleep with whomever one wanted when the occasion arose.

After dinner, Susan came to the purpose of her visit.

"Jim Bob, I appreciate the time you spent gathering information about the Botox injection business, and the time you spent visiting with Dr. Warner, Dr. Goldfarb, Sandy's personal physician Dr. Stevens, and Hamilton Bowles Jr. And while the scenario you fashioned of Phyllis Reardon having killed both Sandy Lowell and Hamilton Bowles Sr. with timely overdoses of Botox to gain control of his will and further enrich herself is intriguing, there just isn't any proof. The FBI has to operate on facts, and evidence, and in this case, we may be wrong, but we are not going to bring charges against her. I'm sorry. That decision didn't just come from me, but from my higher-ups in Washington. The case is officially closed. I know that will make you very unhappy, because you like to see justice done, but that's just the way it's going to be.

"If it makes you feel any better, think about the logic of Phyllis Reardon having constructed a bathroom in her new home housing facilities to do Botox and filler injections. If she planned to overdose Sandy with Botox, what would be the point? She upgraded the camera system to a miniature camera with digital audio transmissible to her smart phone. I think her plan was for them to continue their illicit love affair and record their sessions together. Otherwise, why bother?"

"Or maybe that's what she wanted you to think, which would give her the benefit of the doubt in case she ever became a suspect in the deaths of Sandy Lowell and Ham Bowles. That it was a ruse."

Susan stared at me for a moment, then said, "I guess we'll never know for sure."

She stood. "I'd like to thank you both for dinner, and for your hospitality, but I must get back to Austin this evening. I treasure our friendship, and don't know what I'd do without it. I hope that the FBI's decision not to pursue criminal charges against Phyllis Reardon doesn't cause you any more sleepless nights. We're all going to have to just let this one go."

Susan gave each of us a hug and was out the door.

A couple weeks later, on a beautiful Sunday afternoon, after a round of golf with my best friend and lover, my cell phone and pager went off simultaneously, suggesting some urgent matter. I answered the cell first, and it was Cynthia Stiles.

"Doc Brady, I'm so sorry to bother you, but I need you to come over right away."

"Cynthia, I'm—"

"Please. It's urgent."

I checked the pager, and it had instructed me to call Cynthia's number. Mary Louise and I left our beverages unfinished, got in the car, and went to Jennifer Lowell's home. The front door was open.

"Cynthia," I yelled. "We're here."

"Oh my god, oh my god," she screamed. "Please help!"

Mary Louise and I ran toward the kitchen. Phyllis Reardon was lying in a heap on the floor, coughing and spitting blood. I looked at the random wounds. They were deep, and blood was flowing from seemingly everywhere. Cynthia was leaning over Phyllis, kitchen towels in hand, only able to stanch some of the wounds. If the EMTs didn't arrive quickly, Phyllis would be dead soon. I grabbed another nearby kitchen towel and joined Cynthia in trying to stem the blood flow, but it was of little help.

"Tell me you called 911."

"Yes, I didn't know what else to do. Then I called you."

"Shit. Mary Louise, can you find some more towels, please? What the hell happened?"

"The doorbell rang, and it was Phyllis. She said Jennifer had called her and wanted her to come over right away."

"Jennifer called her? Has that happened before?"

"Not to my knowledge. But her number is posted on the fridge in case we need to contact her for something, and Jennifer knows how to use a phone in case of emergencies. Anyway, I let her in, we walked into the kitchen, next thing I know Jennifer has a butcher knife in her hand and starts stabbing her mother every-where. That's when I called you."

Mary Louise found more towels, but Phyllis continued to bleed out. The EMTs arrived quickly, within ten minutes, but Phyllis didn't make it. Too much blood loss.

While we waited for the police to arrive, I asked Cynthia where Jennifer was.

"Lord, I don't know. She stabbed her mother and ran off."

Mary Louise and I walked back to Jennifer's TV room. She was sitting on a couch, watching a show with a lot of bells, whis-tles, and gongs.

"Jennifer, I'm Doc Brady. Do you remember me? And this is Mary Louise, my wife."

She still had the bloody knife in her hand, and we could see blood all over her, so we didn't approach. She continued to stare at the television.

"Jennifer, what happened to your mother? Did she hurt you or something?"

"The TV said that Mama killed Daddy, so I killed Mama. I love my Daddy."

CHAPTER 31

VACATION

A month or so later, we found ourselves in Sun Valley, Idaho, where cool nights and warm days prevailed. Friends of ours owned a resort property, and we were their guests in a luxurious cabin, complete with a spacious living room, bedroom, kitchenette, and his-and-hers baths.

I had been chosen to spread Sandy Lowell's ashes at the Links at Spanish Bay in Pebble Beach. That came about through Buck Owens, who Sandy had thankfully appointed the executor of his estate. Hamilton Bowles Jr. had himself a mess of legal trouble going on and I was happy we didn't have to bother with him in completing Sandy's request. I felt a connection to Sandy as a result of my meddling in his affairs, and no one else seemed to have any interest in carrying out his wishes. Mary Louise and I had chartered a private jet the day before, courtesy of Sandy Lowell's estate, and checked into the inn in the early afternoon. We had pre-arranged the bagpiper and the necessary permissions, and right on time at sunset, my bride and I distributed Sandy's ashes onto the links while "Amazing Grace" was being played. It was a poignant moment for both of us. We spent the night at the inn and flew to Sun Valley the following day.

We had heated up the outdoor hot tub after a perfect day of golf, referring to the weather and not our quality of play at the Valley Club. We were surrounded by beautiful meadows, not amber waves of grain, but there were purple mountains, as our national anthem describes. I had poured us each a glass of cold Ridge chardonnay, and we were soaking in the buff with the jets on, made possible by the construction of a privacy wall around the spa area.

"This is certainly a lot more fun than it was walking into the mess at the Lowell house," said Mary Louise. "In all my years with you, I'm not sure I've ever witnessed a crime scene quite like that one. That time Beverly Richard was going to shoot us, and Susan Beeson rescued us at the last minute, was the worst thing I had experienced prior to this. I don't really need to see another one, either."

The crime scene at the Lowell house was a disaster. The local police had arrived shortly after the EMTs. The two officers that showed up had no clue how to handle a mentally challenged person forty-three years of age. Their first thought was to arrest her, take her into custody, and put her in the local jail, but Jennifer was having none of that. She was no wilting violet physically, and with knife in hand, she was a formidable force, screaming at the top of her lungs. Cynthia could not calm her down.

The County Social Services was called to evaluate the problem and make a recommendation. An absolutely stellar social worker named Marian Roth arrived after an hour or so and was, in her kind and gentle way, able to put Jennifer at ease. Jennifer gave up the knife to Marian, who clearly knew exactly how to manage a conversation with someone at Jennifer's level of cognizance. After a time, she felt that Jennifer was not a danger to herself or anyone else at that point, and that she could be left at home in

Cynthia's care, once she had confirmed that Cynthia was willing and able to continue as Jennifer's caretaker.

"I'm glad you were with me. You were able to corroborate my impressions of the scene and confirm that the murder of Phyllis Reardon was clearly an act of Jennifer Lowell, and not of Cynthia Stiles. Have you talked with Susan about the latest with Jennifer?"

"Yes, as a matter of fact. We spoke the day before we left on this trip. Jennifer has been through a lot of testing by psychologists, sociologists, and social workers. Her IQ has been determined to be just under 60. She has the mind of a third grader, or less. She doesn't really understand the difference between right and wrong, and the fact that she killed her mother after having heard for weeks from the television stories that her mother might have killed her father was some sort of misguided protective response. I don't think Jennifer understands it, but then neither do the shrinks."

"Long term?"

"It looks like she'll stay at home with Cynthia, as it should be. There was discussion about attempting to try her in adult court, but with her mental incapacity, she couldn't understand the proceedings. Then someone suggested trying her in juvenile court because of her mental age, but then wiser minds realized she couldn't get a fair trial there either, because she still wouldn't understand what was going on. I don't think the authorities and ancillary workers have encountered a case quite like Jennifer's. Susan doesn't see a trial in Jennifer's future, at least at this time. Fortunately, she thinks life for Cynthia and Jennifer will go on as before, with an occasional wellness visit from Marian Roth, the social worker."

"I think that's for the best, don't you?"

"Absolutely."

"Did Susan give you any insight as to what's going to happen to the money that Phyllis wasted all that time in alleged nefarious activities to get, now that she is deceased?"

"She and Mike had no children, so he is her beneficiary. He has maintained consistently that he knew nothing about Phyllis's activities with Sandy Lowell, and nothing about her manipulations to get the will changed. He knew that she would have some friends over periodically for what's called Botox parties, in his mind harmless fun for adult females. He doesn't want to be trustee of the $50 million. He makes a good living as a heart surgeon, and that is plenty of income to meet his needs. He stated that if he has to take the trusteeship in order to fulfill the terms of Phyllis's will, he has offered to transfer the management of the trust to a reputable banker, lawyer, or investment institution. Also, he will hire his personal attorney to draft documents that specify that once Jennifer passes, any residual funds in the trust are donated to the charities named in Sandy Lowell's original will."

"What about Phyllis's lawyer, G. Hamilton Bowles Jr.? Is he out of the picture?"

"Yes. Mike Reardon wants nothing to do with Bowles and has said he will do whatever he must to keep Bowles's 'slimy hands' off Jennifer's trust—Susan's words, not mine. She also heard through the alphabet agency grapevine that he could be brought up on disbarment charges. Some shady activity might have gone on with the manipulation of Sandy's new trust documentation in order to allow Phyllis Reardon to be the new trust's manager. The word is that the state bar association received an anonymous tip about that, and they are obligated to investigate. You wouldn't know anything about that, would you?"

"Of course not," I said, with as much confidence and pride as I could. "I accept that it can't be proved, and I am required to keep my opinions to myself, but what a tangled web was woven by Phyllis and Bowles Jr. to enrich themselves, and ironically it all came to naught."

"This is role reversal. I'm usually the one asking you questions about the final disposition of a mystery, and here I am, supplying the great Doc Brady with all the answers. You just backed away from the whole thing, didn't you?"

"For the most part, yes. I did my best to uncover a murder, and expose an act of avarice, and I was thwarted at every turn. It was just too much frustration for me. I'm on the straight and narrow path from now on: work, golf, and Mary Louise."

My better half lifted my arm, placed it around her neck, nestled against me, and said, "I love you, Jim Bob Brady."

"Back at you, ma'am."

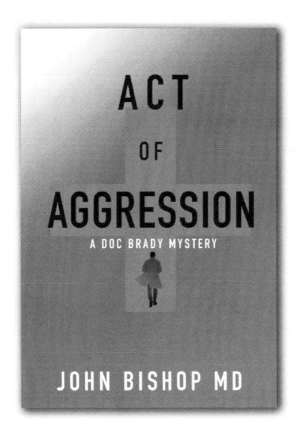

I hope you have enjoyed *Act of Avarice*, the eighth book in the
Doc Brady Mystery series. I'm pleased to present you with a
sneak peek of *Act of Aggression*, the ninth book.

Please visit **JohnBishopAuthor.com** to learn more.

CHAPTER 1

LA CAVA

"**D**r. Brady, I'm sorry to keep you waiting. What a hectic morning. It seems that many of the residents here as well as folks from outside the area have a strong interest in our new club. We are proud of our facilities as well as our new golf course. Do you have any questions prior to the tour?"

I wondered again what I was doing there. We were members at the Horseshoe Bay Golf Club, which was an outstanding facility with four 18-hole golf courses. What else could one possibly need? There were facilities at each course for breakfast and lunch, plus a massive new restaurant for evening events, also servicing all four courses for breakfast, lunch, and dinner, with outstanding Hill Country views at the top of the rock. The services at HBGC were over the top, incomparable in this part of Texas.

Some of my friends, however, had played the new La Cava Golf Club and raved about the artful layout with streams, waterfalls, lush zoysia grass fairways and bentgrass greens. The clubhouse was under construction, but with enough completed to appreciate the beautiful limestone exteriors and vast decks with panoramic Hill Country and Lake LBJ views.

I had been told that the club originally was to be called La Casa Golf Club, signifying a sort of home away from home. Then, when the dredging began, and the developer found old limestone caves on the property, the estimated cost of building the course skyrocketed. Golf course architects say it is much more expensive to move limestone around than it is plain old Texas soil. Thus, the name change from La Casa to La Cava. The limestone was of high quality, so a great deal of it was sold off to pay for golf course construction, with the rest saved for the clubhouse and the restrooms that were to be built on the course, one on the front nine and one on the back nine. Still, in spite of being able to put the limestone to good use, the cost of breaking it down, moving it, and hauling it away took the project off budget significantly, or so my golf buddies said.

"When do you expect the clubhouse to be completed?"

"Within the next twelve months, for sure. I have paperwork for you to review," she said, and went about copying documents on a high-speed printer in her office. Her name was Patricia Simmons, but she went by Patsy, according to her name tag. She was attractive and could probably sell ice to residents of the frozen north. She was close to six feet tall, with auburn hair, fair skin and a shapely figure.

Her office was in a temporary building outside the future main entrance of La Cava. Most of us would call her building a trailer. She had called it a temporary building when I made the appointment for the tour. Meet me at the temporary building outside the new entrance, she had said during our phone conversation. Perhaps the club did not allow the word "trailer" to be uttered on the premises, but "Airstream" was clearly engraved on the aluminum frame adjacent to the entry door.

My wife Mary Louise should have accompanied me for the tour. She was a golfer as well; not to the extent I was, but she played, and loved to dine out, and was a much better judge of how things worked in life than me. She was in Austin for the day for a board meeting. She did a great deal of charity work when we lived in Houston and had slowly resumed that passion over the last few years since we had moved to the lovely little town of Granite Falls.

I had been a high-profile and hard-working orthopedic surgeon in Houston for many years, but as is usual with jobs like that, burnout is always simmering just beneath the surface. I had given up my academic position and the stress of sixty- to seventy-hour work weeks, and moved out to this community west of Austin where I was now an orthopedic surgeon working a reasonable schedule, four days a week. Friday and Saturday were now golf days with my friends, and Sundays were couples golf days with my wife. I was a much happier man and was enjoying my practice and my patients again.

It did not hurt that I had been named a beneficiary in the will of a former grateful patient of mine, an old-time wildcatter who left me 100 acres in an oil-rich area of south Texas. His family was mostly horrified and immediately set about buying me out of the bequest. By the time the legal fees and taxes were settled, I received a nest egg of close to $20 million. That kind of money bought Mary Louise and I a great deal of security and allowed us to move to a beautiful home on Lake LBJ in the Hill Country and allowed me to have a much smaller practice and to play golf two or three days per week.

On the other hand, my schedule also allowed me to get into trouble, as illustrated by my involvement a while back with Mourning Doves, a residential haven for abused and battered women, and most recently, my quest to discover the cause of the mysterious death of Sandy Lowell, whom I had met in a grocery store parking lot the day of his death.

"If you have no more questions, Doctor, let me give you a tour of the facilities. Have you played the course yet?"

"No, I was hoping to do that with my wife, Mary Louise. She wasn't able to make the appointment today. She's in Austin for the day on business. We would like to schedule a round of golf soon if that's possible."

"Of course, not a problem. Shall we?"

Patsy handed me a white hard hat and donned one herself. We exited the Airstream, walked around to the future entrance of La Cava Golf Club, and stepped on to a plywood walkway into the building under construction.

"Are you going to be all right walking in those high heels? It looks like there's ample opportunity to sprain or break your ankle," I said.

"It's not a problem. I have become adept at dodging potholes. Besides, hiking boots really would not do much for this dress, do you think?" she said, turned, and gave me a come-hither look.

Patsy had a point there. She had on a bright-red leather skirt, with a white silk blouse and red heels. She was dressed for a cock-tail party, and with that look she had given me, well, I felt the sudden need to burst out of there and run home safely to mama.

I stayed well behind her as she gave me the tour, far enough back that she had to yell her explanations of various dining areas and party rooms. We walked to what would be the grand patio when completed, and I had to admit that the views of the Hill Country were spectacular.

"Pretty special, huh?" Patsy stated.

"Yes. How many people will the outdoor deck hold when completed?"

"Around two hundred."

"Nice party space. I like that overhang they're building. Looks like it will be adequate to buffer the sun as well as the rain."

"Oh, absolutely. Our architect had specific instructions to design the outdoor space such that the elements could be avoided as much as possible. Let me walk you to the golf shop area, which is partially completed. Then I'll have to leave you. I have another appointment," she said, checking the time on her gold Rolex with a diamond bezel.

The check-in area of the La Cava golf shop was complete, but the large area where men's and women's golf clothes would be displayed was behind plastic sheeting and obviously not ready for prime time. Patsy introduced me to Jason, the young pro staffing the most important area of the shop, which would be where credit cards are used by guests to pay for a round of golf.

"Will the club be fully private?" I asked.

"That is the developers' long-range plan. Of course, the club will need revenue right away, so we will be allowing guest play, both member-accompanied as well as play available to the general public on a daily fee bases. Our accountants estimate that it will take at least two years for the club to become totally private. But it could be shorter."

"Or longer," I said, playing devil's advocate.

She gave me another look, this one not quite so friendly.

"Here is all the paperwork you'll need to complete to become eligible to join La Cava, Doctor. Please call me and I'll arrange a gratis practice round for you and Mrs. Brady. If you don't mind showing yourself out . . ." she said, then extended her hand, gave me a limp finger shake, and sashayed away.

I wandered around for a bit and found a great deal of empty space. I did discover the future men's and women's locker rooms. It was hard for me to tell how ornate they would be when completed, but the ceilings were high and there were huge windows in place with, again, outstanding Hill Country views.

I was very thirsty by then and stopped back in the pro shop and asked Jason where I could find a cold beverage. He directed me to a temporary dining facility one level down, adjacent to the starter area where the golf carts were parked. I found the facility easily. It was the only food truck on the property. I ordered a cola on ice and a ground beef taco. It has been my experience in life that you can tell a great deal about a restaurant from a taco. That may sound simplistic, but for me, the quality of the taco shell, the amount of lettuce, and the thickness and spiciness of the meat and pico de gallo all enter into play in allowing me to decide whether I want to return to the eating establishment or not. The taco was out of sight. That was a good start for an upscale golf club with an Airstream trailer for a clubhouse and a food truck for a restaurant.

As I finished my impromptu meal, I heard raised voices. The food truck sat on a level piece of ground above the practice range, which was at a lower level, and reached by a series of concrete steps. The voices were coming from a man and a woman, both well dressed and carrying a few golf clubs back from the practice range. They reached a high-end private golf cart with a Mercedes Benz hood ornament, put the clubs in their respective golf bags, and sat in the cart. I was sitting at a small table with an umbrella, on the other side of the food truck, out of their line of sight, which meant I could not see their faces.

"How in the world do you think you can get by with that? You don't think the principals are smart enough to figure out what you're doing?"

"I've worked my ass off, and I deserve compensation. I may have to cut some corners, and slightly falsify the records, but I WILL be paid what's owed me."

"Hon, you've been to jail. You know what that is like. And remember what you've told me about those federal institutions, those so-called prison country clubs."

"Yes, and that's bullshit, those white-collar-crime units. I was knifed twice in the last one, up in Colorado. That's why I paid all that money to the forger to get new IDs and a name change. I am clean as a whistle as far as anyone around here knows. New social security number, new driver's license, the works. You need to work on keeping a low profile, and your mouth shut. This will be my big score. We'll be on Easy Street from then on. You just wait and see."

I stood up and walked in the direction of the voices, taking care so as not to be seen. If the male speaker had been to prison and had been knifed twice, he probably would not think twice about doing in yours truly. By the time I reached the other side of the food truck, all I could see was the back of their heads. I did note the license plate on the golf cart, however. It read HIGHROLLER.

ABOUT THE AUTHOR

Dr. John Bishop has led a triple life. This orthopedic surgeon and keyboard musician has combined two of his talents into a third, as the author of the beloved Doc Brady mystery series. Beyond applying his medical expertise at a relatable and comprehensible level, Dr. Bishop, through his fictional counterpart Doc Brady, also infuses his books with his love of not only Houston and Galveston, Texas, but especially with his love for his adored wife. Bishop's talented Doc Brady is confident yet humble; brilliant, yet a genuinely nice and funny guy who happens to have a knack for solving medical mysteries. Above all, he is the doctor who will cure you of your blues and boredom. Step into his world with the first five books of the series, and you'll be clamoring for more.

Printed in Great Britain
by Amazon